"WONDERFUL . . .

Edgerton is such a funny writer that sometimes you just howl. . . . He's a master at catching the language of people who almost get it right. . . . The best thing about Clyde Edgerton is his life is more interesting than most of ours. And he can write it down."

The Houston Post

"One of the niftiest new books around . . . Once again Mr. Edgerton has targeted the snake-oil variety of Southern Christianity for the slings and arrows of his outrageous humor, his outraged sensibilities. . . . A laff riot."

The Raleigh News and Observer

"The dialogue is smooth and rich and the characters are zesty and spicy. In particular, Edgerton produces a wonderful portrait of the kind of evangelist/businessman who keeps his Bible in the cash register drawer. KILLER DILLER is a killer."

The Kansas City Star

"Edgerton has proved himself to be a masterly storyteller, and KILLER DILLER won't disillusion anyone. . . . In a sense, KILLER DILLER is a *One Flew Over the Cuckoo's Nest* in which everyone escapes."

The Virginian-Pilot/The Ledger-Star

Also by Clyde Edgerton
Published by Ballantine Books

RANEY
WALKING ACROSS EGYPT
THE FLOATPLANE NOTEBOOKS

KILLER DILLER

Clyde Edgerton

For Betty
All Best.
C Edgerton
15 Oct. 92

BALLANTINE BOOKS · NEW YORK

"Sour Sweetheart Blues" by Clyde Edgerton, Tom Scheft, and Dudley Jahnke, Copyright © 1990. Used by permission. All rights reserved. "When I Sleep in Class," by Clyde Edgerton and Tom Scheft. Copyright © 1988. Used by permission. All rights reserved.

Parts of this book have appeared in slightly different form in *Southern Exposure* and *Chattahoochee Review*.

Library of Congress Catalog Card Number: 90-42778

ISBN 0-345-37072-4

This edition published by arrangement with Algonquin Books of Chapel Hill

Manufactured in the United States of America

First Ballantine Books Edition: March 1992

For David McGirt and Charlie Garren,
my fishing buddies,
and with fond memories of *Cabin 6*, lost at sea.

He's a ugly little something on a scout
He's a terrible little something, hush your mouth
He's a awful little creature
He's a killer diller from the South

—*Memphis Minnie, singing, "Killer Diller"*

With appreciation to:

The John Simon Guggenheim Foundation; Shannon Ravenel, my editor, whose insights are invaluable; friends who have made suggestions for this and/or other novels— Susan Ketchin, Louis Rubin, John Justice, Sylvia Wilkinson, Margot Wilkinson, Lee Smith, David McGirt, Michael McFee, Bettye Dew, Jan Tedder, Jim Henderson, Sterling Hennis, Grant Kornberg, Laurie Scheft, Tom Scheft, and Catharine Coolidge; my agents, Liz Darhansoff, Lynn Pleshette, Tessa Sayle, and their co-workers; the faculty of Meredith College, Ruel Tyson, Carl Holleman, and those who wrote letters and attended meetings in my behalf; St. Andrews College, for allowing me long stretches of writing time, and for being supportive in other ways; my publishers— Workman, Algonquin, Ballantine, Viking-Penguin—and their staffs; librarians; book sales representatives; bookstore owners and operators who read as well as sell books; Bruce, at the Tulane Jazz Archives; Paul Garon of Beasley Books in Chicago; Perry at Soundtracks Recording Studio, Raleigh, North Carolina; and Mrs. Lucille Ingram, for inspiration.

Summerlin, North Carolina
August 3, 1989
From the *Hansen County Pilot*

Ballard University to Host Project Promise

SUMMERLIN—President Ted Sears of Ballard University announced yesterday that his school has been awarded a $320,000 federal grant to sponsor an innovative project with the halfway house adjacent to the Ballard campus, BOTA House (Back On Track Again).

The project, starting this fall, will be called Project Promise. The innovative aspect of the project will be that residents of the halfway house will be teaching special education students from Hansen County. Skills taught will include masonry, sewing, and plumbing. Faculty and graduate students from Ballard University School of Social Work will provide guidance and support.

"We are aware," said President Sears, "that risks are involved, but correctly overseen, this program will enable us to reach segments of the population we've yet to reach—enabling the Ballard family to continue living by our motto: Witnessing By Example."

Wesley Benfield, a BOTA House resident, and probable participant in the project, said, "Project Promise looks like a good idea to me and I'm looking forward to teaching masonry. It's a good skill. Like they say, if you bring fish to somebody, they just eat fish, but if you teach them to fish, then they know how to fish."

1

VERNON JACKSON SITS ON THE SIDE OF HIS BED IN HIS white Jockey undershorts—which have mostly separated from their waistband. It's six-thirty on a Monday morning in September.

Vernon is sixteen and small for his age. He has short, spikey black hair, and his pointed face looks so much like a possum's that Vernon is sometimes called Possum. His elbows are together in his lap and he rocks back and forth.

He reaches for the wire-rimmed glasses on his bedside table, a large cardboard box with NAPA PARTS written on the side. He puts the glasses on slowly—they are too small—and looks through thumb prints for his T-shirt on the floor. He finds it, picks it up, turns it in his hands first one way then the other, then starts the sleeve opening over his head. It won't go on—too tight. He looks down into the space inside the shirt, gets his bearings, turns the shirt around and pulls it over his head, the right way.

A wind-up alarm clock, on its back in a cooking pot out in the hall, will ring in about thirty seconds. Then after Vernon and his daddy, Holister, find something to eat, Vernon will follow Holister out to the Sunrise Auto Repair Shop in the side yard, and help out until the school bus comes.

Vernon is in Special Education.

The alarm goes off. Vernon hears his daddy's feet hit the floor in the next room. The same thump as always.

The *fact* of Jules Vernon Jackson as a baby, tiny, wouldn't grow, wouldn't walk, wouldn't talk—and his father's sudden obsession with car engines—all this drove Vernon's mother out West. Alone. Forever. So Holister raised Vernon by himself, mostly in the auto shop out back.

It worked like this: Holister would be bent over the front fender of a car, a drop light hanging from underneath the open hood. He would reach down into the engine, work for a few minutes, then stand, wipe his hands and arms with a dirty rag, look around, locate the baby on the floor, shift the drop light to another spot, and bend back to what he was doing.

The baby crawled around under car engines that hung from block and tackle and into turned-over boxes and barrels, black fingerprints usually on his diapers.

In the little hallway, Vernon stands on the grate

over the furnace, finishes pulling up and hitching his overalls, and then studies the face on the clock in the pot.

In the kitchen, his father is sitting at the table, peeling a banana and watching the women do their morning exercises on Channel 9.

Vernon sits down, gets a banana out of the plastic fruit basket and starts peeling. "Why are the numbers on a clock in a circle?" he asks his daddy.

"Huh?"

"Why are the numbers on a clock—"

"I don't know." Holister keeps watching the women. "She's new."

"Seems like they just always put them in a circle. Everywhere you look there they are—in a circle. They ain't ever sideways or in a line or nothing. Just in a circle."

"That's the way the pygmies did it, with sun dials, and it just stayed that way. God a-mighty, look at them muscles. She's got too many muscles. That's just getting sick." A piece of banana hangs on Holister's lip, then drops. He has a large round face. The hair that usually goes from just above his ear up over the top of his bald head hangs loose. "You want some bread?"

"No."

Holister spreads mayonnaise on a piece of white bread, folds it, and puts half of it into his mouth.

Vernon drops his banana peel into the trash can, goes into the living room, shuts the door behind him, and sits in the gray metal fold-up chair at the upright piano. He stumbles through the new song that was playing for the women exercising. On the second try he gets it right.

3

Whenever Vernon sits anywhere—here at this piano, or on the tree stump beside the '61 Ford engine that has been there since '76, or anywhere else—he always rocks back and forth.

Holister brushes bread crumbs off the table and onto the floor and pitches his banana peel into the trash can. Music is Vernon's gift it looks like to Holister, and everything else about Vernon has been a theft, except his arguing, which sometimes comes with force, in great waves.

After breakfast, Holister is walking across the side yard toward the auto shop. At the back steps of the house, Vernon pulls an invisible car key from his pocket, opens an invisible car door, hops in, sticks the key in the ignition, says, "Crump up, baby, crump up," and then with his back stooped, his legs chopping like pistons, he runs past his daddy on over to the auto shop. He drives himself to most places he goes. He's in good physical shape, lean and hard as a new tire.

A little later, bending over a car fender, his morning plug of Picnic Twist tobacco in place in his cheek, Holister says, "Hand me a 7/16th, Vernon."

"Huh?"

"Hand me a 7/16th. Hurry up. . . . That ain't a 7/16th."

"It looks like one."

"Well, it ain't one. Get a 7/16th."

"It looks like one. That's what it looks like, a 7/16th. I got eyes. I can see what looks like a 7/16th and what don't look like a 7/16th. I was just using my eyes. What do you expect?" This is the arguing part. Vernon walks the few steps back over to the tool box. He walks like a duck.

People driving in the neighborhood sometimes see Vernon out beside a road somewhere, working on his invisible car, working on the engine, walking back to the trunk for a 7/16th, then back up to the engine, bending over, standing, shifting the drop light from one spot to another.

Anyway, when Mrs. McIntyre, who teaches mentally handicapped students at Hansen County High School, was asked to pick one of her students to learn masonry over at Ballard University, for something called Project Promise, she picked Jules Vernon Jackson. She figured he was just the one.

Ballard University is a Baptist school. It is nestled on two hundred rolling acres not far from the Sunrise Auto Repair Shop in the piedmont town of Summerlin, North Carolina. On the wide, clean campus, giant oak trees provide early-fall shade for the lawns, brick sidewalks, classrooms buildings, and boys' and girls' dorms. Here and there are sturdy, glass-fronted, locked wooden bulletin boards with short Bible scriptures carved along the top: IN THE BEGINNING GOD CREATED THE HEAVEN AND EARTH. LOVE THY NEIGHBOR AS THYSELF. ASK AND YE SHALL RECEIVE. There is a modern student store where textbooks, stationery, teddy bears, and green-and-yellow Ballard coffee mugs are sold, and where the paperback books are checked by Mr. Burleson, the bookstore manager, for ugly words and un-Christian situations. This is where students and parents buy the green Ballard sweatshirts and the ball caps embroidered with the yellow Ballard bulldog.

The Ballard Bulldogs. Hark, hark, hark, to the bark,

bark, bark of the Green and Gold. Go-o-o-o-o-o-o-o, Bulldogs.

At the same time Vernon Jackson is climbing into the Special Ed. school bus, Ted Sears, "The Father of the Ballard Family," is seating himself at his long blond polished table in the President's Meeting Room to review plans for Project Promise, the brainchild of Dr. Frances Fleming in the School of Social Work. The plans are spiral-bound in light blue. Ted is about to make notes on a fresh yellow legal pad with his $200 Parker ink pen.

Ballard's president is a tall, well-groomed, fifty-six-year-old, clear-eyed, former fighter pilot whose major regret in life is that he never saw combat.

When students' parents see Ted Sears enter a room—parents, some with only one Sunday suit and tie, red skin under starched white collars, thick hard hands, plain dresses and one Sunday pocketbook, black, held with both hands—when these parents see this man enter a room wearing one of his seven-hundred-dollar suits (or the sixty-dollar green school blazer with the little yellow bulldog on the pocket), they know they are in the presence of power. This man is a leader. He looks parents in the eye, he shakes those worn hands firmly, and he flashes that smile that his wife, Lorraine, worries about sometimes. When Ted sleepwalks, and Lorraine finds him off in the den, standing there in his blue pajamas with the little white ships, or the yellow ones with the little brown airplanes, or the solid blues, or the solid greens, when she finds him standing in the dark in the middle of the night, in the den by the bookcase full of leather-bound classics, asleep, that smile—visible in the light through the window from the bugzapper—is frozen onto his face. And he's standing there with his hand extended. That smile on her husband when he's standing asleep in the den with his hand extended makes her nervous.

From his notes on the yellow pad, Ted plans to compose a letter to the Summerlin Chamber of Commerce, explaining the college's relationship to BOTA House, the halfway house. He will do this *before* there are any complaints. He himself hadn't been too sure about Dr. Fleming's plan at first, this Project Promise, but Ted's twin brother, Ned—Ballard's provost— encouraged him to go forward with the idea. Federal money was available, and the school by golly should not refuse federal money if that money could be used to spread the Gospel. Even so, it was a hard decision—this halfway house business— because it involved, even though indirectly, known criminals, black criminals in some cases. However, Ted's difficulty in giving the go-ahead was greatly diminished when the university attorneys determined that the college was not legally liable for any actions committed by halfway house residents—as long as no Ballard employees worked at BOTA House.

Mysteria, Ted's secretary, brings in his seven forty-five cup of coffee and sets it on his personalized leather coaster from Henderson Cadillac.

Ted is musing. He takes a sip of coffee. "Thank you, Mysteria," he says. He stands up from his long table and walks to his long, low window and looks across campus, across University Boulevard, at BOTA House. Dr. Fleming has promised that this Project Promise will bring national attention.

Ted looks farther down the street from BOTA House to the Nutrition House, the diet house he established five years ago when Ballard introduced a master's degree in Diet and Nutrition. A lab school of sorts for the faculty and graduate students, and now, a nationally known Christian diet center.

There, in the Nutrition House, on a bench in the exercise room, sits Phoebe Trent, weighing two hundred and thirty-one pounds, about. She is dressed in shiny white tights, khaki Bermuda shorts, and a dark green sweatshirt. She has thick red hair, freckles, and very bright blue eyes. She's sitting up straight, getting her breath, after tying one shoe. This is ridiculous, she thinks.

Phoebe wishes she had some of those tennis shoes with Velcro straps like her kindergarten students wear.

Other people in the exercise room are holding their hands high over their heads. Some are walking around, bending at the waist. That terribly fat man on the bench across the room looks like he might be unable to stand. The aerobics instructor, a graduate student at Ballard, is putting a cassette in the recorder. "Stretch time," she says.

At BOTA House, the message printed neatly on the blackboard nailed to the housemother's door is: IT'S NICE TO BE IMPORTANT, BUT IT'S MORE IMPORTANT TO BE NICE. Mrs. White is a former Ballard dormmother. Now working for the Federal Bureau of Prisons, she's making three times her old salary.

Upstairs in his room, the front corner room, Wesley Benfield is making up his narrow single bed. His roommate, Ben, has already left for his job at the Texaco.

Wesley takes one last swipe at his tan-and-red blanket, to smooth it, then looks around for something to Xerox. He picks up last Sunday's church bulletin, locks the door behind him, and walks down the old wide, wooden stairs past the weekly message. He signs out in the sign-out book—the rule is, out after eight A.M., in before six P.M., and with special permission, before nine, depending on demerits. He walks out onto the big porch, with its six rocking chairs, and down the street toward Copy-Op, the duplicating place. He takes long strides, slinging his head back every once in a while to throw his long blond hair out of his eyes.

Wesley has a plan—a way to meet a woman. Maybe a student. Maybe not. At twenty-four, he's not too old for students—all the way down to freshmen. As he walks he sings snatches from a blues song he's been writing.

> *What do I do, Lord Jesus,*
> *with the women in my dreams?*
> *Some are dressed, some are not dressed,*
> *da-da, da-da, it seems.*
> *Da-da, da-da, da-da, da-da.*
> *Ah, the women in my dreams.*

Dear Lord, help me on this plan to, to meet somebody I might spend my life with, and be happy with, and have children with, to have fruit and multiply with. Guide and direct my steps. Help me to do what is right, oh God. In Jesus' name, Amen.

9

The Copy-Op is just off campus, on the corner of University Drive and General MacArthur. Inside, Wesley fishes several sheets of paper from a trash can and then stands behind a chest-high counter which cordons off three do-it-yourself copy machines.

Wesley has done this a few times before. He can usually count on somebody stopping at his station, thinking he is a Copy-Op employee. He can usually work up a little conversation. His plan is to meet a beautiful girl needing his help. One thing will lead to another.

Let her come in, dear God. Let her come in.

A young woman comes in carrying a large sheet of poster paper. She walks right up to Wesley. "Can you-all do oversized stuff?"

Not bad, thinks Wesley. "Sure can. Just follow me over here to the oversized machine. The *machine's* not oversized, you know. Well, it actually is oversized but it does the oversized stuff is why it's called oversized. Here you go. Now what you do is—" Wesley has no idea. "Let's see." On and off button. "There you go. It's on."

"I got to do this map for twelve people in my geography class. I worked three weeks on it."

"Yeah. Right. No problem."

Large sheets of clean paper are on the floor under the machine.

"We just need to get one of these sheets right here," says Wesley, "to go right in here, it looks like."

"Have you ever operated this thing?"

"Oh yeah. All the time." There seems to be a place to get the map started and a place to get the

10

copy paper started and both of them will be pulled through at the same time, it looks like.

Wesley starts the blank paper in the far slot, the map in the near slot.

"I worked on that map for three weeks," says the girl.

Wesley presses the COPY button. The sheets are being pulled into the machine. The machine stops and a red light starts blinking.

"Let's see here," says Wesley. "Let's just open this door and see if we can't—" He pulls a handle and the front of the machine opens on hinges. The inside is a mass of rods, little orange stickers, and metal and plastic plates. A piece of map is visible.

"Uh-hummm," says Wesley.

"My map looks like it's hung," says the girl.

I need some fresh air, thinks Wesley. "I'll tell you what you do," he says to the girl. "You wait right here. I need to go out to my car and get a pair of pliers. I'll be right back." Next week, he thinks.

"Pliers?"

Wesley starts for the door.

Another young woman, a big one, with lots of thick red hair comes in. She must weigh close to three hundred pounds. She looks familiar, Wesley thinks. Oh yeah, right. The one from over at Nutrition House. He's seen her—from a distance— walk past BOTA House when he was on the porch, and he noticed how big her boobs were. Stick way out there. But now right in front of him, close up: her face! She's beautiful. Freckles, blue eyes, full lips. Those country freckles. She's got that cornfield look, like she just walked in from a cornfield, wearing a straw hat, wanting to fall in love with

11

somebody like him—some fairly tall, blond, kind of lanky, good-looking guy who knows his way in the world, but is also a Christian. Some guy who has been in trouble but is now back on track, or maybe *really* on track for the first time ever.

"Can we help you?" says Wesley.

"I need to duplicate some pages from this book."

A Yankee or something, he thinks, and she's probably in college, maybe a freshman.

"No problem. Which pages would you like done?"

"I've got them marked there. The ones with a paper clip and a piece of paper."

"Okay, if you will just go over there and get that little black counter box, and bring it on back over here to me, I'll fix you right up."

"Thank you."

"And ask them if they can help that girl over there with the oversized stuff." Wesley steps toward the oversize machine and says to the girl waiting, "My buddy's going to help you out. He's the expert on repairs. I already had an appointment set up when you came in." He moves back to his post behind the chest-high wall, looks at the new young woman over at the main desk. She sure is fat, he thinks, but maybe it's just more *big* since her proportions are about right. Nothing is hanging anywhere. Everything looks pretty firm. Wesley imagines his hands on her bare skin, roaming all around all over the body of this great big old young woman, probably a virgin, his hands just sort of venturing around, finding a bunch of little bitty freckles like a bunch of stars up in the night sky there under one of her breasts where the skin is the whitest, following a little line of star-freckles right

12

up to the sun—her nipple. Her nipples are probably bright pink, not dark brown or black, he thinks. He blinks, hard. Dear God, please forgive me. Help me free my mind of things that I'm not supposed to think about.

It's weird that I should feel this way about some girl who's fat, thinks Wesley. He's been trying *not* to think about women and sex. Maybe what's going on is that he'll just be thinking about kind of weird and different women, unusual women, like this one—for awhile. Then, after that, no women, no fantasies. Maybe God is slowly changing the way he thinks about women. Kind of slowly getting him out of the habit. Now, if he had a wife, he could think about her all he wanted to. That wouldn't be a sin.

This business of stopping thinking about women and stuff has been harder than stopping drinking and cursing. Wesley doesn't like to hear cursing any more. It's wrong. When he couldn't get his room-mate, Ben, to stop, he had to finally insist that Ben please at least start all his curse words with an *n*, or at least do it with the main ones. Wesley has had a hard time figuring out which are the main ones. He figures damn and hell are okay. They were okay with Mrs. Rigsbee, the old Christian lady he used to live with, the one that got him to become a Christian himself.

The Christian life has not been an easy life, but Wesley knows it's the right life.

The big girl with red hair returns, hands Wesley the little black counter box and her book. "I just need a copy on the sides where the little piece of paper is clipped on," she says.

Wesley takes the book to a machine. He reads a little from each page before he copies it. It's some kind of education thing, about teaching kindergarten. There are diagrams of a classroom, several lists. He finishes, removes the counter from the machine, puts the sheets inside the book, gives it all back to the fat girl.

"You pay him over there," he says. "And ah, come back to see us. I'm usually here on Monday mornings."

"Thank you." She smiles at him.

"I believe I've seen you over close to where I live."

"I'm at the Nutrition House."

"Yeah, I live close to there. I'm Wesley Benfield. Pleased to meet you." Mrs. Rigsbee taught him to look the person in the eye, reach out with his hand, use a firm grip.

"I'm Phoebe Trent," the young woman says.

She's still smiling, thinks Wesley. A lazy kind of smile, full lips. Those eyes and those freckles and that thick red hair all together. Wow. He can't believe how much he wants to see her all over. "Well," he says, "I hope you'll come back."

"I will."

"You a kindergarten teacher?"

"I'm an aide at Mt. Gilead Kindergarten, but just for this year."

"You got to be kidding. I go to church there!"

"Really? Well, I'll be going there, too. I've been there for the last few Sundays."

"I haven't seen you. Do you have a ca—?" He feels himself moving too fast. Car. He can find that out later, if all the other stuff works out.

14

"Excuse me?"

"Nothing." I bet she does have a car.

A man in a suit and tie walks up and says to Wesley, "Do y'all sell paper clips?"

"There's some in a plastic cup over there on the counter."

"I need about a hundred."

"Check with them over there." Get *out* of here, man.

The first young woman is raising her voice to the Copy-Op employee. "But I worked on that map for three weeks. It won't do me any good in three pieces. It goes on display. It was *his* fault," she says, pointing to Wesley.

"I got to mail out this flyer," says the man who wants paper clips, "and I decided to add this letter that explains what my business is all about."

"Over there." Wesley points toward the counter without taking his eyes off Phoebe.

Then Phoebe is walking away. As she opens the door to leave, she looks back at Wesley and smiles, holds up her hand and says, "Bye."

The Copy-Op boss is walking up. "That map is ruined. Did you tell her you worked here?" he asks.

"I'll be right back," says Wesley. He walks around the counter, out the door into the hot air outside, calls to Phoebe. "Hey. You headed to the Nutrition House?"

She stops, amazed. A man is calling out to her. But it's daylight, a city street. She will be in daylight, walking home. It's all probably okay. And he's cute. This is a surprise. She can't remember when she was last pursued in any way like this.

"I'm heading home, too," says Wesley, catching

up. "I'm not far from where you live." The hot sunlight glints off car fenders. Wesley feels like jumping into the air.

Phoebe decides to make a little joke. "You're not at the halfway house, are you?"

"Actually, I am." Wesley reaches up to his nose, pinches it, eyes her. "I'm a counselor there." Wesley knows his residency at BOTA House is a kind of mistake. He was already a Christian when somebody left their keys in the ignition of a white Continental with a tan interior. And now he's asked God for forgiveness. And he's been forgiven. And he's been in enough institutions—the orphanage, the rehabilitation center—to know how to be a counselor. He knows the ropes, more or less.

"Oh. Well," says Phoebe. "That must be an interesting job."

"Oh, yes. Very interesting."

Phoebe notices Wesley's shoes. Sneakers, with the laces undone. They don't seem to be a counselor's shoes, she thinks. But you can't always tell about counselors. "Do you know Celia Boles—one of the counselors at Nutrition House? The graduate student?"

"Actually ... actually I'm not actually a counselor." Wesley tries to smile, but the smile doesn't come onto his face just right. Half of his mouth stays down. "I just ... I mean ..." Honesty is the best policy. "I didn't want to scare you off. I'm a resident at BOTA House." Christians are honest. THE BEST CUNNING IS NO CUNNING, Mrs. White had up on her blackboard one time.

Phoebe moves her hand up to the top button of her blouse. One of those! She knows about the halfway house—where it is and . . . and everything. At the Nutrition House people sit on the porch and joke about it.

"But see," says Wesley, "I got in some trouble a couple of years ago, but it was an accident. Honest. Like a honest accident. See, I been going to church for several years—still do, regular—and up until this trouble I was living with this woman, this old lady. And I was going to church then, too. This old lady, she took me in, see, and she got in trouble on account of it, and had to change churches and all just because she took me in, and so we both ended up at Mt. Gilead, and she was like my grandmother, and so anyway, I'm going to be getting out of BOTA House in three or four months. What happened was I went and took this Continental for a ride and had already been in trouble when I was a teenager about cars. I was a orphan. Still am. But see they won't take you in at the halfway house unless you're really okay. The other clients are just embezzlers and women and stuff, people that don't pose no threat at all. My roommate might pose a little threat, but he's the only one. No, I'm kidding. He don't pose a threat. He plays guitar. It's really a normal place, pretty lax, like a dormitory or something. We got a band and everything. Just a few people that had bad breaks."

"I see." Phoebe *has* seen normal kinds of activities going on over there—people cutting grass, painting a shed out back. And anyway, he's a musician. "What instrument do you play?"

"I play bass. But I'm learning bottleneck guitar on my roommate's six string. I'm going to get me a

National Steel Dobro when I save enough money. It's a—you know what they are?"

"No."

"It's made out of aluminum or steel or something like that and has a chrome finish—looks like a guitar but it's really a Dobro. And they made these National Steels back in the old days, the thirties and stuff, and since. Same people that made those big old cash registers. Anyway, they were built to be loud, before there were microphones and stuff. Had these little speaker things built in front of them. What you do is put a bottleneck on your finger, see. Then you slide it up and down the neck and you fret kind of light and it's a great sound." Wesley slows his walking, reaches in his pocket and pulls out a bottleneck. She seems interested, he thinks, and she's slowing down. "You get them made out of glass or metal. Some of the guys that play that way are Bukka White, Son House. And Bonnie Raitt. It's a great sound. And Johnny Winter. And there's a guy that plays in Raleigh, Clifton Dowell. I already got some books that teach you."

"Oh, I see." He is definitely sincere, Phoebe thinks, and polite. She wonders if he'll want to see her again. She wonders why he is so nice to her. As big as she is. It's unusual, she thinks.

By the time they get to the halfway house, Phoebe has learned that Wesley, besides being a musician, is a part-time brickmason over at the university. Clearly he is not someone she would ever think about marrying, or even getting overly serious about, but on the other hand, she has been hoping for some kind of adventure here in North Carolina while she solves her weight problem. This may be the start of it. A Short, Gentle Adventure with an Interesting Young Man.

"You from around here?" asks Wesley.

"I'm from Michigan. I'm majoring in elementary education up there, but I'm taking a year off, you know, to be down here."

"Oh, yeah. Okay. I thought you sort of sounded like you were from somewhere up North. How do you like it down here?"

"Fine. Just fine so far."

It's time for Wesley to cross the street. "I'll see you later," he says. "Nice to meet you."

Phoebe lifts her hand and wiggles her fingers. "Nice to meet you."

Crossing the street, Wesley wishes he'd told her he could cook. Maybe he could have arranged to cook her a little something in the BOTA House kitchen—get her over there. He's about to call out to her about cooking her some cornbread and stuff but as he opens his mouth, he remembers she's in town to lose weight. He crosses the curb, walks along the sidewalk. Maybe she's rich, he thinks. He's heard that a lot of the clients at the Nutrition House are. Maybe if it all works out, she'll see how much he needs a Dobro, and buy him one for Christmas.

As she walks away, Phoebe worries about Wesley looking at her rear end. In the past, before she really faced up to her weight problem, she was learning to look in the mirror and convince herself that she was rather large, but not fat, really. She would turn and look at herself at different angles in the mirror. But all the Nutrition House literature, sent to her home back in Michigan, emphasized—and helped convince her—that she had a real weight problem and had to take control of her life and solve it with the help of Jesus—changing in the process her whole style of life.

Her own personalized chart now hangs on her wall. It shows projected weekly weights and blank spaces for actual weights. All tailored to her personal situation. And she has little sayings taped on her wall, to say aloud and silently over and over. "A closed mouth gathers no food." "Count, count, count and the calories won't mount."

And now, there's a new dimension to her life down South. An Interesting Young Man.

Wesley runs his song through his mind:

> What do I do, Lord Jesus,
> with the women in my dreams?
> Some are dressed, some are not,
> and they come at me, it seems.
> They come at me through soft satin doors.
> Lord, what did you do with yours?
> Lord, what did you do with yours?

2

LARRY LEDFORD IS SITTING BEHIND HIS DRUM SET in the basement of BOTA House. He touches a cymbal with the tip of his drumstick—ching, ching, ching. He's getting his distance from the cymbal just right. He moves his stool back a few inches, touches the cymbal again. Now forward a couple of inches.

Larry has been out of BOTA House for several months and drives a bread truck. His girlfriend, Shanita, is sitting beside him. She is hardly ever more than two feet away from him—when the band is practicing *or* performing.

Shanita does not like the bass player, Wesley Benfield, or the lead singer, Sherri Gold. Because they are white.

Wesley comes down the outside basement stairs and in the door carrying his guitar in a battered case covered with bumper stickers. Wesley plays bass guitar but he doesn't own a bass guitar. Instead he owns an old six-string electric hollow-body. He has taken all the strings off and put on four bass strings, creating a sort of homemade bass guitar, for the time being.

Shanita watches Wesley open his guitar case. Honky-dude-cracker. Larry told me he wouldn't *never* play music with no white-assed-cracker. Pale man. I tell you.

To Shanita's dismay, Ben, the lead guitar player and Larry's good friend, turned to blues over a year ago, when she and all of her friends were getting into rap. And then Ben had to come across this white boy, his roommate Wesley, who liked blues, and this white girl, Sherri Gold, who had this thing for blues. Shanita doesn't understand it. Then her honey, Larry, *he* got into blues. Blues is just not where it's at. It all sounds the same, for one thing. It's got soul, but it's just not where it's at in this day and time. It's from a different age.

Ben comes in, speaks, sets his guitar case on the floor and starts opening it.

Wesley gets out his guitar, straps it on, watches Larry tighten his cymbal. "New cymbal?"

"Naw. Just shined it."

"Hey, Shanita."

"Fine."

Sherri Gold, the lead singer, hasn't come yet. She's late. She's been out of BOTA House for a while now too, like Larry, and is working at Winn

Dixie. She has a gold front tooth and a good, scratchy blues voice. Her goal in life is to sing like Joe Cocker up high.

Wesley and Ben hang the blankets. Four over their heads flat out, and four around them, to soak up noise.

The BOTA House band is a gospel band, the Noble Defenders of the Word, waiting to become a blues band. They've got the loan of an old sound system from Ballard University for as long as they play gospel. The band's plans are to—in a few months, oh, maybe six, when Wesley and Ben are out and get full-time jobs and the band can afford their own sound system—expand to blues, maybe some rhythm and blues, change the band's name from the Noble Defenders of the Word to the Fat City Blues Band and head to Myrtle Beach or Key West—or somewhere like that—and a future that includes long nights of playing the blues to hot, dancing crowds, playing till they drop, sleeping late, making albums and videos, and getting rich. Wesley figures he can work all this in together with being a Christian.

The band practices very quietly when they're playing blues—loudly on the gospel music.

Larry touches the cymbal again, adjusts it, moves his seat forward, touches the cymbal, moves his seat back, touches another cymbal, moves a cymbal stand toward him a few inches. Larry has a small chin, a long nose, and wears three gold chains around his neck. He stands and leans over, adjusts the height of a cymbal stand. The chains hang loose.

Shanita thinks: I love to see his chains dangle.

The band is planning to work up a blues song, "If It Looks Like Jelly, Shakes Like Jelly." Ben's cassette player, dark gray, long and low, with a speaker at each end, holds the tape—a Charlie Hicks recording. Ben has just pressed the start button when Larry, positioned so he can see Provost Sears or Mrs. White, the housemother, coming down the outside stairs, says, "Red alert, red alert, red alert."

Shanita looks through the glass in the basement door and sees Ned Sears's pasty-white face. Oh, God, she thinks. Another honky.

Ben punches the cassette player off button with his foot and starts singing. Wesley and Larry join in.

Just a closer walk with Thee. Precious Savior—

Sears walks in. Shanita watches the smile play on his face. Fooling this dude. The provost, the university president's twin brother—except they don't look alike. This one's almost bald. Shiny white head. He snoops sometimes. They're that kind of twins that ain't identical.

The band sings while Sears stands, listening. When the song is over, he says, "Gets better every time."

Larry adjusts a cymbal. Ben gets a rag from his guitar case and wipes down his strings.

"Good work, good work," says Sears, glowing, but uncomfortable. It's difficult to glow here in the basement—now—because neither of the three blacks present will look at him. The whole BOTA House band idea started out as a white gospel quar-

24

tet, and Mrs. White got him to get Philby in the Music Department to find them some sheet music and a sound system. A wonderful idea, he thought. But then two blacks joined, and they started singing Negro spirituals, never checking with Mrs. White. Well, of course black gospel music—the spirituals—is all right, as long as they don't move on over into rock and roll or any of that bong-bong black stuff.

Sears knows Ballard's black enrollment is climbing every year. A mind is a mind and a soul is a soul, regardless of that Ham business in the Bible. But as a matter of fact, he can hardly think of *any* young blacks who will look at him. Certainly, he glows around them just like he glows around white people. He's never tried to glow less around one group than another. And he's supported BOTA's acceptance of young black criminals. He's on the BOTA House board, where he's had to listen to all sorts of views about that topic, including one board member's preference for small-nosed instead of large-nosed Negroes.

"Keep up the good work," says Sears as he turns to leave. His rounds don't allow loitering. But one of his personal responsibilities has been to advise Mrs. White, the housemother, since even before this Project Promise agreement came about, and he feels good about how he's been able to drop in and offer advice.

"We got to get a new red-alert song," says Ben, when the door closes behind the provost.

In comes Sherri Gold. Sherri Smith, really. Gold is her stage name.

Lord God, thinks Shanita, what the dogs drug up.

Sherri, wearing tight jeans, boots, a red shirt and a Durham Bulls baseball cap, backwards, believes the band should eventually do *four* kinds of music: gospel, blues, rhythm and blues, and country club standards. "I'm talking money," she told Larry at the last rehearsal. "Country clubs is where the money is. You might have a good *time* playing The Continental Club, but you can't make the kind of money you can in country clubs, especially if you learn a few standards. And they got country clubs in Myrtle Beach, and Key West, especially Miami."

"We asking for trouble," Larry had said, while Shanita thought, No way can we add all this *country club* honky shit. Lord, help my time.

"You're late, man," says Ben.

"I ain't no man, man," says Sherri. "Howdy, Shanita. Hey, boys."

"Fine," says Shanita.

"I'm sorry I'm late. Let's get to work. Play the blues." She clinches her fist and draws her elbow into her side.

"We're going to work up the 'Jelly' song," says Wesley.

"What about the radio show?" asks Sherri.

"Just those five gospels for the radio show."

"Can we go over those first?"

"Okay with me."

"I mean, you know," says Sherri, "the radio show is a big deal. We need to be ready. There ain't no re-takes on a live radio show.

What time we supposed to be out there, any-way?"

"Seven-thirty A.M.," says Wesley.

"I ain't ever been up that early," says Sherri.

3

On Tuesday, a month later, Wesley stands at the snack bar on the Ballard campus. It's lunchtime. He's been laying bricks, helping build a wall for the new addition to the vet school. His denim jacket and jeans are cruddy and dusty at the elbows and knees.

"What do you need today?" says Robbie, the small woman behind the counter.

"I need a new car—a Trans Am, or a Continental."

"Me too. And a good man. You must already have a good woman."

"Sort of."

"What kind of food you want?"

"A barbecue with slaw, a bag of Nachos, and a Mello Yello."

Robbie pulls a Mello Yello from the drink box, pops the top and sets it on the counter. As Wesley takes a sip, he pulls a folded letter from his back pocket, shakes it open, checks the room number over in Morgan Hall where he's supposed to have this first Project Promise meeting—meet this Vernon Jackson he's going to be teaching masonry to. It's 231 Morgan Hall.

Wesley eats as he walks across campus. He thinks about Phoebe, about Phoebe and him. They talked on the sidewalk in front of BOTA House yesterday, the fourth time they've met. Twice she's driven him out to the mall, where they sat together on a bench and talked about things. She talked about how she had been addicted to food. She seemed to enjoy telling him, talking to him. She said she used to go into a 7-Eleven and eye a bag of Nacho chips and say to herself that she was not going to buy them, yet deep inside she'd hear a whisper—yes, yes you are, yes you are, yes you are, and she would way deep down know with one hundred percent certainty that before she could get out of that store, she would buy that bag of Nachos, the giant bag of Nachos, go home and eat them up with a big hunk of hard cold cheese put in a little pot on the stove, melted, and then poured all over them.

She finally had to stop going into any store where there was food. She did a lot of shopping at hardware stores. But she kept finding ways to eat. Once food got into her mouth, all resistance was gone, she said. She'd always have to eat all of whatever was in front of her.

Wesley sees Phoebe in his mind. She is so . . . she looks so good. Her face. Those freckles, that thick,

29

soft red hair, and blue eyes. He thinks—yet again—
about this whole business of sex before marriage.
Maybe he should read up on it in the Bible—this
love and sex stuff. There is supposed to be something in there about David and some women or
something like that.

Being *too* strict can't be right. That's for monks
and all them.

Wesley walks up the steps at Morgan Hall. He's
done some masonry work on these steps and has
been inside a few times. Little gold plaques are beside each classroom. The John H. Collins Classroom, says one plaque. The Bertha Swain McDuff
Classroom, says the next. A broom closet with no
plaque. Then the Tina Johnson Dillworth Classroom. He's ten minutes early. There is no one in
sight. He pulls his screwdriver from his back pocket.

Wesley looks both ways, covers a smile with the
back of his hand.

The broom closet becomes the Tina Johnson
Dillworth Classroom.

Upstairs, Wesley sees a side view of Dr. Fleming
through her open office door. He's seen her before,
in the snack bar. She's not so old, and she's sitting
in a chair that's out in front of her desk, wearing
glasses, a turtleneck sweater, short brown hair.
Cardboard boxes and stacks of books and papers
are all around on the floor, on a table, and on her
desk. As he moves on into the doorway, Wesley
sees, on a couch, a white man with big grimy hands
and a—Wesley stares ... damn ... he looks like a
possum. A boy sitting there rocking back and forth
with his elbows tucked between his knees.

"You must be Wesley," says Dr. Fleming, standing, extending her hand.

Her hand—small, soft. Wesley again thinks about Mattie Rigsbee, how she taught him to shake hands. He squeezes firmly, looks Dr. Fleming in the eye. "Yeah. Yes, ma'am. That's right."

"I want you to meet Holister and Vernon Jackson," says Dr. Fleming. "Wesley Benfield."

Holister stands, starts his hand forward toward Wesley, stops it. "My hand's pretty dirty."

"That's all right."

Holister's hand is rough. He holds firmly, turns loose fast.

Vernon still sits, rocking himself forward and backward, looking at his hands, then up at Wesley.

"Stand up, boy," says Holister.

Vernon stands up, looks down, puts his hand forward. Wesley gives it a shake. The hand is limp, little, no grip at all.

"Wesley, you can sit over here in this chair by the door," say Dr. Fleming. "I was just telling Mr. Jackson and Vernon about Project Promise, about how we hope to set it up and run it. Did you get a letter?"

"Yes ma'am."

Dr. Fleming sits in her chair again. "We believe this can be a positive experience for everyone involved. Mrs. White speaks very highly of you. We will be able to pay you for your time, and our graduate students will be able to assess how these kinds of programs might work in other, similar settings.

"There will be three of you at BOTA, working in the program initially. Carla McGhee and Linda French are the others. I think that's in your letter.

31

We hope to involve more later on. Today I want to set up a tentative schedule for meetings and so on."

"That's the messiest desk I ever seen," says Vernon.

Holister jerks his face toward Vernon. "Who you talking to?"

Dr. Fleming smiles and looks at her desk over her shoulder.

"Her," says Vernon. "I mean, I mean I seen messy stuff in the shop and all, tables, but I ain't ever seen nothing that messy. That is messy.

"Well," says Dr. Fleming, "you probably *haven't* seen anything like that. Occasionally, I—"

"I mean, how do you find something under all that stuff? What if you had something under there you just needed to pick up, just, you know, pick up?"

"You'd be—"

"Something you just needed to pick up, like a pencil or something like that." Vernon's rocking is constant.

"You'd be surprised at how easy it is to—"

"I mean you'd have to climb down *in* all that stuff."

"Shut up," says Holister. "Let her finish."

"I was letting her finish. I was just telling her what—"

"No, you won't. Now shut up, I said."

"I usually know where the important material is," says Dr. Fleming. "Most of it is—"

"Why don't you just throw it—"

"Shut up. I mean it."

"Away."

* * *

"I always wanted to be a carpenter-brick thing," Vernon says to Wesley, outside after the meeting. "That's one of the things I've always wanted to be."

"Well, I think I can teach you some bricklaying," says Wesley.

"Carpenters and stuff are killer dillers," says Vernon.

"I tried to teach him about automobile engines," says Holister, "but it didn't stick. He has a unusual approach to things. But he can flat play a piano. That's one thing he can do."

"Yep," says Vernon. "That's one thing I can do."

Ted Sears is on his 1:45 to 2:05 lunch break, standing at his office window, eating the ham and cheese sandwich made by the Sears' cook, Aunt Polly. He watches a threesome walking along the brick pathway under the shade of the big oaks, now turning gold and red. He recognizes Wesley Benfield from church and from the picture of him that was in the paper, along with the article on Project Promise. And that must be the retarded boy with him. This whole business with BOTA House as a lab is certainly bold, thinks Ted. But not too bold—Ballard will be free of any liability. The relationship is just right for full impact at low risk. He might even be able to entice this Benfield boy, since he's a Christian, to take a class or two—firm up the relationship—so the world can see that Ballard is taking an active part in his transformation from sinner to Christian.

Parents would love it. A direct result of the foresight of the university president who was once poor, too. Yes, one of them. They all know Ted was raised

33

in a poor family. They know he paid his own way through college, joined the Marines and flew jets—was an officer in the military—and then came home and went back to school, earned a Ph.D. in physical education, became a nutrition scholar and a professor at Ballard. Then a dean. And now president. He manages to work this information into speeches and into interviews, whenever possible. He believes that his constituents should know him as thoroughly as possible. If they feel that he's one of them, they will trust him. If they trust him they will freely and in good conscience support Ballard University. Without the support of parents and friends, Ballard's mission will fail.

And most people know that he's the author of two full-length books on nutrition: *Food and the Bible* and *Nutrition for a Christian*.

Now with Project Promise, parents will see a form of Christian education at Ballard that actually touches the criminal, the Negro criminal even. And this new Project Promise may attract money sources as yet unrealized—*liberal* money sources. Ballard's boldness, spurred by his leadership, and a few key Washington contacts are keeping the grant money coming, while it's thinning for schools with less bold, less farsighted leaders.

Yes, this Project Promise will be his latest in a long line of victories. The trustees approve all of his plans. They are loyal almost to a fault. His most recent victory was the Marilyn Massy Hargroves School of Veterinary Medicine, now regularly sending young Christian vets into the coastal, mountain, and piedmont towns of North Carolina. And South Carolina, where they're needed even worse.

And earlier, when Ted realized it could be just the thing for home missions, he founded a school of social work, a grand opportunity for Ballard to enter a field dominated, sadly, by liberals and secular humanists. By golly, somebody needed to cut into all that mumbo-jumbo government social work business with bedrock free-enterprise Bible-believing Christianity—why hadn't he thought of that before? And so he established the Horace B. Groves School of Social Work, offering a master's degree. And Ballard College became Ballard University—a dream come true.

Along the way, Ted has learned to raise money. He raises money by talking to God-fearing Americans who are sincerely afraid—in these strange times—of losing America, if not from without, from within. He preaches quietly, neatly, about the American flag, democracy, about the Bible, Jesus, about heritage, his heritage, his family's heritage, the sacred heritage of Bible-believing Baptists and the sacred heritage of Ballard University.

And Ted Sears knows he's not hurt by his looks, neat and clean—strong-chinned, clear-eyed. And he knows exactly how to slap an admiring American man—rich or poor—on his back and talk in confidence about long hair on men and about the dread danger of unions, and about what takes place on the campuses of state-supported schools, talk in such a way that this American man, rich or poor— a man who suddenly realizes that this college president is his *friend*—can hardly wait to pull out his checkbook and support Ballard's bold mission of making the world more American, more Christian, more union-free in the best sense of those words.

And Ted knows (grew up with the knowledge of) how to get along with elderly widows—when to visit, what to say, what to eat, how much, and how long to stay. He knows when to go himself and when to send someone else. And he knows that many of these elderly widows will, in appreciation for maintenance men dropping by and mowing their lawns and tending their plumbing needs for the remainder of their days on earth—he knows that for these thoughtful services there are a few elderly women who'll leave the university their houses and property.

And he has a sense of humor. He can tell funny jokes, funny clean jokes. And he does. He's even got a written record of which ones he's told at which Kiwanis or Lions or Elks Club, and when. And he has an idea that before too long, he may have the opportunity to tell some of these jokes from Washington, D.C.—if everything falls into place.

4

Iт's Work Task time at BOTA House. Ben is raking leaves, Don and Dennis are painting gutters.
Wesley is inside, building a wall—a waist-high brick
wall in the den, designed to hold plants along its
top. He is working with mortar, brick trowel, hawk,
chisel, level, bricks, and a canvas floor cover.

Carla and Linda, the two female residents, are
sitting on the front porch, sewing curtains. Carla
has a scar across her nose. Linda has a scar running
from the corner of her mouth down her neck.

"What's yours like?" Carla asks Linda.

"She's a Mongolian idiot."

"No. They don't call them that any more. It's
Down's syndrome."

"Mongolian Down syndrome?"

"No. No. Plain Down's syndrome. That's the disease."

"I thought diseases were something you catch."

"I don't know," says Carla. "This is something you're born with."

"They call the person 'retarded,' don't they?"

"That's what they used to call them. I think it's mentally handicapped now. Or exceptional. My sister is one. We got mail calling her all sorts of things."

"Does she have the Mongolian thing?" Linda bites a thread.

"No. She got some kind of brain damage when she was born. Not enough oxygen, or something." Carla bends over and sifts through the shoebox of sewing gear on the porch floor.

"It's terrible, ain't it."

"Yeah. It is. She was older than me so I didn't know too much about it when it happened. She was in the County Home for a long time."

Linda looks across the lawn. "Look at that."

A boy dressed in overalls and wearing wire-rimmed glasses is running down the sidewalk toward them, pumping his legs, making good time. He sticks his arm out straight, turns and runs across the lawn. "Eeerk," he says at the front porch steps as he stops. He opens his car door, gets out, slams the door with both hands, saying "Blam." He looks up at the two women.

"What you driving?" Carla asks the boy.

"Plymouth."

"Looks pretty good."

"It'll go about a hundred miles a hour. Is this where Mr. Wesley Benfield lives?"

"Sure is. Go on in. He's in there."

Vernon studies the two women as he comes up the steps. He stops on the top step. "What happened to your face?" he asks Linda.

"I got cut."

"Yours too?"

"Yeah, I got cut too," says Carla.

"How did that happen?"

"Accident."

"I mean *how*, how did it happen?"

"It's private."

"You can't tell nobody?"

"Listen boy, Wesley's inside—if he's the one you come to see. If you come to see me, it's time for you to go back home."

Inside, Wesley has only two more rows of bricks to go on the wall, up top. "I'll just watch," says a voice right behind him.

Wesley turns and looks. The possum. "Sure, that's okay."

Vernon pulls an ottoman to a spot near Wesley. He sits, tucks his elbows between his legs, crosses his arms, and starts his rocking.

"This is the wall I was telling you about," says Wesley. "See, you got these strings up so that you keep everything level. You just put the mortar on the brick here, like that, lay this on like that, tap it till it's level, scoop off the extra, and that's all there is to it. You got your basic trowel, your basic hawk, and a jointer to smooth the mortar. You mix the mortar outside and bring in a little at a time. And that's about all there is. You got to practice, that's the main thing."

"What's a hawk?"

"This thing right here."

"You call it a hawk like a bird?"

"Yeah."

"Why do they call it that? Looks like there'd be some kind of reason for calling it something like that, don't it?"

"I don't know. I guess so. I guess you can call it whatever you want to but what it is is a hawk."

"I mean if they're going to name it a hawk it ought to have something to do with a hawk."

"Maybe so."

Wesley works.

"Can I do one?"

"Sure. In a minute."

Provost Sears—Ned—the tips of his fingers held together in front of his chest, appears in the doorway. He is glowing. "Good morning, Wesley."

Wesley looks over his shoulder. "Morning, Dr. Sears."

"And you, son, I don't believe we've met."

Vernon looks at a button—chest level—on the man's shirt, and keeps rocking.

"This is Vernon," says Wesley. "He's in that Project Promise thing, with me."

"Oh, of course," says Ned Sears. He bends his head forward a bit to catch Vernon's eye, reaches out his hand. This one looks like he might bite, thinks Sears. Reminds me of . . . of something, but I can't place it.

Vernon hands Sears two of his fingers, and looks down.

An opossum! That's it. Sears shakes the boy's hand, turns to Wesley. "That's good work, son. You obviously know what you're doing. It's always a

40

pleasure to watch you work. But, ah, my wife dropped in for a—"

"He's going to let me do one," says Vernon, looking Sears in the eye for the first time.

"Excuse me?"

"I get to lay a brick."

"Oh. I didn't know Project Promise was actually up and running."

"It's not," says Wesley. "This is just extra."

"In any case," says Sears to Wesley, "my wife was over here with a casserole the other day and she had a very good suggestion. If this wall were moved a little toward—"

"You mean I *don't* get to lay one?" asks Vernon.

"Son, I'm one of the BOTA building and grounds committee members and this wall is my little project and I've got to explain something to Wesley, then I'll be on my way. So as I was saying, my wife suggested that if this wall were moved a little toward the middle of the room, that extra couch in the upstairs hall could be placed in the space over here." Sears walks around the wall. "In this area, and we'd be killing two birds with one stone. So, if you don't mind, I'd like for you to dismantle it, and start again about three feet over this way, right along here."

Wesley looks off—out a window.

"If we get it right this time," says Sears, "we won't have to worry about it again. This will be it— absolutely the last time."

Wesley shakes his head back and forth. He's trying to think of a Bible verse that will keep him calm. *Jesus wept.*

"It's just a matter of patience, son—until we get

41

it done the way it will be most beneficial. Patience is something we all have to learn. And until we learn it, we strive to learn it. Here, I'll help you get started taking this one down. This cement hasn't dried, has it?"

"It's mortar. No, no sir, it hadn't."

"Let me give you a hand." Ned Sears is proud that he's had a hand in turning Wesley Benfield around. On the other hand, as a college dean, and then provost, Ned has seen a seamy side of life he never knew existed. Students, some graduate students even, say g. d. They drink, they lie, they have sex with each other. Homosexuals get through Admissions—even after he and Ted have explained at length about how to detect them, male *and* female. As a man of God, it's sometimes all he can do to stay on the job. But as a man of God, it's his duty. He has been called by God from that little church back in Focal, North Carolina, to the college classroom, and then from the classroom to administration—the deanship, then from there on up to provost. His good brother, Ted, with whom he sees eye to eye on most things, and God, with whom he sees eye to eye on everything, have done the calling. And who knows, Sears thinks, where I might be called here on earth before I arrive in heaven to reap my heavenly reward on those long, deep streets of gold.

"Here, Vernon," says Wesley. "You sit right over here and scrape the mortar off these bricks I pile up. I'll go get a bucket of water to wash them in. Sit right over here. No, don't pull that thing over here. You'll have to sit on the floor, on the canvas."

"That's an ottoman," says Sears. *Thing*, he

thinks, is one of those words that usually has a better word to take its place.

Vernon sits on the floor, gets into his rocking position, and rocks. Wesley piles a few bricks in front of him on the canvas.

Ned Sears looks at his watch. "You boys keep at it. Nice to have met you, son," he says to Vernon as he leaves.

"This is easy," says Vernon, raking wet mortar off a brick into a little pile.

"Yeah, it's pretty easy. That's why it gets hard sometimes." Wesley looks at Vernon to see if he got it. He didn't. This boy may not have what it takes to be a brickmason, Wesley thinks. There's more to laying bricks than laying bricks.

Two hours later, Vernon jumps off the porch, opens the door to his Plymouth, steps in, cranks her up and and roars out across the lawn, headed home.

Wesley sits down on the couch in the TV room, puts his feet up on the coffee table, and starts thumbing through a *Newsweek*. Carla and Linda are sitting on bean bag chairs watching wrestling on Channel 9. Wesley looks at a picture of a girl in a bathing suit. He thinks about Phoebe. She has this kind of intelligence, Wesley thinks, but at the same time she seems so soft. Her light skin with those freckles, her blue eyes, her thick, fluffy red hair all combine in a way that speaks of magic and love. He thinks about being married to Phoebe, crawling into a big soft bed with her every night, on up onto her big soft breasts—and then sort of crawling all over her big soft body, finding places

43

to stop and settle in, massaging, kneading, before moving on to another place to settle into for a while, perhaps getting lost, not realizing which port he's in this time, all the while bringing her great joy, making her giggle and move all around.

She's got to be muscular in some parts, carrying all that weight around. That'll be good. He thinks about her making love with him, abandoning her senses. Going crazy. He tries to stop thinking about that—he knows it's not Christian—but he can't get it all out of his mind, her, these things, these forbidden things.

Then he wishes he could just make love to her without having to go through all the trouble and paperwork of getting married. But getting married is the Christian thing to do. That's final. He thinks about how she will look when she loses all that weight. He's not sure how much difference it will make. He thinks about the Bible, women, wet dreams. Whoops. He sings softly from the song he's still working on.

> *What do I do, Lord Jesus,*
> *with the women in my dreams?*
> *Some are—*

"Can you please be quiet?" says Linda. "Can't you see I'm trying to watch this?"

Dennis comes in with a ball cap in his hand, rubbing his forehead with his sleeve. White paint is on his sleeves, hands, face, hair. "Let's watch the football game," he says.

"We're watching this," says Linda. She looks up at Dennis. "Did you get any paint on the gutters?"

Dennis stops, stands, looking at the wrestling. "That stuff is fake, man."

"I seen blood on there," says Linda. "Blood ain't fake."

"They don't even hit each other," says Dennis. "Look, see that. Stand up, Wesley, come here."

Wesley slings *Newsweek* onto the coffee table, stands, walks around the table to face Dennis. Wesley is taller, thinner than Dennis.

"Now, when I swing," says Dennis, "you snap your head back. Watch this."

"Blood don't lie," says Linda. "I know."

"No, watch this. Okay, you ready?" he asks Wesley.

Wesley spreads his legs. "Yeah, I'm ready."

"First I'll do it kind of slow motion." Dennis draws back his fist and starts it slowly toward Wesley's face. When it reaches Wesley's chin, Wesley snaps back his head, ducks, grabs Dennis around the waist, lifts him and starts staggering around the room, holding him off the floor.

"Get out of the way," says Carla. "I'm watching television. Get the hell out of here."

"No profanity," wheezes Dennis.

Wesley drops and pushes Dennis down onto the couch, and starts out of the room toward the stairs in the foyer.

"Where you going?" says Dennis.

"Somewhere else. I got to get somewhere to think."

"That's a joke."

"Go cook us something," calls Linda.

"Go buy something. I'll cook it."

"I got to see this."

45

Wesley stops at the blackboard on Mrs. White's door: WE USUALLY FALL THE WAY WE LEAN. Not a very good one, he thinks.

He starts up the wide wooden stairs, up three steps at a time. He slows down, thinking. Did Jesus dream about women? He stops on the steps, turns slowly, and sits down. Jesus was a human man. He was flesh and blood—so he had food feelings. He got hungry. He must have *had* to have sex feelings—or he wasn't a man like the Bible said he was.

Dennis is coming up the stairs toward him. "This your new room?" he asks Wesley.

"No," Wesley says absently, standing. He turns and starts up the steps again, slowly, one step at a time.

This sex business can be a real problem, Wesley thinks, for somebody who becomes a Christian after screwing Patricia Boles and them other four. It's hard to forget how good that was. Nobody was getting hurt or anything. Maybe the Christian rules were made when it meant having a baby was automatically liable to follow making love with somebody. That must be what it was in the Bible times, before rubbers. Or maybe they had rubbers back then. Sheep bladders. Or maybe it's just a plain fact that you're supposed to stay away from somebody unless you're married to them.

He walks into his room, flips on the light. Ben's not in.

Wesley bunches his pillow against the dark pine headboard of the bed, sits on the bed and leans back against it, crosses his legs. He thinks about how he can tell Phoebe about his life so far. About how hard it's been. But good, too. About how Mrs.

Rigsbee got him out of the rehabilitation center and then on the road to salvation.

Now, how should he think about Phoebe and sex—sex with Phoebe—and be a Christian at the same time? Is he *supposed* to think about sex and her at the same time, he wonders. Maybe tonight after they ride over to to the mall they can go somewhere to neck. Lake Blanca. If he could just get his lips on those red lips of hers and then sort of wander over to her cheek and kiss one of those freckles, then another one, and another one, and tell her he wants to kiss every single freckle that's ever been born on her body. . . . Neck a little. It'll be all right with her, probably. He stares straight ahead at the two photographs from an old 1986 blues calendar that he's had since 1987: Son House playing bottleneck on a National Steel Dobro with the Clifton Dowell Blues Band, Bukka White playing a National Steel solo. And then he looks over at the two posters he ordered over a month ago and just got: Taj Mahal playing a National Steel solo, and Skip James standing, eating from an ice cream cone in one hand, and holding a National Steel by the pegboard, the bottom resting on his foot.

He'll have to try to describe to Phoebe what makes him feel like he's going to die if doesn't get to play bottleneck blues on a National Steel Dobro. That'll be a good thing to talk about. Feelings. But how can he sort of talk about sex? Maybe he can find something in the Bible that could get him started.

He picks up his Bible from his bedside table, removes his Sunday school quarterly from inside, turns to the concordance. Mrs. Rigsbee, sitting on her faded green couch that she kept saying needed covering, taught him how to to use the concordance. He finds "love." The first entry is "passing the l. of women," II Samuel 1:26. He looks it up.

I am distressed for thee, my brother Jonathan; very pleasant hast thou been unto me: thy love to me was wonderful, passing the love of women.

Is this guy a queer? thinks Wesley. He reads back a ways to see who this is, talking. David. It looks like David. The one who killed Goliath and went on to be a king or some kind of head man. He was the shepherd who wrote poetry and played the harp. David is one of the main guys in the whole Bible. Wesley adjusts his pillow behind his back. David likes Jonathan's love better than women's love. He's got to be talking about friendly love, not the other kind.

He reads the first twenty-five verses of the chapter.

He reads them again. What David is doing doesn't seem fair at all. Wesley reads the chapters one more time. David has gotten somebody to kill a man with a funny name who a day or two earlier had been *ordered* by Saul to help Saul commit suicide. It looked like Saul knew he was fixing to get killed anyway by this army that was on the way, and what happened was Saul asked this young guy to help him kill himself, and so he did, and then he took Saul's crown and bracelet to David and gave him the bad news. David was so sad he tore all his clothes off, but then instead of *thanking* this guy, he told somebody to *kill* him, and somebody did—right on the spot. David wouldn't even do it himself.

There are all these names and all this stabbing—people lined up facing each other across a pool and then "they caught every one his fellow by the head, and thrust his sword in his fellow's side; so they fell down together. . . ." *Killing their buddies who are killing them.* Committing suicide—a sin. All kinds of wild stuff here. He hadn't read any of this before—hasn't even heard about it, even though he's been sitting in Sunday school and church every Sunday, regular, for over five years.

Wesley pushes himself up higher against the headboard. There is a war going on. Then something about David having all these sons. But . . . wait a minute. He rereads carefully. His second son, Chileab, was "of Abigail *the wife of Nabal the Carmelite.* . . ." Now *David*, Wesley thinks, the one Mrs. Rigsbee had all the time gone on about writing poetry and all that, is here having a son by somebody's else wife, and whoever was writing all this down didn't have nothing to say about it, nothing, and whoever was writing it down was getting it straight from God, which seems like it means that God must not have found any big problem with David going to bed with another man's wife. Else, God would tell the man who was writing it down and there'd be all kinds of excitement washed up.

Wesley closes the Bible slowly on his hand. He looks up at the poster of Son House, his sunken cheeks, the bottleneck on his ring finger. If God didn't get upset with all that with another man's wife, Wesley thinks, then maybe I shouldn't worry about what I been thinking about doing with Phoebe, especially if we're going to end up getting married. At least I shouldn't worry about *thinking* about it. I'm getting this stuff from the Bible, the very Bible, where every word is true. He reads chapter 3, verse 14:

And David sent messengers to Ishbosheth, Saul's son, saying, Deliver me my wife Michal, which I espoused to me for an hundred foreskins of the Philistines.

Gosh almighty! he thinks. This is amazing. The *Indians* weren't all that bad. They at least scalped your *head*. But these guys. . . . Yow.

And then this: "And Saul had a concubine." What was a concubine? Wesley lays the Bible down, open, gets up off his bed, goes over to Ben's desk, opens a drawer. There's a pocket dictionary in there somewhere. There. There it is. Concubine. Concubine. . . . Well, this is . . . this is amazing. It didn't make any difference if you were married or not. Why hadn't they read all this in the Sunday school class at Listre Baptist, or down the street at Mt. Gilead!?

He starts back toward the bed, stops, stands in the middle of the room. It's coming to him. Of course! He looks straight up at the ceiling—at the water stain shaped like Florida. *The people at Sunday school were just reading what they wanted to.* He gets back on the bed. This part is as much the inspired word of God as any of the other parts. And for sure David and Saul, since they were some of the main people in the Bible, didn't die and go to hell. If David and Saul did all that with that young man that brought the news, thinks Wesley, and all that with all those other people's wives and concubines, it don't seem to matter too much what me and Phoebe might do on a little old date. The people that would get upset would be Dr. Sears and people like that. And what they've been doing is skipping all this other stuff in the Bible: not telling what all is in there, just reading what's in those Sunday school quarterlies, so that none of this other stuff gets read by anybody.

Wesley decides to check out another reference to "love." Sol. 2:5—"I am sick of l." What is "Sol."? He remembers going over all those abbreviations with Mrs. Rigsbee. The book of Solomon? Is that it? Has to be. Where would that be? He finds it— it's only a few pages long. He reads a little. He is astonished—they weren't even married as far as he can tell, and this girl was black. It's. . . . He reads the whole thing again, gets a pencil from his bedside table, and reads it once more, underlining.

5

*P*HOEBE IS EATING POPCORN. SHE USUALLY GETS A red-and-white bag of popcorn from the Popcorn Palace beside the pet shop. It's not in the Ballard Nutrition Plan, but it's only a matter of a mere ounce or two. She and Wesley are at the mall, sitting on a bench across from the pet shop, in front of Dean's Delicious Cookies. Wesley has his foot on a big clay tree pot. A little girl sits on a bench across from them, eating a cone of chocolate ice cream.

Wesley pulls his heel up onto the bench and grasps his knee with his arms. "Do you know what a concubine is?" he asks.

"Yes, I do."

"Well, *David* had one."

"Most kings in the Old Testatment did."

"Are you . . . did you join the church in Michigan?"

"Yes. When I was twelve. Methodist."

"Did they call it 'getting saved'?"

"I think some did and some didn't. But we changed to Baptist after my mother died. Father likes the Baptists. It's a good thing he does because he's trying for a job at Ballard."

"Here?"

"Yes."

"Oh. But don't that strike you as funny?" says Wesley. "About the concubines and all."

"Why?" Phoebe reaches into her bag and gets three pieces of popcorn. Three pieces is not a handful. She's trying not to gobble a handful at a time. She's about to starve. She's supposed to eat in small amounts and chew well—one night last week the president of Ballard University gave a talk called "Chewing for Health Means Healthy for Jesus."

"It didn't seem to bother nobody then, but it would now," said Wesley. "I mean the kings won't married to all them girls."

"That was the custom."

"Custom? Well, somebody needs to preach about customs. Why don't somebody preach a sermon about customs, about how that was okay then, okay with God, because whoever wrote about it in the Bible didn't mind about all that going on—and they were getting it straight from God and they didn't write down anything about God not liking it. But you let somebody set up a concubine today and Sears and them would go crazy. But it don't look

53

like God would say anything—now—because he didn't then."

Wesley reaches for some popcorn in Phoebe's bag. Phoebe draws back, catches herself, offers the bag.

"Sears and them might could go straight to somewhere in the Bible," says Wesley, "and show what a sin it *is*. I can show what a sin it *won't*." Wesley takes popcorn into his mouth from his flat palm. "Or maybe they're saying God changes with the times. Do you think that's it? They're not saying that, are they? Maybe I ought to figure out how to preach about it myself."

Phoebe has never known a boy who got excited about religion. Randy, fishing. Pete, army things. Maybe he'll suggest we park somewhere tonight, Phoebe thinks. He's good looking, good looking in an interesting and intriguing way, and his feeling for me seems genuine. More and more people will be appreciating me as I get smaller. I'm down eleven already. Eleven! All I have to do is lose that much about nine more times. I won't know myself. And here's a man, Wesley, intriguing and rather mysterious, who seems to love me like I am, right now. While I'm in North Carolina there is no reason I can't spend some time with him, perhaps even become slightly intimate with him. Maybe he'll suggest we drive somewhere. I need somebody to touch me. It would feel so good, just some soft touching.

Wesley is watching the kittens in the pet shop window. He feels Phoebe's hand slide over his. His eyes widen. He wets his lips. Oh, man. Oh, man. This is a sign. Everything is going just right. He feels salt on her fingertips. She wants some loving.

He needs to say something that's about sex and at the same time not about sex, and then they need to ride out to Lake Blanca to look at the moonlight. He's got to think how to set things up.

"Have you read Solomon?" he asks.

"Maybe a verse or two." That piece of popcorn looks like a man with a long beard, she thinks. It looks like God.

"I had this operation one time."

"Operation?" She puts the piece of popcorn in her mouth.

"On my, ah, thing." I need to get back to Solomon. This is not exactly right. But if I just say 'thing' it'll be all right. We can talk about it. Maybe she'll talk about it. Who knows?

" 'Thing' ?"

"You know, my thing."

"Wesley!" Her fingers, holding another piece of popcorn, stop in front of her mouth. She stares at him.

"It was so big it was causing my shoulders to slump."

"Wesley!"

"They had to trim it down."

Phoebe looks away and then back at the boy who is suddenly talking so wild.

Wesley hesitates. She seems a little bit alarmed or something. "No, I'm, I'm kidding. Phoebe. Okay? Okay, Phoebe? I really did have a problem in there though. When I was little. A little boy, I mean. And they had to look in there."

"Look *in* there? Wesley . . ." Phoebe is frowning, shaking her head back and forth.

"I was about ten. It hurt so bad they had to give

me a towel to chew on. I think it's when I started snapping my fingers when I hurt."

"Snapping your fingers?"

"Instead of hollering when I hurt, I just kind of moan and start snapping my fingers. I got that habit somewhere, and I think it was then, when they gave me a towel to chew on."

Phoebe sees a little boy, pain in his eyes. "Oh, Wesley. That sounds horrible. What caused it?" She realizes she shouldn't have asked. This is very odd. She shouldn't have asked. He'll be encouraged.

Wesley is encouraged. "I don't know. It all started at the orphanage. They had this swimming pool and I was in the shallow end one day. I was about six." Wesley doesn't remember telling this to anybody before. "And I tried to pee and I could feel it just plain stop, about halfway out. So I went up to Terrone, who was taking care of us—this black guy—and told him and he says, 'You just need a commode.' So I went inside and tried the commode, but it was the same thing. I was just plain stopped up. So I went back outside and told him and he went inside with me and stood there and watched while I tried to pee. Not a drop. Nothing."

Wesley is sure he's never told this before. He's going too far. This is private stuff. But he can tell that Phoebe is interested—she's watching him, her blue eyes wide.

" 'I got to go *real* bad,' I told him. I could tell he was scared. He drove me to the hospital in the bus. There weren't no cars. I was starting to hurt—I had to go so bad.

"We got there and the doctor came in, pulled my pants down, and there was this nurse in there too.

56

They put me on a table on my back. He went over and washed his hands two or three times and came back with this little pan of water, or I guess maybe it was alcohol, and in there was this thing that looked like a wire." Stop here, Wesley tells himself. She's looking funny.

This is certainly not about religion, thinks Phoebe. What's going on here? Do people down here tell these sad little stories about their . . . their members?

"He took that and he took my, my pisser in his cold hand"—Wesley crosses his legs—"and stuck that wire in the end and it scared me and I started crying again and he went all the way down in there with it, then he pulled that out and stuck a little tube in there—"

"Wesley!" Phoebe slides away on the bench a few inches.

"—and once he got that all the way in—"

"Oh, goodness, Wesley!" She looks away and then back at him. "I don't think I should hear any more. I'm sorry."

"—he. Well, anyway. Then every one or two months—"

"Wesley, please." This is so strange.

"Okay. Okay. That's all." Maybe he can finish telling her some other time. Or maybe that's it on that subject. Closed. Over. Done with. He feels a little bit lonely. He ought to move along to something else sort of on the same subject. "But it's never affected my, ah, you know, sex life so to speak. Everything's in order, except nothing's been *used* really since I joined the church. You know what I mean. But I've been trying to figure out if

57

that's the way God wants it to stay. I mean, like what we were talking about. I *am* a Christian. And I've stopped everything like cussing and stuff—even got my roommate to stop, pretty much. But you know, people had sex in the Bible when they won't married and it didn't seem like no big deal."

"But it's one of God's laws." Phoebe's hand stops in the popcorn bag. He's very odd, she thinks. I wonder if he's just interested in sex things, and operations, and for sure my breasts, and nothing else. I wonder if he's one of those. Something is getting dangerous. Phoebe thinks of some of those crime shows she's seen on television, pictures of a woman's partly nude body. "I'm a little tired," says Phoebe. "I think I'd better get back to the Nutrition House."

Tired! Get back! thinks Wesley. Oh NO.

This could be a horrible danger, thinks Phoebe. He *is* in a halfway house. A halfway house. Why has it taken so long for the red flag to go up? There is something rather 'smooth' about him.

"Okay," says Wesley. "If you think so." What did I do wrong? Why can't you just tell women things. You can't do nothing right with women. Oh, well. Maybe she is tired. She's got a lot of weight to carry around. "Want to get a little supper somewhere?"

"No, I'd better get back, thanks. I'm sorry. I just need to get back now. I have some things I need to do."

In the Nutrition House parking lot, Wesley looks across the car roof at Phoebe as she gets out. She won't look at him. Should he follow her in or what? Go on back to BOTA House now? See if she'll sit on the porch for a while? Where can he go now?

It's not even dark, not even suppertime. He was hoping to have her at the lake soon after sundown, getting her hot and bothered while he got hot and bothered. Sort of like old David.

Wesley follows about two steps behind Phoebe to the back door of the Nutrition House. He's trying to think of something to say. "I'll see you later," he says. "I'm supposed to get on over to see this boy I'm going to be teaching bricklaying to, anyway. Retarded boy."

"Oh, okay." More strange stuff, thinks Phoebe. "Good night, Wesley. I, I enjoyed it."

You sure got a unusual way of showing it. "Yeah, me too."

As he walks along the sidewalk, taking extra long strides, he thinks hard about what he can say to Phoebe the next time. Something to get things rolling again, to get things changed back around so they can get on out to Lake Blanca. Get some loving going. He thought for sure all the Bible stuff would work, but it didn't somehow. I shouldn't have said a word about my pisser. Why did I get off on all that? I should have talked about movies or Mrs. Rigsbee or something.

Dear God, guide me to do Thy will. Direct my thoughts in ways pleasing to Thee. Help me to know what to say. Wesley tries to sense God up there through the trees passing over his head, way up there somewhere in the dark blue and yellow sky where some stars are already appearing. He buttons his denim jacket.

But what about David and them? I'm probably going to end up acting more like David and them

59

than like Jesus. I don't see how I can help it. I can't expect to be like Jesus. He was perfect.

Wesley decides to walk on over to the Sunrise Garage where that Vernon boy and his daddy live. As he walks by the Ballard campus, he thinks about going to the library to look up "love" and see what he can find that might help out.

The sidewalk changes to a dirt path. Wesley comes to a small sign nailed to a post: "Sunrise Auto Repair Shop," with a rising sun painted on it. An arrow points down a dirt street. They said there would be signs. In a few hundred yards, he sees a bright light at the top of another, larger sign. Just beyond the sign is a tree stump, then a car engine on the ground, then the garage. Cars are parked around. A light is on inside the garage. A light burns on the front porch of the little house next door. That must be where they live, Wesley thinks. They said it was just the two of them. Living there inside four walls. No long halls with boys and boys and boys.

Somebody is working in the garage—Vernon's daddy, probably. As he gets closer Wesley hears some blues music—bottleneck guitar, maybe Dobro—coming from inside the garage. The garage is just big enough to hold an old orange GMC school bus. The top of the bus almost touches two long sets of fluorescent bulbs shining from the ceiling.

Wesley stops at the garage entrance, leans against the door jamb, looks around. The floor is packed black dirt. He remembers his old habit of looking at windows and back doors to see how they were locked. He lets himself look for a back door, doesn't see one. Two windows, one locked, one he can't tell. No nails. He could pop a pane. Too easy. Mr. Jackson is standing on a chair, bending over the bus fender and looking down on the engine. Wesley starts toward him.

"Howdy."

Holister Jackson looks up, steps down off the chair, grabs a rag and wipes his hands. He has a big plug of tobacco in his cheek. He spits into a dirt-filled bucket near his foot. "Hey. 'Wesley,' is that right?"

"That's right. I like that music you got on there."

"Yeah. Me too."

Wesley walks on over, wondering if Mr. Jackson is going to offer his hand. He doesn't.

Mr. Jackson drops the rag onto the fender. "That's about all I listen to. Blues. I play a little country for variety, listen to the radio once in a while."

"That's a tape?"

"Yeah. Son House."

"I got a poster of him," says Wesley. "I'm learning to play bottleneck myself. I'm going to buy a National Steel Dobro when I save up enough money."

Holister grabs his rag, wipes away a grease spot on the fender, then spits. He looks at Wesley. "I got one of them."

"You got a *National Steel*?"

"Yeah, I got two or three guitars and things I traded for car work. The National Steel is back there in the corner."

"Damn—I mean namn." Wesley steps over engine parts, a stool, heading for the back corner,

61

looking, staring, seeking the outline of a National Steel.

"It's behind that oil barrel, under them rods, in that yellow shammy bag. It ain't been played in ten, twelve years and the strings are off it. Did you say, 'namn'?"

"I just put *n*'s on the front of cuss words. A habit, kind of." There. Wesley sees the bag. It's deep in the corner. "Can I . . . ?"

"Yeah. Get it out. Just be careful."

Wesley grips the Dobro neck through the bag.

"Be careful with it. It's the real thing."

Wesley lifts it. "This is yours? A National Steel?"

"This guy traded it to me for some car work—a guy from Alaska. Hand it here."

Outside there is a noise coming—somebody making a sound like a car. Vernon. He comes running into the garage. "Eeerk." He stops right up close to them, opens his car door, gets out, stares at Wesley, and sticks out his hand. "Oh, it's Mr. Killer Diller." Vernon's wire-rimmed glasses, smudged with fingerprints, reflect fluorescent lights.

"Yeah, I guess so," says Wesley. "How you doing?"

"Tolerable."

Holister has laid the Dobro on a table, and is pulling it out of the yellow shammy bag. There are no strings and no strap on it. The chrome body has no shine, no luster.

"Can you play that thing?" Vernon asks Wesley.

"Not like it is." A golden, precious idea suddenly blooms in Wesley's head. "What if I shine it up? Put some strings on it, maybe practice on it a little bit, give it a little use?" Wesley stops breathing. The entire weight of the universe is waiting to collapse onto a "no," to lift and fly with a "yes."

Holister spits, wipes his mouth with the back of his hand, looks hard at Wesley. "I guess so. It ain't doing nothing back there in the corner. Just be careful with it."

Wesley raises both hands over his head, clenches his fists. Joy to the world, the Lord is come, let earth proclaim the sound. "I'll have to wait until tomorrow to get the strings and ..." Wesley touches the guitar—picks up a rag, rubs out a little circle, which shines.

Vernon looks at Holister. "There ain't no food in there except them tomatoes."

"And a strap," says Wesley. "I already got some bottleneck teaching books. I've been—"

"How about in the freezer?" says Holister.

"Nothing in there except that froze fish. I don't want no fish."

"Go get something then." Holister reaches in his pocket, pulls out a wad of bills, separates a ten and several ones. "Get some of that ham and a loaf of bread and some other stuff." He looks at Wesley. "You want to eat with us?"

"Well ... I was going to cook something at BOTA House. I usually cook my own meals. I could ah ... could cook here. If it's all right with you." Wesley sees himself inside four walls cooking for this family of two.

"All right by me. I just got to get back to work. Just don't let Vernon around no electricity by himself—cooking and all that." Holister spits into the can. "Yeah, I wouldn't mind eating something that

63

was cooked. You want to drive the truck—to get something?"

"Well, yeah." I don't have a driver's license, the voice in Wesley's head says. But no words come from his mouth. He's looking at the National Steel. He can't keep his eyes off the National Steel. "You're going to just leave that there?" says Wesley, nodding toward the Dobro.

"I'll bring it in the house when I come in. The truck's parked right around the corner, there in the parking lot. It's the red one. Keys are in it."

As Wesley walks to the truck, the National Steel is in his eye, lying there on the table—its body out of the yellow bag, with the little shined spot near the resonator. By the time he gets some Semi-Chrome polish on that thing, rubbed in, let set, wiped off, it'll shine like the sun and moon together. And the sound. He already hears the sound.

Wesley and Vernon get into the red-and-white '65 Ford truck, slamming the doors. Wesley places both hands on the steering wheel, his feet on the clutch and brake, checks their resistance. The inside of the truck smells wonderful: tobacco, oil, gas, and dirt. A *National Steel.* Thank you, thank you, Jesus.

"It pops out of second gear," says Vernon. "Daddy goes from first to third. You put it in first, then put in the clutch, then you put it in third."

"Yeah, okay. I know how to do that."

"Daddy lets me drive it in the parking lot sometimes, but I don't ever get out of first. He lets me drive cars in and out of the shop, too. And when he finishes working on that bus, he's going to let me drive that. It's ours. We're going to drive it to

64

the Grand Canyon and live in it on the way and on the way back."

"That ought to be fun." Wesley cranks the truck, drives out of the parking lot toward Food Lion. He is sitting high off the ground, higher than he's ever been in a car. He can look down on the roofs of cars from up here. And this truck is loud, the busted muffler making a sweet, deep, powerful sound.

"This thing is fun to drive."

"It's a truck," says Vernon.

6

IN FOOD LION, VERNON PUSHES THE CART. WESLEY takes his time, picking through the okra until he gets enough small tender shoots for three people. Then he gets three big Irish potatoes, flour, cornmeal, and Wesson Oil.

After he's selected the pork chops, Wesley heads across the store along the pet supply aisle to see if he can find Vernon, who has wandered off. He needs to know what kind of dessert they like. He sees Vernon standing at the doughnut display, with one of the little doors slid back, reaching in.

Vernon grabs a doughnut, looks at it, puts it back and gets another one, inspects that one.

"Hey," says Wesley. "You're supposed to use those little sheets of paper. Right there."

"For what?"

"To pick up the doughnut. You're not supposed to use your fingers."

"My hands are clean."

"Just use one of those papers, Vernon."

"What about the people that makes them. Somebody makes them with their hands. Everybody handles everything with their hands." Vernon nods toward produce. "Ain't you ever seen people pick up fruit over yonder and look at it and then put it back?"

"That's different. That's fruit."

"People eat fruit. People eat fruit; people eat doughnuts. The same naked hands that pick up fruit pick up doughnuts. What's wrong with that?"

"Just get some doughnuts and let's go."

"I already got them. Lined up right in there. Those are the ones I picked. We need to get one of them apple pies and some ice cream, too."

Back at the garage, Wesley follows Vernon across the yard toward the house. The screen is loose and torn and the porch is very small, just large enough for three aluminum lawn chairs. As they go in through the screen door Wesley remembers the day he first saw Mattie Rigsbee's porch, the day he came to steal the pound cake and was trying to open the inside screen latch with a match book cover through the crack when she came out there, not even catching on to what he was trying to do. He still visits her, and her porch is closed in with tight solid screen and is roomy, with potted plants, lots of chairs and a swing.

Here at the Jacksons', the light green front door to the house is soiled—a black halo around the door knob. One of the three little windows in the door—the bottom one—has no glass, and is covered from the inside with duct tape. The bottom corner of the door has been sawed off, to make a hole for a dog or cat, it looks like.

Inside, a bare light bulb is in the middle of the living room ceiling. On a bare wooden floor sit two slipcovered chairs with ragged armrests, a couch, and against the wall, a piano with a metal folding chair at the keyboard. There's a hole in the wall above the light switch near the entrance to the kitchen. On top of the piano is a cassette recorder and a stack of newspapers, and on top of the papers is something that looks like a hammer—with a funny head. On the wall is a picture of a boy in tight blue pants from the Middle Ages or something. It is in a plastic frame and covered over with clear plastic.

Vernon and Wesley unpack the groceries in the small kitchen, and soon Wesley is working at the kitchen counter beside the sink. Vernon sits down at the power-line spool turned on its side for a kitchen table and rocks back and forth.

"We just eat sandwiches mostly," Vernon says. "One week ham, one week chicken salad, one week ham. Sometimes we eat bacon or frozen pizza."

Wesley is cutting okra on a dinner plate. "Y'all need some kind of cutting board," he says.

"We use knifes."

"No. I mean something to cut the stuff *on*. I know you use a knife."

"We got all the stuff Mama left, but we don't use it, hardly."

"Come over here and I'll show you how to do

this okra. It's fun. Where are the pots and pans? I need two frying pans, and a pot."

"Under there. Daddy don't let me touch the stove or nothing that has electricity to it. I blowed up some things."

"Come here. Here, see how I've cut these up? Just little hunks about that big."

Vernon stands beside Wesley, watches, rocking.

"This old lady taught me," says Wesley. "I got to live with her for a few years. She gave me some great food, and told me about Jesus. Then . . . See? Like that. You just pour them in a paper sack like that and then pour in about . . . that much flour. See? Then you just shake it up." Wesley shakes, puts the sack down. "Then . . . the pots and pans are under here?"

"Yeah." Vernon steps back while Wesley squats down and looks into the cabinet.

Vernon stands with one hand on the counter, rocking.

"Can't you hold still?" Wesley asks. He finds a frying pan.

Vernon freezes, breathes faster. "What do you mean?" he asks, looking down at Wesley.

"All that rocking back and forth," says Wesley, sitting back on his haunches and looking up at Vernon, whose eyes are getting bigger and bigger behind his thick wire-rimmed glasses. A redness is creeping up into his cheeks. A sneer comes to his mouth—which suddenly springs wide open. Vernon leans down toward Wesley's face. Wesley leans back on his heels, loses his balance, then catches it. And then Vernon roars in Wesley's face. He roars as if he were falling off a cliff. Wesley smells his breath, faint onion, something else.

Then Vernon turns and runs out of the kitchen, through the living room, out the front door.

Wesley, holding the knife and frying pan, goes to the front door, steps out on the porch.

Vernon is standing in the middle of the yard, screaming, turning around and around in little short steps, his fists against his chest.

Holister walks rapidly from the garage. When he reaches Vernon, he yells, "Hey! Hey. Hey," right in Vernon's face.

Vernon blinks hard, once, twice, looks at Holister, stops turning, starts rocking. But he's still crying out softly on each breath. Then all of a sudden, he screams again. Holister grabs his elbow and starts him toward the house. "Hey! Hey!"

Wesley stands back as Holister pulls Vernon, screaming again, onto the porch, by him, into the house.

"He just went crazy," says Wesley as they pass by him.

"He went crazy before he was born," says Holister. "I got to go slice him a tomato."

"A tomato?" Wesley follows them in. Holister releases Vernon and Vernon heads toward a back room, stooped and swaying, moaning.

"Yeah. What'd you say to him?" says Holister, going into the kitchen. "Something about his rocking?"

"That was it." Wesley follows.

"Don't do that anymore." Holister opens the refrigerator, pulls out a tomato, gets a dish, looks

70

around, takes the knife from Wesley and slices the tomato.

"Okay. Sorry. I didn't know. A tomato?"

"A tomato. Got to slice him a tomato. You can hunk it if you ain't got no plate."

Holister starts toward Vernon's bedroom. He carries a plate holding a sliced tomato and a fork.

There is a loud scream-yell from the back of the house.

"I got it! Here it comes," shouts Holister, headed for Vernon. "Hold it! Hold it."

Wesley stops in the living room, sits on the piano bench, waits, looks around. In the corner there's a cat's basket. Inside is a navy-blue pillow covered with yellow fur.

Holister and Vernon walk back into the living room. They both sit down on the couch.

In through the hole in the bottom of the door comes a bony yellow cat with a crook in the end of his tail. Holister lifts both feet, slams them onto the floor. "Git!" The cat scrambles, springs for the hole.

Vernon, rocking while he sits, eats the sliced tomato, cutting off pieces with his fork.

"Tell him," says Holister.

"I'm sorry I got mad." Vernon, rocking and chewing, looks at the floor.

"That's okay."

"It's something we don't talk about," says Holister. "I should have told you. If you get in that problem again, a tomato will usually straighten everything out. I try to keep one in the truck. 'Course I forget and they rot." He goes out onto the front porch.

Wesley rubs his fingers along the piano bench.

71

He hears Holister open the porch door and spit. Wesley looks around, takes the hammer-looking thing from the top of the piano. "What's this?"

Vernon looks up. "That's a piano tuner."

"He tunes the piano," says Holister, coming back in. Then to Vernon: "You all right now?"

"Yessir. Just need to finish this." Vernon cuts off a piece of tomato with his fork, puts it in his mouth, chews.

"I got to get back on that carburetor," says Holister. "Behave yourself, now."

Back in the kitchen, Vernon watches as Wesley opens the bottom cabinet door again and gets out another frying pan and a small pot and places them on the counter and looks in them.

"What's that in there?" says Wesley. "Rat—"

"Rat turds," says Vernon. "We got roaches, too."

"Yeah? Well, we'll rinse it out. You got any detergent?"

"Over there."

"That's soap."

"That's what we use."

"Well, yeah, but ... you think you got a bigger piece than that?"

"No."

"Okay, let's just clean this out and I'll show you a little bit about cooking."

"That cat catches them rats but other'ns keep coming."

"That's okay. You boil or fry something, it's clean. Heat kills germs." Wesley places the frying pans on the stove eyes. "There we go. Okay. Now. You can put some flour in a plate and kind of dunk these pork chops. About this much flour. See. Then we'll fry them. Pour some of that Wesson Oil in that frying pan. Right there, that's Wesson Oil."

"Why?"

"To fry the pork chops."

Vernon picks up the bottle, stands there rocking, pours a few drops.

"Fry, like french fries, fried chicken, fried whatever. You got to pour some more. That's—WHOA. WHOA! No. No, man. Look. Now, we got to get rid of some of that." Wesley's hands are white with flour. "Can you pour that back in the bottle? Go slow. No. No. Use that little spout on the side of the pan. WHOA, it's . . . here, let me do it." Wesley pours the oil back into the bottle. "Now." He looks around. "You need some paper towels to clean up that oil."

"We just got that rag hanging over there."

Wesley looks at the rag, looks around for something else.

"We got some old newspapers, too."

"That's okay. The rag's all right. Let's just get these pork chops on. Now, see the thing is we got to cook them so they don't dry out. The way you do that is, once they get going good, we can put a little water in there, and leave the lid cracked on top so they don't get soggy, but they don't dry out either. Then we can turn up the heat at the end to crisp them up a little. See what I mean?"

"I don't think so."

"Well, you'll see. Now we got to get this okra started. Now watch. You just cover the bottom of this pan good with oil. Turn it on medium high. Let it get hot. It'll just take a minute. Now when it gets hot we'll pour the okra, with the flour on it, in there and stir it up so the grease and flour kind of mixes and then they'll fry and we'll put a little salt on there and they'll be the best things you ever eat. Okay, let's drop one in there to see. . . . Yeah, see, it's fizzling a little bit so we pour all of them in there, stir around a little bit. That's going to be good." Wesley does a drum roll on the counter.

"Now we can mix up the cornbread. You can do that. Get a bowl out of there. . . . No, bigger than that. . . . That one's good. We can cook it where the pork chops are when they get done. So now, pour some cornmeal in there. No. Cornmeal. Yeah, that's cornmeal. Go ahead and pour some in there. Wait a minute. What was that?"

"What?"

"In the bottom of that bowl."

"I don't know. You gone fry it, ain't you? You said heat kills everything."

"Yeah—it'll be all right. Now, just run some water in there from the faucet. Okay. . . . No, it'll take more than that. . . . Good. . . . Now pour some salt in there and mix it all up. . . . That's right. That's it. Just mix it."

"That's easy." Vernon's rocking is getting faster and faster. His head is rocking back and forth rapidly, his body rocking very slightly.

"Oh hell, I forgot the potatoes," says Wesley. "Can you peel a potato?"

"I think so."

"Well, here, peel this, and I'll peel these. Go ahead. I got to put some water on."

Wesley rinses out the pan. "These things ever been washed?"

"They just been sitting in there since Mama left."

Vernon's body is still while he peels his potato, but his head rocks back and forth rapidly.

Wesley puts the pan, with water, on the stove, turns the eye on high, then peels and slices two potatoes, puts them in the pan, turns to get the potato Vernon has peeled. It's on the counter: once the size of a baseball, now it's a grape.

"Yow, you peeled it all right. Now, maybe you can just peel those peelings. Look, see, just get the peeling off here. You can eat all this. See, you want to leave all the white stuff you can—that's the potato part."

"I know that. I know what the potato part is. I just had to get down deep to get everything off."

"I didn't know you were doing that. Now, we'll slice it and put it in with the others, and ... you don't have a potato masher, do you?"

"Maybe over in that drawer."

Wesley opens the drawer, looks around. "Here's one. Now let's do that cornbread."

"Does that mean my mama used to cook mashed potatoes?"

"I guess it does."

A short while before lights-out at BOTA House, Wesley gets comfortable on his bed, his back against a pillow which is against the headboard, the National Steel in his lap. He polishes slowly, carefully, with Ben's Semi-Chrome polish. Then he shines the aluminum with one of his own undershirts.

Ben, sitting by the window in the cane-bottomed chair, tilts back, pulls a joint from his shirt pocket, puts it in his mouth, and lights it with a kitchen match. He takes a drag, thinks about this white boy.

He at least don't look at you funny, don't snoop around. He leaves your stuff alone, don't steal, it seem like. Plays good bass. Crazy about the blues. Crazy about that old Dobro.

"You going to get caught smoking that stuff," says Wesley. "You get caught and you be in trouble sure enough." Some people have a hard time learning when to grow up, he thinks. If it hadn't been for Mrs. Rigsbee, Wesley is sure he'd still be involved in growing up. Mrs. Rigsbee and Jesus got him grown all the way. Got him mature about love anyway, he figures.

"Anybody who knows what it is ain't gone tell," says Ben, "and Miss White, she think it's pine straw burning." He takes a drag, holds his breath, releases. "If I hear some strange footsteps I eat it. If I get burn it won't be no worse than pizza." Ben thumps ashes into a gold-colored glass ashtray on the radiator. "I got the stuff hid so good I can't even find it myself."

"You just better be careful. You could get on to something that'll kill you." Wesley thinks about how good a cold beer would taste, then pushes the thought from his mind. It comes back.

"This stuff just make you feel good," says Ben. "Relax you a little bit. You don't go crazy to have it, and it ain't no three hundred dollars a day. I seen too many like that, man."

"Did you have some kind of drug problem, you know, with the other stuff?"

"Well, yeah." Ben looks at Wesley. "I had some problems, and I took some dope. Yeah, that's right. Don't give me no—"

"Hey, I won't say nothing. I didn't mean noth-

76

ing." Wesley gently applies some more of Ben's polish to the Dobro.

"People got wine, liquor and coffee and shit, shnit, nit, whatever," says Ben, "to get them away from the cold. You got people zonked out on caffeine, nicotine, all over the place. You got secretaries brewing it up and serving it to gray-suits in every office building in the United States, man. They on drugs all over the place. Glassy-eyed all over the place." Ben drops the front legs of the chair to the floor, thumps ashes in the ashtray. "Then the man come down on me. But I admit in the long run it would have ruin my life. But this stuff ain't nothing," he says, looking at the joint between his fingers.

Wesley thinks about how his own life used to be. Those three or four acid trips. The pot. Coke. The beer, grain alcohol and grape juice—Purple Jesuses. He thinks about David and the concubines, eyes Ben, wonders whether he should bring up something about Phoebe. He has roomed with Ben for six or eight weeks, knows him pretty well. Ben don't mind talking about things. And he agreed to Wesley's cuss words rule—put an *n* on the front.

"You ever dated a big woman?" Wesley asks.

"Yeah, I dated some big women. Then, too, I dated some that's big in parts."

"I'm talking about big all over. In parts, too."

"Yeah. My cousin. In the eighth grade. Skating. She'd run into the damn wall and shake the whole place, the whole skating rink. I remember that, man." Ben pinches the joint between his thumb and forefinger, puts it to his lips and draws. Then, holding the joint under his nose, he sniffs the drifting smoke. "Why? You thinking about taking out that rather large chick you been talking to over at the Fat House?"

"I just did. I mean she gave me a ride to the mall. But if I had a car we'd do something else. She's really good looking in the face. I mean *good* looking." Wesley shines a spot on the back of the Dobro. "She's got these blue eyes and thick red hair and freckles, and I've dreamed about a woman like that all my life I guess, but never, you know, met somebody I could get my hands on—somebody I know. I mean I seen some in the movies. Like that Ringwald. What's her name?"

"I don't know no Ringwald. But that woman you're talking about has got big tits, too. *Big.* I don't have to say 'nits,' do I?"

"Naw. It's just, you know, the bad words."

"I got so I'm putting *n* on that stuff when I'm at work. I'll be working on a tire and I'll say, 'Nod-namn.' People look at you funny."

"Good. Cussing is a bad habit."

"You're crazy, man."

"But about Phoebe. You know, she's like, proportioned well."

"Yeah. But man, she's fat. She's real fat."

"She's losing though. She's already lost right much, around ten or fifteen pounds, I think." Wesley gets up, stands the National Steel in the corner, takes off his shirt, throws it into the closet. He sits down on the edge of the bed in his white T-shirt, looks over at Ben. Ben's eyes are closed, his head is back.

"What I do," says Wesley, "is I just think about her in one place at a time. Like her hands look regular, and I figure you get a small-enough place, it's just like any other girl. Know what I mean? But it's them blue eyes and all them freckles and that thick bushy red hair that I like. And I don't mind the big tits, either." Wesley gets back up on the bed, adjusts himself against the headboard.

Ben picks up an old *Sports Illustrated* and fans smoke out the open window. "Them big, giant, mountain tits. You let her fall on you and you be dead. You better be careful. She roll *over* on you she mash you flat. My brother broke his back one time on his motorcycle with this fat man riding behind him. The fat man landed on top of him and broke his back. This actually happened. He's still hurting from it, and that happened in, let's see, 1981. He gets pain so bad he can't eat, can't sleep, can't nothing." Ben presses the joint in the ashtray, pulls a toothpick from his pocket and puts it in his mouth.

"Most I ever hurt was when I was ten and they went up my pisser," says Wesley. Maybe he shouldn't tell Ben either. "I was stopped up. Man, you talk about hurt." Maybe he should. "They had something that looked like a fountain pen on the end of this long tubelike thing that was hooked to a machine," says Wesley. "They touch that thing to the tip of your pisser, and it's ice cold, and then they stick it in and start it up the channel."

Ben crosses his legs—tight—takes his toothpick out of his mouth, covers his crotch with his hand. "Nodnamn." He looks out across the empty lot and on across the road to the lights on the front porch at Nutrition House.

"It got me started to snapping my fingers when

79

I hurt. And you know what? Listen to this. You know what they give me for pain?"

Ben looks back. "What? Bufferin?" He smiles with half his mouth. He's thinking about when he hurt most. Easy.

"They give me a towel—to chew on," says Wesley. "I tell you. I was telling Phoebe. Got her attention. I think I might have told her too much. Upset her or something." Wesley leans forward and repositions the pillow behind his back, leans back again, tucks a strand of hair behind his ear. "She couldn't take it."

"Most I ever hurt," says Ben, "was when I sprained my ankle and got it put in this cast. Next day it started swelling and it didn't have nowhere to swell to."

"Yow."

"I even got shot in the back one time and that didn't hurt like that ankle."

"Shot in the back?"

"Yeah." Ben props one foot on the radiator. "This guy sideswiped my car one time and kept going and I chased him down in my car. I had this honey with me. He was stopped at a stoplight, so I got out and opened his door. He turned sideways, holding onto the steering wheel, and kicked at me. So we got in a fight. His car was running, you know. He kicks me outen the car and then tries to run *over* me—with the car. I start running down the street and finally he gets me pinned in this doorway to this building—I think something snapped in him, you know. We were downtown Bishopville about two A.M.—and he starts ramming the building trying to get at me, but I'm back up in there where he can't."

"You mean he's in his car?"

"Yeah, he's in his car. It was the craziest thing I ever seen. I could see him in there behind the steering wheel, you know"—Ben holds a pretend steering wheel—"and his eyes were great big like this and he was going ram-bam, then he'd throw it in reverse, burn rubber, hit the brakes, drop it in drive, burn rubber, them eyes great big, and come at me again, ram-bam."

"Like a cop show, sounds like, don't it?"

"Well, yeah, sort of. Except it won't. This was real. Then he leaves, and before I can walk back down to my car, he pulls up beside it—he's done drove around the block and there he is, down the street in this parking lot beside my car. I start running, because the honey's still in my car, you know. When I'm almost there he opens his car door, and he's got a pistol in his hand but I don't believe it's real at first, see. He aims it at me and I keep running at him because I couldn't believe this was like real. He shoots." Ben stands up, spreads his legs. "And the bullet goes between my legs through my pants, man. I feel it zip through. Zip. Right there." Ben zips his finger between his legs. "So I turn around and start the other way, dodging left and right like they do on TV—like this, you know—and he shoots twice more. The second one gets me down low in the back. Felt like somebody kicked me. I didn't know it at the time but the bullet came out my stomach and fell in my underwear." Ben turns around, sits again. "They found it when I got to the hospital. So, anyway, I round the corner at this building and turn down another street still running and get up on this porch and knock on the door. I'm feeling the blood down in my *shoe*, man. Slushing. This woman comes to the door, great big old eyes in these thick glasses looking like she's looking every which way with both eyes, you know, and I tell her what's wrong, and ask her to call me a ambulance. She goes in and, and comes back out with a mop handle and starts hitting me with it. No shit, no nit, man."

"Hitting you?"

"Yeah, this is like some kind of nightmare."

"Yeah."

"So I leave there, and next I'm in this back yard where there's a light up on this little deck. I get up the stairs and knock on the door and two guys come and I tell them what happened and then I lay down on their deck beside this little steak grill. They called the cops, and the last I remember is laying there on that porch, and blood swooshing out my shoe, and the lights from the cop car swirling all over the place. I tell you, I felt bad. Yeah, I felt bad." Ben puts the toothpick back in his mouth. "But it won't *nothing* like that ankle, as far as sheer pain is concerned."

"Did they catch the guy?"

"Yeah. He got five years." Ben puts his other foot on the radiator.

"That don't seem like much. Seems like it was attempted murder."

"They said they proved it wadn't premeditated, that it was a 'fit of passion' or something. Damn." Ben picks up the *Sports Illustrated* again and fans smoke out the open window.

Wesley reaches over, turns on the fan, stands up, empties change out of his pocket and puts it in the top dresser drawer. "I guess that did must of hurt— the ankle." He gets his toothbrush and tube of Colgate off the dresser. "I'm turning in. I'm tired."

"When I *die* it won't hurt that bad."

Wesley walks down the hall toward the bathroom and thinks about Phoebe. He wishes he hadn't rushed things. When she loses that weight she just might turn out to be the most beautiful woman in the world. The Nutrition House has a good record. People come from all over the United States to that place.

Wesley squeezes toothpaste onto the brush. Just a tiny, tiny bit. It costs money. Project Promise should make a difference with his money situation—it pays minimum wage. And might be a bridge to a full-time job or something.

He smiles in the mirror and looks at the teeth Mrs. Rigsbee gave him. They look good. Four crowns up top in front, and a partial plate on bottom—a little wire with two teeth on it. He keeps it in a handkerchief on his bedside table—takes it out after lights out. It gives him trouble when he's eating sometimes. Tries to pop out.

Mrs. Rigsbee paid for it all. Decent teeth meant almost as much to her as Jesus. He sees her walking along her back sidewalk toward the garage, her sweater hiked up in back, going to feed that little dog. That little dog she's still got, Perkie, and talks to like he's got some sense.

He thinks about his job, jobs. There is something in laying brick that he can't get from playing music, and there is something in playing music he can't get from laying brick. By the time he's twenty-seven or twenty-eight, he'll be a full-time blues guitar player and maybe married. Phoebe will be down to fighting-weight by then, and even if she's not ... those blue eyes and freckles, light skin, and red hair go together like magic.

She won't stay stuffy too long, he thinks. He can write her a song or something.

He leans over the sink and takes water in his mouth from the faucet, being careful not to touch the faucet. That's another thing Mrs. Rigsbee hammered in—don't put your mouth on the faucet. He rinses, spits, turns off the water and heads for bed.

> *I got teeth growing in my head,*
> *Some have gone their way.*
> *Othern's came to fill the gaps,*
> *I'm glad I didn't have to pay.*
> *Oh, Mrs. Rigsbee, thank you thank you*
> *For everything you do.*
> *Now when I smile, now when I eat,*
> *My mouth is just like new.*

7

SUNDAY, IN THE MORNING SERVICE, PHOEBE IS INTRO-
duced as the new kindergarten teacher at Mt. Gilead Baptist Church, just off campus. Wesley had
planned to sit with her, but he has decided not to
push his luck. He watches her from his seat in the
back. She sits way down front.

After church, Ted Sears, standing with some
other men by the front steps, calls out to Wesley
and walks over to meet him so they can talk in private a minute or so on the church lawn, here beside
the trimmed hedges in the warm fall sun.

Sears holds out his hand. Wesley takes it, remembers to squeeze firmly. Wesley feels this guy's
power, and is wondering why in the world he would
want to talk to him, Wesley.

"Wesley, son, it's good to see you, and I felt like I ought to mention to you that your name has come up in my office as an example of some of the things we're trying to do at Ballard in the name of Christian Education."

Wesley looks into Sears's squinting eyes, then notices tiny specks of white spit in the corners of his mouth.

Sears moves to avoid the direct sunlight. "If you'd be interested in taking a class or two, we want to help you out, see if we can't sign you up. And I must add, in all fairness and sincerity, that I am a bit concerned about your faith while you're living in the midst of people who don't necessarily choose the Christian life."

"How do you mean?" Wesley throws his hair back out of his eyes.

"Oh, just that the backgrounds of some of your fellow clients at BOTA House are not necessarily conducive to a Christian lifestyle."

"Oh, yeah, well, they've had some weird things happen to them and all that. I, you know, try to help them with things about the Bible and all. My roommate has about stopped cussing."

"That's wonderful. Sounds like you're witnessing by example. Did you know that that's the Ballard University motto?"

"Yes sir. I seen it up at the top of some letters I been getting about Project Promise."

"Right. And that looks like it's going to be a darn good project, if I say so myself." Sears glances over Wesley's shoulder. "Well, son, just know that we're thinking about you, praying for you. Every day."

"Yes sir. Thank you. I'll pray for you, too."

"Good. Good. Stop in to see me sometime." Sears is looking at Sally Lattis, who's in charge of the flower arrangements. He needs to let her know he noticed the arrangement today—and appreciates it.

"Maybe I will," says Wesley.

"What's that, son?"

"Stop in to see you."

"Oh, yes, you do that. I'll be seeing you. I need to get over and speak to Mrs. Lattis."

Wesley watches him walk off. He looks like he's in pretty good shape, a fighter pilot, an old fighter pilot, but still a fighter pilot. Somebody said he swims a half mile every day.

On this Sunday, as on most Sundays after church, Wesley rides home with Mattie Rigsbee for Sunday dinner. When the weather's good they sit out on the porch and eat ice cream.

"Good ice cream," says Wesley, raking off the bottom of his spoon on the bowl's edge.

Mrs. Rigsbee is sitting in a cane-bottom rocking chair with her arms resting on the rocker arms. She's eighty-six years old, and seems to Wesley to have gotten a little smaller in the last few years. She's wearing her old brown sweater with several sewn-up holes. "It's Breyers," she says. "I don't usually get Breyers, but they had it on sale. If you bring your girlfriend from the diet house, we'll have to hide it. Do you want a little more?"

"Yeah, if you got it."

Mattie starts to rise from the chair, stops. "I thought I taught you to say 'ma'am.'"

"Yes, ma'am. I just don't get much chance to practice it. Except with Mrs. White."

"You ought to have a chance to practice it around the college." Mattie stands, starts for the kitchen, stops. "What did I get up for?"

"You asked me if I wanted some more ice cream. I can get it."

"I got it. Sit down. Give me the bowl."

She is a good old woman, thinks Wesley. He looks down the road at where he parked the car that time he was with his old girlfriend, Patricia—how many years ago?—when he was going to steal some of Mrs. Rigsbee's pound cake. That was the day he was trying to open her screened-in porch door—the same day he had some of that pound cake which was better than anything he'd ever tasted.

"There you go," says Mattie, handing Wesley the bowl. "You want a glass of water?"

"No ma'am."

Mattie sits. "How's your work coming?"

"Okay. I'll be teaching this mentally retarded boy to lay brick. We start tomorrow."

"A college student?"

"No. High school. Retarded."

"Why are they teaching *them*?" Mattie rocks slowly in her chair.

"I don't know."

"Looks like they'd be teaching the ones who can learn something."

"This one's pretty smart, I think. He plays the piano, and can tune one. But he looks like a possum."

"A problem?"

"A possum."

"Oh, a possum. He looks like a possum?"

"Yes, ma'am."

Mattie sits still, looks at Wesley with an absent stare. "These are strange times." She seems lost for a minute. "What about your new girlfriend? When you going to bring her by?"

Wesley thinks Mrs. Rigsbee looks more tired than usual. "Oh, I don't know. I think you'll like her—better than Patricia, anyway. She's real nice."

"Patricia was okay. If she just hadn't wore so much make-up and had come out a little more. What's the new one's name?"

"Phoebe. She's the one they introduced in church this morning—new in the kindergarten."

"The big one?"

"That's her."

"She looked right nice."

"How come you never told me about David sleeping with all these concubines and all that?" Wesley asks. "And Song of Solomon?"

"What about it?"

"Don't you know about Song of Solomon?"

"Well, I know a little about it. It was written by Solomon. It's about Christ and the church, I think."

"Oh, no it ain't."

Mattie hitches her skirt out from under her, smooths it on top. "Listen, before I forget it—I got so I can't remember nothing much—let me tell you what happened to me yesterday. I about got hurt sure enough.

"It was so nice out I decided to sit out on the porch steps and cut my toenails. It wadn't too cold, you know, for late October. Use your napkin, son. One of the worse things about cold weather is that

89

you don't have no place to cut your toenails without flinging them every which way in the den. And I'm getting so about the only way I can get to my feet is to be sitting down on some steps.

"Well, I was over there yesterday, top step, clipping away when the phone rang. Of course I had to get up. Well, scrunched down on those steps it takes me forever to get up, so finally I got straightened out, and you know those steps are pretty high—eight or nine steps up and I was at the top—so when I was turning around, my heel slipped over the edge of one and I started losing my balance backwards. The only thing to grab was the screen-door handle. I did, and pulled it open, toward me, you know, but I was going on backwards so I had to grab onto the door with my arms and legs and everything, and I want you to know I rode that door right on around until it was all the way open and I was up against the porch screen looking down in that rhododendron that's there beside the steps. So I kind of kicked against the porch and the door goes swinging back till I can get back down on the steps and in the kitchen and answer that phone—on the last ring. It was Alora. She always lets it go nine rings. I was counting the whole time."

Wesley spoons out the last of the ice cream from his bowl. "Well, it's a good thing you didn't fall down the steps. You ought to be more careful."

"I am careful. I take about twice as long to do everything as I used to, and I get in Roses or somewhere and forget what I came in there for. And lose things. My Lord. Worse than Eloise Rymer. Did I tell you about that?"

"I don't think so."

90

"Poor thing's getting so she takes those little bitty steps, you know, and she was walking down Compton Street with Dot Jenkins, over there close to the bakery I think it was, and she walked right out of her underpants. Man standing there calls out and says, 'I think you lost something, ma'am.' She stops, turns around. He points. She walks back and looks at them for a minute and says, 'Oh, no, they ain't mine.' "

Wesley laughs, puts his hand to his mouth—in spite of the fact that he's had new teeth for four years now.

Later, Mattie Rigsbee and Wesley pull into the parking lot of the Shady Grove Nursing Home. They've come to visit Mrs. Rigsbee's sister, Pearl. When Wesley lived with Mrs. Rigsbee, she brought him out here to the nursing home before Pearl was ever over here and got him talking to these people, so he feels pretty much at home. He feels like he's doing good, visiting. Sometimes he feels like he's doing too much good, so sometimes if there is no attendant in the TV room he walks through and changes the channel just to hear the canes bang on the floor. Somebody *threw* a cane at him the last time he did it.

Before they leave the parking lot, Wesley points to the front tire on Mrs. Rigsbee's new Plymouth. "You're over the line two feet."

Mattie stops, turns, and stands, holding her pocketbook with both hands in front of her stomach, looks at the wheel, then at Wesley. "Listen, son, when you get your driver's license you can complain about what I do with mine. This parking lot has several hundred parking places and about twenty cars, so if I were you I wouldn't worry about it."

Wesley holds the lobby door open for Mrs. Rigsbee, then follows her in. She's getting more stooped, he thinks. Grumpier, too.

Old people, mouths open, look up at them. One old woman gets up and follows them—at a distance—down the hall.

Miss Emma sits in a wheelchair tied to the handrail along the wall. "Sonny, can you untie this thing, please?" She smiles broadly at Wesley.

Wesley knows that Miss Emma has twice wheeled her chair down Interstate 40. "How are you, Miss Emma?"

"Want an M&M? Untie me and you can have an M&M. Did you know I used to have everything I wanted?"

"Yes ma'am. No, thank you. I got to get on down the hall—and see Mrs. Turnage."

"How are you today, Miss Emma?" says Mattie.

"I'm fine. Did you know I used to have everything I wanted?"

"You told me that."

Pearl is sitting in a rocking chair in her room. Her hair is white, and she is heavier, even sturdier looking, than Mattie. Pearl's face has always reminded Wesley of an Indian's. Her skin is still tough and dark. She rarely talks any more, so Mattie talks mostly.

"I went in Revco yesterday to get some corn pads," says Mattie. "You know you used to could get twelve for thirty-nine cents. Did you know that?" she says to Wesley.

"No, I didn't know that. I don't buy corn pads."

"Well if you get corns you will. Anyway"—Mattie looks back at Pearl—"this was a box of nine for $1.44, marked down from $1.99. But the saleslady was some foreigner and I was thinking so hard about *her* I didn't notice until I got home that she had charged me $1.99. If I hadn't needed one so bad I would have taken them back. Well, they were just the right size for this bad corn I got, so last night I got one out to put on. You pull off this backing and there's this thick, sticky part that goes all around the edge, you know." She looks at Wesley. "You ever *seen* a corn pad?"

"Not that I know of."

"You'd know it if you had. Anyway, about the time I got ready to stick it on the corn, for some reason I had to get up to do something, and I thought to myself, I'll finish this in a minute. Well, when I got back to the couch I couldn't find the pad—you know, the one I'd got ready to stick on— so I looked all around—under me, under the cushion. I went over to the kitchen, looked all around the sink, come back, and on and on. Couldn't find it nowhere.

"Finally I decide I'm going to have to get another one out of the package and take the backing off of that one and all that. The first one was sure enough lost. Well, I want you to know that while I'm pulling the backing off the second one I feel something stuck to the heel of my hand and bless pat there it was—the lost one. When those things stick, they stick. I didn't think I was ever going to get it off. When I did there was a red circle on my hand for over an hour. So—I saved it. That one. Used the other one. I'm not about to throw away a—what would that be?—a twenty-cent corn pad."

Wesley studies Pearl's room to see if there are any new pictures up. She's got family pictures sitting all over the place. Her mother, her father, her mother and father together, her brothers and sisters individually and in groups. The one of Mrs. Rigsbee is when she must have been about twenty, with lace up around her neck and her dark hair piled on top her head. No smiling. No smiling in hardly any of the pictures, except one of the late ones of Pearl and Mrs. Rigsbee together. There are early and late pictures of Pearl and Mr. Turnage, and a wedding picture.

Mrs. Rigsbee is talking about what she had for lunch at the K and W yesterday. She talks about every item, separately. Fish, the fish sauce, peas, which were mushy, though not as mushy as they have been, carrots, slaw. Next she talks about what Netta Gilbertson had, and then Savannah Smith. Then she starts in on what the people at the next table had. Pearl follows the stories with her eyes on Mrs. Rigsbee's face.

Wesley decides to wander around. He stands. "I'll be back in a minute."

"We don't have too much longer. I want you to visit some with Pearl. She's happy to see you. I want to tell her about what all you been getting involved with at the college. Why don't you tell her?"

Wesley pushes his fingers through his hair. "Well, they're starting this program thing where I'll be doing some teaching, and they might let me take a class over there, too."

"He's doing real fine," Mattie tells Pearl.

Pearl manages a weak smile and nods her head. She nods her head at a picture of Robert and Elaine, Mattie's children.

"Oh, they're doing all right, I think," says Mattie. "Elaine called the other night. She's thinking about changing jobs again. She's had a good offer."

Wesley walks down the empty hall toward Miss Emma.

"I'll give you an M&M if you'll undo this wheelchair," says Miss Emma.

"Okay."

"Oh boy, you're such a nice young man." She starts to sift through the M&Ms in her lap.

"I'll just get a few myself," says Wesley. He reaches down and gets a handful of M&Ms. "Whups, I hear Mrs. Rigsbee calling. I got to get on back. Sorry."

"You said you'd untie me."

"I got to get on back down the hall."

"I used to have everything I wanted."

"Yes ma'am. See you later."

Wesley sings the blues:

> *Old people, old people, all over the earth.*
> *If old people could turn new,*
> *Just think what they'd be worth.*

8

THE BOTA BAND MEMBERS, PLUS SHANITA, PULL into the WRBR parking lot in the BOTA House van at seven twenty-five and pile out. "The Good Morning Charlie Show" starts at eight A.M.

WRBR is housed in a small brick building, without windows, in the middle of a field.

Sherri Gold stretches and yawns. Shanita hooks three fingers inside the waistband of Larry's black pants and follows him along toward the building. Wesley holds the door for them all, tries to trip Ben as he goes in.

There is a man in an office straight ahead, a small sandy-haired man with his feet propped up on a desk. "Come on in here," he says. He has a deep radio voice.

The band files in.

"My name is Jake Davis," says the man. "Oh, I didn't know there'd be but four."

You'd better get another *chair*, honky-face, thinks Shanita. I ain't about to stand while Goldyass sits.

"My name is Jake Davis," says the man.

Shanita looks around. "We need another chair," she says.

"Oh, hey." Jake Davis hurries out, and brings back another chair. He sits behind his desk and pushes up the sleeves of his yellow V-neck sweater. "I'm the general manager here," he says, "as I guess Sherri told you. All I need now is just a song, or a piece of a song, since there hasn't been any audition. Buddy told me about—Buddy Loggins— told me about Sherri and all, and he's got great judgment, so I'm not worried, but as a matter of procedure we need an audition, you know, technically."

The band starts singing "Time Ain't Long." After a few bars, Jake Davis holds up his hand. "That's great. I just needed to know, you understand. Procedure. So . . ." He picks up a clipboard and mechanical pencil from his desk. "What was it? 'Noble Defenders of the Word'?"

"Right," says Sherri. "This radio stuff'll be good for exposure. But I gotta admit I ain't used to being up this early. I bet you ain't either, are you, Shanita?"

What you say, bitch? "Oh yeah, I get up early all the time." What is your *prob*lem, you cracker? Shanita slides down in her chair, folds her arms.

"Radio separates the men from the boys," says Jake, filling out the form. "Now, let me tell you something about Charlie." Jake lights a cigarette with a metal flip-top lighter, leans back in his chair. "Charlie knows you guys are going to be here, but he won't get here until about five till. Like I say, he's not a morning person. But listen ..." Jake draws on the cigarette, blows smoke, looks at each band member, and at Shanita.

Don't look at me, you pasty-faced white boy.

"Here's the important message," says Jake, "that I need to get across to you folks. 'The Good Morning Charlie Show' is a call-in show. But there aren't that many calls, usually. So Charlie gets excited about a call. *Real* excited. If you're in the middle of a song and that phone rings, you can forget the rest of the song. Charlie will snap the phone up and start talking, and you folks will have to get quiet. Okay?"

"It ain't especially okay with me," says Ben, looking at the others. "I don't especially like my music interrupted."

"I'm sorry. It'll have to be that way."

"Maybe we could start up where we left off as soon as the call is over," says Wesley.

"I don't know about that," says Jake.

"This exposure will be good," says Sherri, "either way."

Exposure my ass, thinks Shanita.

Over on the Ballard University Campus, the sun shines warmly. The dew sparkles on freshly mowed grass—probably the last mowing of the season. Lumps of grass will be sucked up into the appropriate machine before ten A.M.

On Monday mornings, Ballard U. exudes a special air of importance and confidence. Monday mornings are set aside for the weekly breakfast meetings, when President Ted and Provost Ned meet with the executive committee to discuss the charting of Ballard University's course through another week of witnessing by example. Ted's secretary, Mysteria, Miss Summerlin 1939, has picked up the doughnuts at Dunkin' Donuts on her way in to work. Mysteria Montgomery is a faithful and loyal secretary. She's short, a bit baggy, and wears excessive lipstick. Her hair is dyed a very dull red. This Monday morning, as usual, she has made the coffee—regular and decaf—and has set out pencils and legal pads on the big meeting table in Ted's pine-panelled Executive Meeting Room. The leaders meet at seven-thirty A.M. sharp. Sharp.

The oldtimers on the executive committee are able, dedicated men. They mean to save Ballard University from wayward and sinful trends brought on by the modern world. Each of them wears, with pride, at least one day per month, his green blazer with the yellow Ballard bulldog emblem on the breast pocket.

Stan Laurence, the new assistant treasurer at Ballard University, arrives at the meeting at seven-twenty, sits at his usual spot at the table, and stares out Ted's wide, spotless picture window, studying the differences in the grilles of Ted's silver Chrysler New Yorker and Ned's white Lincoln Continental. I wish I had one payment on either one of those cars, he thinks. Stan, a former trade book sales representative, has been at Ballard less than a year. He read in *Business Week* last week that, with his four children and Ballard's salary for beginning administrators and professors, he now lives below the poverty line. Just last night he and his wife decided that to avoid embarrassment about using the food stamps that they are now eligible for, and plan to use, they should shop at the Listre Winn Dixie, ten miles away, rather than at the Food Lion near campus.

Present for today's breakfast meeting are six men: the Sears twins; the acting dean, Bob Reynolds; the treasurer, "Big Don" Summers; athletic director and special projects coordinator, Coach Mack Guthrie; and assistant treasurer, Stan Laurence—the new man.

Under discussion is the filling of the academic dean post. Two resumés have survived the cut. The faculty senate had asked for three finalists, but Ted and Ned decided the budget would not allow travel funds for three men to come for interviews.

This business of faculty senate power gets to be a problem at some universities, Ted knows. Professors and such deciding policy. He knows that parents, at least Ballard parents, want their children ultimately—in terms of overall policy and so on—in the hands of a few good administrators, not in the hands of dozens of faculty members and instructors who have come onto the campus from out there in the world where no telling what has influenced them in no telling which ways—politically, as well as theologically. You can't be too careful. Carelessness on these kinds of matters will come back to visit you on a cold dark night. At Ballard, final authority rests with final responsibility, the president's office. And this, Ted knows, is the way trustees and parents want it, or would want it.

"Seems to me, all things being equal," says Big Don, the treasurer, "we should go with the military man, this Trent fellow. He's going to have some experience with a chain of command behind him. And he had those three tours in Vietnam. Plus, he gets about $23,000 a year just for waking up every morning. Money we won't have to pay him."

"That's right," says Ned. "And this other fellow's wife is a Methodist."

"They must go to separate churches or something," says Bob Reynolds.

"She might not go at all."

"What?" says Big Don, turning up his hearing aid.

"She might not go at all."

"That's right," says Bob. "She's a Methodist."

"Find out about all that, Don," says Ned, "and let me know."

And this other fellow, thinks Stan, this military man, could wear a Mickey Mouse hat and chew shrapnel.

Stan misses sales more than he ever thought he would. He actually gets to spend *less* time with his children now than he did, and he's beginning to feel pretty certain that he's going nowhere in this new job. All the benefits, as in "salary plus benefits," were supposed to round out the low salary, but that hasn't happened. And Big Don, his boss—the man he will be replacing—has recently mentioned that he'll probably stay on an extra year before retirement. Stan was told—by Sears, the provost—about the impressive qualifications of all the applicants he beat out for the job. But Coach Guthrie, the athletic director, told him the main reason he got the job was that he was the only applicant who'd been in the Marines.

President Ted, steely-eyed, strong-chinned, glances at this fellow Stan, this new fellow—who could, should, be jumping in and agreeing, and he's not, thinks Ted. You'd think he'd say something agreeable about this military thing. He's a Marine. Or was. But he just doesn't speak up enough. He looks out the window too much. And darned if he doesn't need a haircut. Ted decides to kid him about that after the meeting. Maybe he can take a hint. Some long hair on faculty is unavoidable. But on administrators? Not at Ballard. Long hair on the outside of the head is a clear sign of confusion on the inside of the head.

"Let's go with Trent," says Ted, "unless the interview goes bad. We don't need to be taking chances. But let's bring both men down so the search committee can interview them both. Any discussion or objection? Good. Can you see about getting plane reservations and meeting them at the airport, Coach? Ned, you handle it with the senate and trustees if they ask about it. Tell the senate we have a 'private and confidential' on the reasons for two instead of three finalists."

"What's a 'private and confidential'?" asks Stan.

Ted looks at him. Why is he asking that? "It means private and confidential."

"For what kinds of things?"

"I'm not at liberty to discuss it—it's private and confidential."

"Oh."

"This Trent fellow has a daughter at the Nutri-

102

tion House, he said in his letter," says Ned. "That's another plus."

"Mysteria was saying something," says Ted, "about . . ." He presses his intercom button. "Mysteria, what were you saying about—"

"His daughter's name is Phoebe," says Mysteria, "and she's gone out several times with the brickmason at BOTA House, the one in the Project Promise who got written up in the newspaper. Mrs. White was telling me all about it."

"Yes, I couldn't—"

"He's one of the ones in the Christian band they've got over there with the blacks in it."

"Yes, I knew I'd heard something about that. Thank you, Mysteria."

"How's that band working out, anyway?" Coach asks Ned. "What kind of music are they doing now?"

"Working out good," says Ned. "They're doing just gospel music."

"Do they jump around when they sing? Anything vulgar?"

"Oh, no. I dropped in the other day while they were practicing. They sound very good, in fact. They do nice harmony. And that Benfield has turned into a real nice young man. The one they did that newspaper article on. He's a darn good bricklayer, too."

"I talked to him at church the other day," says Ted. "He goes to Mt. Gilead, you know. And he's there every Sunday. How are those blacks working out, by the way? In the band."

"Fine. Far as I can tell. There are two of them.

They're supposed to play on 'The Good Morning Charlie Show' one morning this week."

"That's what I heard," says Coach.

"I think it might be this morning, in fact," says Ned.

Ted presses his intercom button. "Mysteria, do you—"

"This morning. They're on now. I got it turned on. WRBR. Mrs. White left that message yesterday for you to listen in."

"Oh yes. Turn that radio on over there, Coach." Ted tilts back in his high-back leather office chair and folds his hands under his chin.

When Good Morning Charlie arrives, the band is waiting in the studio, sitting around a long, battered table with four microphones.

"Good morning, folks," says Charlie. He's tall and thin and wears a straw hat and white shoes. His face is too full and red for his thin body. He drops a manila folder on the table, sets his briefcase in the corner. "This the gospel group?"

"The Noble Defenders of the Word," says Sherri.

Charlie sits down in his swivel chair at the panel, picks up the clipboard from a small table beside him. "Let's see," he says, "we've got an extra here. I only count four on the program brief here."

"She's with me," says Larry.

"Could I ask you to sit back against the wall there, ma'am, if you don't mind," Charlie says to Shanita, "so I don't get confused about who I'm talking to."

"Fine with me," says Shanita. You red-faced-queer-fag-honky-cracker shit.

"Well, gang, I'm sure Jake has covered it all," says

104

Charlie. "In about, ah, one minute thirty—" Charlie presses a button. "Jake, did you set the clock?"

"Check."

"Yes or no?"

"Check—yes."

"In about one minute and ten seconds I'll hit the music switch, theme song will come on, and we'll be on the air." He reaches to the wall, flips a switch and a red ON THE AIR light comes on over the door.

Jake's voice comes in over two speakers, up on the wall: "How do you read?"

"Loud and clear," says Charlie.

". . . two, one, zero."

An instrumental version of "Nothing Could Be Finer Than to Be in Carolina in the Morning" comes over the speakers.

"Morning out there, fine neighbors, this is Good Morning Charlie, bringing you 'The Good Morning Charlie Show,' from WRBR, 1310 on your radio dial, straight from the outskirts of Summerlin, North Carolina, the field pea capital of the South. We've got a fine gospel group with us today that you've heard of for sure. The Noble Defenders of the Work. If you haven't heard of them, it's oooonly a matter of time."

Charlie's shoulders are twitching. He's spraying the words, thinking ahead, getting the timing, the intonation, the rhythm all moving together. He picks up an index card. "Speaking of field peas, Pickett's grocery is the place to pick up all those fresh items on your grocery list. Mr. Pickett packs them in daily from local farms only. If you don't want those old cardboard tomatoes, cucumbers, and green peppers from who knows where, then you shop at Pickett's, where quality and local freshness make the difference." He slips a tape into a tape recorder. "And now, before our first number from the Noble Defenders of the Work, a message from Bethel Hardware." He hits a button and the commercial starts.

"These mikes are cold now," he says.

"It's 'Word,'" says Sherri.

"Excuse me?"

"Noble Defenders of the Word."

"Oh, it says 'Work' here. Let me change that. Now, let me just see if I can pronounce these names." He picks up the clipboard: "Sherri Gold, Ben Ashley, Wesley Benfield, and Larry Ledford. Easy enough."

The commercial is over. Charlie hits a switch. "Remember," he says into his microphone, "if you've got a question for the Noble Defenders this morning, or a song request, or if you've got a recipe to share, or an item for sale, or if you're looking for a special item of interest to purchase, give us a buzz at 667–6627. That's 667–6627. We'd love to hear from you. All lines are open. . . . All lines *are* open. And now let's hear from the Noble Defenders of the Word. We've got them right here in our studio—WRBR, 1310 on that radio dial and don't you touch it. Now. Our guests. Welcome to 'The Good Morning Charlie Show,' folks," Charlie says to the band. "First I'd like to ask—"

The phone rings.

"Wup, hey, we've got a call—already."

Ben looks at Wesley, rolls his eyes.

Charlie picks up the receiver. "Stand tall, reach high, look far. This is Good Morning Charlie with the, the, ah"—he finds his clipboard—"Noble Defenders of the Word."

The voice comes clearly over the speakers. It sounds like a woman without teeth. "I've got a whole batch of tomatoes that didn't seal, you know, when I was canning them, and I, and I want to sell them."

"Okeedoekee. What's that name and number?"

"Erma Phillips. 667-4831."

"Okay, Erma. That's 667-4831 for those of you who didn't have a pencil ready—which has already happened to me once this morning. Several jars of tomatoes that didn't seal. And how much are you asking per jar, Erma?"

"Oh, about fifty cents. 'Cept they'll have to pick them up."

"Okeedoekee. Give Erma Phillips a call at 667-4831 for some freshly canned tomatoes that didn't seal. She'll tell you how to find her house. Thanks much, Erma."

"You're welcome. I . . . I would have give them to my mother and them but they've all gone to the beach for two weeks. Myrtle Beach."

"Right, Erma. Thanks for your call. And good luck with your tomatoes."

"I don't know why they didn't go to Caro—"

Charlie presses the phone receiver button. "Wups. Mrs. Phillips? Sorry Mrs. Phillips. We lost Mrs. Phillips there, but you give us a call at 667-6627. 'The Good Morning Charlie Show,' straight to you from WRBR. 1310 on your dial. And we'll be back in one minute with more from the Defenders of the World, a gospel quartet from the Summerlin area." He picks up an index card. "But first

107

a word from Husky Pesticides. Husky. The strong but safe pesticide. 'Acts against the pest, but doesn't hurt the rest.' Strong, quick relief from corn-ear worms, soybean pod worms, cotton boll worms, and tobacco bud worms."

Sherri fingers her little two-holed pitch pipe. "We might not get to sing at all," she says to Wesley.

Charlie swings around in his swivel chair, his index finger to his lips. Wesley notices tiny blue blood vessels all over his nose.

After the commercial, Charlie introduces the band and they sing, uninterrupted by a call. After "Never Turn Back," and two commercials, they sing "Time Ain't Long," and then "Twelve Gates," which is interrupted by two calls. One is for a car for sale, the other is a request for "The Old Rugged Cross," which the band doesn't know.

"They sound almost professional," says Ted, his hands still folded under his chin. "Do you think you could get them to learn 'The Old Rugged Cross'?" he says to Ned.

"I don't see why not."

Ted thinks about the possibility of a Ballard University–sponsored gospel band. There is a formal link-up with BOTA House now—Project Promise. He could funnel a little piece of the Project Promise grant to cover expenses. He catches sight of himself in the gold-framed mirror on the opposite wall. "Here's an idea," he says. "What if we sent these people on a little tour here in North Carolina. A *little* tour, inexpensive. We could see about using the BOTA House van—Ned, you could check with Rittner at Prisons. Maybe send Mrs. White along.

'The Noble whatever-it-was—from Ballard University.' We could more or less sponsor them—and downplay the halfway house thing until the Benfield boy gives his testimony in the middle of the performance, say, or at the end. Check with Legal, Ned, and see how much we can do of this and still not be liable for any, you know, problems that might arise. But anyway, this Benfield boy could represent what we're doing here for the underprivileged. The boy is intelligent. I've talked to him."

"What about a grammar class for him?" says Ned.

"Yes. Get on that, but even if he comes across a little underprivileged in that department, that might not hurt."

Charlie takes off his headphones, turns and looks at the band members—a moment of pleasure. He's been in the business twenty-eight years. He's come in here at seven fifty-five A.M. five morning a week for the last twelve years. He's had winners from the National Hollering Contest, banjo pickers who couldn't pick banjo, barbershop quartets, whole Baptist choirs, one Methodist choir, a cassette tape from the Episcopal choir, declamation contest winners from the high school, the junior high, and the elementary school, giving their speeches. He's had students on the show talking about their science projects, people calling in to say they don't know what the hell the students are talking about. He's had a man on who had his eye taken out. That man's daughter was along and she said, "He had his eye took out on the same day I had my cyst took out."

And then here, suddenly, one Monday morning,

is raw talent. He's had a part in a real discovery. He could almost . . . almost weep.

"A tour is just the thing," says Ted. "With this lab set-up at Social Work, we should be able to use some of the grant money—or even use the recruitment budget," says Ted. "There's plenty in there for something like that, isn't there, Don?"

"Oh, yes sir, but that's what we usually do with the choral group on the Hawaiian trip."

"Well, yes, but—"

"I see what you mean," says Coach. "We got these criminals over there, and these Negroes, blacks, and we're working with them directly now."

"Well, we'd focus in on the Benfield boy. He's already gotten some good press. Then too, it'll be obvious that these people in the band are getting second chances through BOTA House, with our lab program and everything. But the safe one, since he's a Christian, is Benfield. It's a powerful image. A young member of the Ballard family who's been given a second chance. We could send them to a few churches, schools first time out—cater to the youth. And then to finish it off they could play for the Eastern LinkComm Christmas luncheon—you know, for the nursing home people. Snaps has been wanting us to help them make a bigger event out of that anyway."

Stan raises his hand, weakly. "Who is Snaps?"

"He's the president over at Eastern LinkComm. A good friend of the university. And—"

"Mr. President," says Mysteria over the intercom. "You asked me to mention about Leroy Yates."

"Oh, yes, Y'all heard about Leroy's passing away. Twenty-five years in maintenance, wasn't it, Ned?"

"Twenty-seven."

"Fine worker. Never complained once about the first thing. Always had a smile, a good word. No problems of any kind. Put his heart into his work. Don, did you send the family something?"

"A dozen roses and some chicken."

Ted frowns, looks at Big Don. "I thought we usually sent just one or the other."

"Better make a note of that," Ned says to Big Don.

Ted swings his chair back straight ahead, drops it forward, quickly checks his hair in the window reflection, puts his arms on his desk. "Now, let's see, I guess that's about it. We do have one more little item which we need to cover in executive session, so, ah, Stan. . . ."

"Sir?"

"We need just a brief huddle on an unrelated matter—you can wait outside or head on back to your office."

"Oh. Okay."

Stan leaves. Mysteria is not at her desk. If he waits here, maybe he could hear some of what they're saying, he thinks. As he starts to sit, Mysteria comes in from the hall and Ned closes the inside office door. Stan says bye to Mysteria and leaves.

In the inner office, Ted says to the men remaining, "I've been talking to Snaps. He needs an airport and he was going to buy the Thornburg property but they wouldn't sell. I told him they wouldn't before he asked them. Anyway, he's asked

111

me if we can expand our little airstrip. He's wanting to get his own jet—well, it would be LinkComm's—and our field would be the perfect place for it if we expanded and repaved the runway and so on. He's dealing with some companies that have their own jets too, and if we expanded, it would make life simpler for him."

"What about finances?" asks Big Don.

"That's settled. He's willing to donate to us whatever the expansion would cost, plus some. Plus a good bit, in fact. So we can't lose, and we'll be sitting pretty if we ever find ourselves in the position of needing a jet ourselves."

"Right," says Ned. "Sure thing."

"We could get a turbo-prop for a while," says Coach. "They're cheaper."

"In any case, our whole Washington connection will be enhanced with an expansion," says Ted. "So we need to get Legal in on this, Ned, and let's keep it under our hats."

Jake Davis's door is closed as the band members leave the WRBR building. The door opens as they file past, and Jake sticks his head out. "Sherri, could you step in here just a second." He closes the door behind her, goes around behind his desk, picks up a cigarette off his desk as he sits, lights it, blows smoke. "Darned impressive," he says. "Darned impressive. Have a seat and let's talk for a minute."

Wesley is outside the door when Sherri comes out. The others are in the van, waiting. "What'd he want?" asks Wesley as they go through the door, on outside.

"It's big news. Big," says Sherri, clenching her

112

fist, pulling her elbow to her side. "Album. A-L-B-U-M."

As soon as Sherri is in the van, she turns around from the front passenger seat, her eyes wide. "Listen, guys, listen. This Jake guy has got connections with BirdSwim Records. BirdSwim! He's getting the ball rolling on an album, this very minute! It'll be gospel, but it'll be a great set-up for another one, blues, then another one and on and on."

"Yeah," says Ben, cranking the van, "and when I see the green, I'll know what you mean."

"He said we sounded great. He's going to get on the phone. I tell you, it's going to happen."

"Yeah," says Larry, "sure, but the problem was that ending to 'Time Ain't Long.' Somebody didn't make that chord change at the end." Larry has four gold chains around his neck this morning—three with medallions.

Ben says. "Somebody's going to cut off your head and steal them chains."

"How did you think it sounded, Shanita?" Sherri asks.

"Fine."

Wesley sees himself in a record studio, standing behind a microphone with the National Steel around his neck, looking through a plate glass window at several producers behind a board with hundreds, maybe thousands of dials. Phoebe is sitting nearby, holding a dozen roses, watching him.

Sherri sees lights on a marquee—in San Francisco or Chicago: "Sherri Gold and the Fat City Band." She sees hands, holding slips of paper and

113

pens, reaching out to her as she's jostled and pushed by a crowd. She sees a white tablecloth, wine, a rose in a clear vase, a man ... a man owning a beach house, a British racing green Jaguar, and a big boat—one of them that has a lot of rooms in it.

9

WESLEY TELLS PHOEBE ABOUT HOLISTER AND THE auto shop, the National Steel—what it's like, the little Hawaiian figures brushed on the chromed aluminum body. About how he's put strings on it. How it sounds.

They're sitting on their bench at the mall. He's cute when he gets excited, Phoebe thinks. That little red spot on his neck heats up. And he gets excited rather often. And he has been so many things—an orphan, a somewhat-thief for awhile, then on the mend—and a college student at the community college. It's so intriguing, almost exotic in a way. He might even be a genius—and after all, a genius might get carried away, telling about a medical problem and not really mean anything by it. Thank goodness he called and apologized. Thank goodness he realized his mistake.

And there's his guitar and all. Phoebe has heard a tape of Wesley's band. Gospel music. And he's written several songs himself. He's actually a composer. And now it looks like he might be in an album. He's invited her to band practice.

But I'm not sure I want to be around the black men in the band, she thinks. I've never been around black men and I'm not sure what they might say about my weight. People have made awful remarks. But now Wesley has asked me to be with him in front of his friends. He's passed that test. Pete and Randy would take me straight somewhere to park. And then there'd be a tussle. They never wanted me for me. All they wanted was the same thing every other girl in America has. I think Wesley is different maybe.

Just after dark, Wesley and Phoebe pull into the upper parking lot at Lake Blanca. Wesley's just finished a Big Mac and Phoebe an Oriental chicken salad. They are in Phoebe's dark green Chevrolet Citation and Phoebe is driving.

The moon is low and reflects from the water. "What time do you have to be in?" asks Phoebe.

"Nine-thirty. I got thirty extra minutes because I didn't get any demerits for two weeks."

"They're kind of loose over there, aren't they?"

"Some people are more restricted than others. Everybody has to go to all the meetings and group counseling, and we split up chores, but after that it pretty much depends on demerits and what the judge said—or whoever it was put you in there."

"It's all very interesting."

"Yeah, it's pretty interesting."

"That's a beautiful moon, isn't it," say Phoebe.

"Sure is." Wesley slips over toward her. He's not used to being on the passenger side. It feels awkward like this. Backwards. What can I talk about? What can I talk about?

"Sometimes," says Wesley, "when Vernon's sort of by hisself, doing something quiet, he's got this low hum. I've heard him do it twice. It sounds almost like a wolf howling far, far off. Then you realize it's him. He does it on every breath. It sounds like this." Wesley makes an owl-like sound, but with his mouth closed. "It's lonesome. I didn't know what it was. He was cleaning off some bricks. I looked around before I finally realized it was him."

Phoebe is wondering whether to rest her hands on the steering wheel or in her lap.

"I think he's had a hard life," says Wesley. "We had the first Project Promise meeting and went over the names of the masonry tools and all. He catches on pretty fast but there are these blank spaces you come to every once in a while. He's one of the least of these my brethren."

"That's in the Bible."

"I know." Got to stay away from the Bible this time, thinks Wesley. And my pisser.

This is wonderful, thinks Phoebe. Hard to believe. A boy talking about the Bible while we're parking. He seems to be staying away from all that about his . . . member.

I need to get onto some pretty things, soft things, thinks Wesley. "That really is a pretty moon, ain't it?"

117

"Sure is." Phoebe puts one hand on the steering wheel, one in her lap. But that still doesn't feel right. She would feel better on the passenger side. "When does Project Promise start up?" she asks.

"It's already started." Wesley rubs the back of his neck. "Looks like little diamonds on the water, don't it?"

Phoebe puts both hands in her lap. "Yes, it does look like little diamonds."

Well. Well this is it, thinks Wesley. Kiss time. He turns to face Phoebe, leans over toward her. She doesn't move. He slowly moves his head in front of hers. In the pupils of her eyes he sees tiny moon reflections. She's looking at the water. He moves on toward her face. Contact. She smells so good. Her lips are closed but there is absolutely no resistance. He closes his eyes, and starts his hand to her far side, but while he thinks he's still got a way to go before touching her, he's touching her—a silky blouse. Then he starts his other hand behind her— she shifts forward to give him room. She *is* a big woman, Wesley thinks. And she is kissing back. Ah, and turning toward him. A hand on his side. Pulling him to her. Yes. Yes. Yes. *Okay*. Ah ha, this might move right along.

Then she draws back, pushes him away a little.

"Wesley, I enjoy our time together, and, and it's important to me that you like me the way I am. I just wanted to tell you that."

"Well, I do like you the way you are," says Wesley. "I sure do. It's not like you're fat either, you know, because everything is in the right proportion—you know?" Wesley sees the freckles on her cheek in the moonlight, thinks about freckles in all

118

those other places, especially down there on the inside of her thighs.

"Well, thanks. I guess. But at least I am doing something about the, you know, extra weight." She takes a deep breath. "This really is nice out here."

"It sure is. It sure is."

Phoebe, in order to take three pieces of popcorn from her bag, which is on the dashboard, leans forward. Wesley, with both arms around her, moves forward with her, then back with her.

She can't start eating now, thinks Wesley. "Phoebe?"

"Yes?"

"We need to change places."

"Change places? Why?"

"I'll tell you what. I've got a great game. It's called 'army.' What happens is I give an order and you follow it."

"Wesley . . ."

"Just try it. It's fun."

"Wesley, I—"

"What I'm going to do is slip over this way a little bit." Wesley slips toward the passenger door away from Phoebe. "And I want you to slide over in the middle here. Go ahead. . . . It's okay. I'm not going to bite you."

Phoebe moves over toward the middle of the car.

"Now, that's right. Now all I've got to do is just sort of get over the top of you onto the other side. I can kind of pretend I've been driving."

"Wesley!" Phoebe, with Wesley sitting on her lap, starts to slip back over toward the steering wheel.

"ATTENTION!"

Phoebe stops. Her feet are on the hump in the middle of the floorboard. "Wesley!"

"Quiet, soldier."

"Wesley, you're hurting my—"

Wesley's legs are caught between the dashboard and Phoebe's legs. He gets them loose and slides down off Phoebe to a spot almost behind the steering wheel. "Now," he says. "Now we can relax a little. Whew. That won't as easy as I thought it'd be."

"You were just kidding about pretending to drive, weren't you?"

"Well, I . . . yes." She is very close now.

"Wesley, listen, I just need to be careful. You know what I mean. My mother and I had talks about this, about how it was going to be when some boy tried to talk me into something, and I promised her I'd remain pure. I mean that's just the way it is with me and I think you ought to know."

"Phoebe, what do you think I've got in mind? I'm not just some boy. I'm a Christian. You know that. I'm just talking about relaxing a little bit."

"I just—I don't know. I just needed to say that. I always try to say that."

"You mean there've been others?"

"Wesley. Of course. I mean not in the way you're making it sound. Oh, Wesley." Phoebe lowers her head onto his shoulder. She feels some kind of melting. He's really cute—in his own sort of mysterious way.

Wesley puts his arm around her up on the back of the seat and turns some to face her. His problem is that they're leaning the wrong way, toward the driver's door. He was planning on their leaning toward the passenger door, so he could get more or less on top, but here they are, headed toward—he looks down and sees cleavage, in the moonlight. Her perfume is so, so full of sex, so sultry—it's pulling him to her.

"Oh Wesley." Phoebe closes her eyes, meets Wesley's lips. She feels very relaxed, opens her lips just a little.

Wesley tastes a popcorn taste. He can tell she's relaxed—OH HAPPY DAY, OH GREAT GLORY, WONDERFUL MUSIC—so relaxed that her weight is falling upon him, forcing him back toward the steering wheel, where he doesn't want to be, but perhaps.... He closes his eyes. His shoulder . . .

RRRROOOOOOOONNNNNNKKKKK!

Phoebe jumps back. She moves very fast for a big woman.

But Wesley goes right after her, and manages to end up sort of on top, sort of at the side, almost where he wanted to be to start with. He doesn't want this kiss to stop. He knows this kiss is the beginning of the beginning of the world. He tries to find her mouth again with his, lands on her chin. He moves it on up, and they seem to be back where they were. His left hand begins to awaken to life. As if with a brain of its own, it heads to a spot below Phoebe's knee and starts moving up slowly. The kiss is going very well. With his hand he'll move on up between her legs and settle in at a spot just above her knees, see what happens.

But at her knees the skin is all bunched and pressed together. So the hand burrows like a mole toward home, and Phoebe suddenly scrambles

121

backwards, away from Wesley. Moving back as if in waves.

Everything has shifted somehow, Wesley realizes. Feelings too. He straightens his collar, tries to think about David in the Bible. Should he say something about David?

"Wesley!" What in the world is wrong with him? Phoebe asks herself. Why can't he just kiss a little bit and let that be it, for heaven's sake. He'll try to have me in bed within the week and I'll be pregnant within the month just like Mama warned if I don't put my foot down. Solidly. "Wesley, I think we'd better go."

"Phoebe, I . . . it . . . it was my hand's fault."

"Wesley. I'm sorry, Wesley."

A dull ache settles in Wesley's chest as he watches Phoebe turn her back, open the passenger door, manage to get out, wade around the front of the car to the driver's side. He slips back over to the passenger side. Phoebe opens the driver's door, gets in. There is a coldness in her movements. She puts the key in the ignition and starts the car. The headlights come on. The panel lights seem to Wesley to be a very sad green. Phoebe drives across the parking lot toward the highway, slows not quite to a stop at the stop sign, turns onto the blacktop country road and heads for home.

Wesley stares out the passenger window, watches dark houses go by. He sees lights in windows dimmed by shades and curtains. People are doing all sorts of things in there, he thinks. He decides he should have told Phoebe the truth before things got out of hand. He should have told her he loved her. I'll behave differently next time, he thinks. I do love her. We'll have a little talk. That will be the proper thing to do. I'll remember that I'm a Christian in every way.

When they pull into the Nutrition House parking lot, Phoebe turns off the ignition, looks at Wesley. "I'm going on in now. I'd rather you not call me for a while." I must send the correct signal, she thinks. I can't let him think I am what I'm not. She starts getting out of the car.

Wesley gets out, stands by the passenger door, watches as Phoebe walks toward the back door. The porch light is on. "Good night," he calls.

She doesn't slow down or turn her head. "Good night, Wesley."

Wesley watches her, aches to see her face turn toward him, studies her rear end—two big, very smooth pillows under her dress, moving all around side by side. He watches her open the screen door, and with some effort get up the two steps and onto the porch. Up and in.

That's one group of a woman, thinks Wesley. Man, she is *in* the world. What now? He walks down and across the street. Dear God, please forgive me if I have done the wrong thing. Help me understand the way Thou would'st have me behave. Help me study to make myself approved in Thy sight. Amen.

He walks across the empty lot beside the Nutrition House, thinks about walking to the Sunrise Auto Shop. Naw, not tonight. Vernon would get on his nerves, asking about everything. He walks on to BOTA House, in the door, past YOU WILL EARN TOMORROW WITH WHAT YOU LEARN TODAY, up the stairs and to his room, where he finds a pamphlet stuck

123

in the crack of the door. It's from the university. The title is "How the Free Enterprise System Exposes the Dangers and Immorality of Unions." Wesley tosses it in the trash can. What *is* a union, anyway? he wonders.

Before supper the next evening, Wesley is sitting on his bed playing his National Steel. His instruction book is open beside him. The sound is sweet through his ears and through his chest, like honey, with lemon juice added, just a bit, so that it's not heavy, doesn't get sticky. The sound doesn't get tiring. He has been practicing for almost three hours. The green glass bottleneck feels natural on the ring finger of his left hand. He is precise with its placement on the strings, exactly over the fret. He has learned several steady blues bass riffs, which he plays with his thumb. Then he moves up high on the neck to play a solo break with the bottleneck doing the fretting, his thumb keeping the bass line going.

He practices the riffs over and over and over. When he gets a riff just right, he stands with the Dobro strapped around his neck and walks from the bed over to the mirror. He turns so that the late evening sun through the window flashes off the Dobro. He watches his left hand work, watches the clear green bottleneck making vibrato on a solo break.

Back on his bed he plays a few bars, practices, replays, practices, building until he's got a whole solo break. He's learning to stress off-beats, move around the beat, and the sound from the bottleneck against the steel strings is like cool water on something hot—it keeps feeling good. Patterns and formations in his mind break up and reassemble into others, blend, work in ways he couldn't have dreamed. One little pattern will work in all chords of a verse or bridge. He loves to keep the pattern, the riff, going, while the chords—the structure underneath—are changing. He loves this Dobro, which takes him through doors into rooms of precious sound.

After he's tired of practicing, he gets a yellow legal pad and a pencil from his bedside table. He has decided to do the proper thing, and has already written all but the last verse of a song for Phoebe. He will use his talents in the name of love. He's got a good start for the last verse.

I know you feel mad, I know you're feeling sad.
There ain't nothing I can do,
but sit right here and get blue too.

I could make it about what I want to happen, thinks Wesley.

I'd be so nice, if you'd call me right now,
and talk about the weather
telling me whether
you still love me like before—that you do.
Wish you were here, at my front door right now
to ring my doorbell—

Ben comes in.

"Ben, listen to this."

Ben sits down on his bed, listens as Wesley sings through what he has written.

"You need some more words in there at the last," says Ben. "*Ring my blank-blank doorbell.* See what I mean?"

Wesley sings. "*Ring my dusty . . . ring my dirty, dusty—rusty,* rusty, yeah, *ring my rusty doorbell . . .*"

"Now get something about, like 'smell' in there, man," says Ben. "Like *close enough for me to smell you.* You know?"

"Yeah, that'll work."

"Love song, huh?"

"Well, yeah. For Phoebe."

They work on the song for awhile and get it right. "Let's record it," says Wesley.

Ben starts playing the tape that's already in the recorder—Wesley playing bottleneck with back-up on bass. "Who's that playing bass?" says Ben.

"That's Vernon—the one I'm teaching in Project Promise. He's some kind of music genius. I brought him up here to see if he could play bass. He could play everything I showed him. I'd show it to him twice and he'd have it. You heard him play some piano downstairs."

"Yeah. Pretty good."

"I was thinking about him playing some keyboard with the band, then I figured we might to do some stuff with me on bottleneck and you on lead, and we—"

"Larry ain't going to want nobody else in the band. Especially no retard."

"Well, let's just see. Here, let's record this."

They record Wesley's song to Phoebe, then Wesley writes a note to go with it, asking her to let him know if she would like to go with him to the

126

Project Promise banquet next Tuesday night. He pauses, thinks. He needs to make the letter better. He thinks about Song of Solomon, wonders if he could work in some of that. He gets out his Bible, reads for a minute.

"I'm hungry," says Ben.

"Wait a minute."

> Dear Phoebe, here's something else.
> Love is as strong as death,
> Passion cruel as the grave;
>   it blazes up like a blazing fire
> fiercer than any flame.
> Many waters cannot quench love,
> No flood can sweep it away,
> If a man were to offer for love
>   the whole wealth of his house
>   it would be utterly scorned.

There. He reads it to himself, then reads in Solomon for something to add. A clincher. Ah.

> You are stately as a palm-tree,
> and your breasts are the clusters of dates.
> I will climb up into the palm to grasp its fronds.

"I got to go over and put this in her mailbox," says Wesley. "I ain't supposed to call her or nothing—until she calls me."

"Why not?"

"We had this misunderstanding."

"She told you not to call her or nothing?"

"Call her, see her, anything, until she calls me."

"Hey. She got you by the balls, man." Ben stands up, walks over and looks out the window.

"Naw, I wouldn't say that."

"She telling you what to *do*."

"She's telling me what *not* to do."

"Don't make no difference—it mean the same thing. She got you by the balls. What'd you do to her, man?"

"I didn't do nothing. It was what I *tried* to do."

"Which was?"

"Just kind of, you know, get to know her a little better."

"Ha!" Ben looks around the room, then back at Wesley. "You mean you tried to *nuck* her."

"Naw, man. Look. I been through all that. I mean I done that. I been through that. With other girls. All you got to do is just do it. It's too easy. But, listen, you know . . . see, there's a proper way to go through all this. See, you know, I had a pretty big thing happen to me four, five years ago."

Ben picks up his pic, pics his hair, looks in the mirror, pats his hair down.

"But it's not like you're thinking," says Wesley.

"Hell, that's all right. All my aunts and uncles are Christian. I told you." Ben puts down his pic. "They go to church and everything."

"I ain't talking about church. I'm talking about man-woman stuff."

"I got to go eat, man."

"I'll go with you. I want to tell you about some of this."

Headed outside, Ben reads the new quote of the week out loud: "THE FAMILY ALTAR ALTERS THE FAM-

ILY." Then he says, "Now, that's something I was wondering about. What the hell's a family altar?"

"Some kind of vase, I think."

They sign out, walk on outside into dusk, down the street toward The Columbia Grill. On the way Wesley leaves Phoebe's tape and note across the street in the mailbox on the front porch of the Nutrition House. Walking down the sidewalk again, he tells Ben a story.

"See, I was in the YMRC, and I'm sitting out at the picnic table one Sunday afternoon trying to find a hole in the fence, you know, when a lot of people are visiting, families and stuff, and I see this old lady at the gate. Just this old lady with a black purse and this other stuff. So the guard lets her in and she starts coming straight at me like she knew who I was, and I look all around to figure who it is she really wants, but she keeps walking straight at me and right up to me and stops and says, 'Wesley?,' and it freaked me out, man, so I figured she must be my grandma because I got one somewhere. So I asked her for a cigarette because I was out and needed one bad and she hopped all over me, told me I ought to quit smoking and everything. What was good was she had this ice tea in a jar and the best pound cake you ever eat, *plus* a piece of this apple pie with this real light crispy crust and this cinnamon flavor, and it was the beginning of me being a Christian. She was sort of mean but at the same time she took care of you like you was her own. I mean she cut my hair, and I got my first tub bath at her place. You ever had a tub bath?"

"A tub bath? Oh yeah. Yeah, I had a tub bath."

129

They stop at a side street for a car to pass. Then they cross the street.

"But the law was after me, see, and they finally got me, but in the end, after she took me in and everything, she got me to thinking different about women, and people, you know. She's the one I usually go see on Sundays after church."

Ben doesn't say anything.

Wesley knows what's wrong with Ben: He hasn't learned to *respect* a woman. He's like most guys. They don't see women as real people. That's the way it used to be with him. It used to be that he couldn't have fallen in love if he'd tried. He might have thought he was in love. Now there's Phoebe Trent, and he is *really* in love. The kind of love that keeps you from doing just whatever suits *you*.

The Columbia Grill is built onto the back of the Columbia Tobacco Warehouse. Inside are high-backed booths and two chalkboards almost too slick for chalk, where daily specials are written: four meats, six vegetables—pick one and two or one and three. The owner, Mr. Jimmy Champion, sits at a table near the cash register, smoking a cigarette. He looks up at Ben and Wesley. He has big bags under his eyes. He tells them to go ahead and find a seat, anywhere.

"Three hot dogs all the way," Wesley says to Mary, the waitress. "And a Pepsi."

"Me too," says Ben.

"We'd have these little practice sessions," says Wesley. "And I learned about how a man is supposed to respect a woman. We'd be walking down the street, downtown, and if she was walking next to the street, she'd walk closer and closer to me until I finally switched sides." Wesley demonstrates with two fingers on each hand walking on the table. "It was like a real education. And see, she connected all this stuff up to Jesus, and that got me interested in all that, you know. Accepting Jesus, and the stuff in the Bible and, you know, heaven and hell and all that. See, like I never had a family."

"How'd you get born?"

Mary brings the Pepsis.

"I don't know. I mean, I ain't sure. I just ended up part-time with this uncle because my mama and daddy won't married for some reason—or something. But mostly, it was just the orphanage and the YMRC, and then Mrs. Rigsbee. She got me to thinking about the whole part of people that's below the surface—the soft spot, the soft area."

Ben looks at Wesley, raises an eyebrow.

"No, not that. Not that. I got to thinking about the whole part of people that's below the surface. I even got to thinking about the communists—I mean, you know, they're people. They understand about being in love just as good as people in America—or they could if they was taught. They got potential. Chinese, too."

"You better watch that shit, man," says Ben, looking at Wesley. He raises both eyebrows, sips from his Pepsi, lowers his head, wipes his thin mustache. "Communists."

"What I mean," says Wesley, "is in theory like." He picks up the glass salt shaker and turns it in his hand.

"I don't know about all that," says Ben. "I don't know about 'theory.' I just know about facts. You can't count on nothing but bare facts—and there's no better bare fact than ... than a good looking, firm bare ass. Nass."

"Everything's got a theory. Everything. Anyway, you see what I'm talking about. And that got me to thinking about women and all, about how on the inside they've got the same feelings as me, and so I figure I don't want to just up and crawl them anymore."

"You mean you got to do it *Christian*?"

"Well, no, not exactly. That ain't what I mean. But there *is* stuff in the Bible which makes it all okay. I was reading some stuff about David the other day, the one with the slingshot, killed Goliath? You know about him?"

"Yeah, I heard of him."

"Well, he had this illegitimate son, see. But the thing is, didn't nobody blink a eye, not even the one writing the Bible, the one getting it all straight from God."

"I don't know about that."

"Oh, yeah."

"You serious about all this, ain't you?"

"Well, yeah, but I'm starting to think about it different than they do at church. A lot of the people there don't seem like they could understand about falling in love—all of that. They don't mix in stuff like that from real life when they talk about things. And anybody that wears the kind of clothes they do can't understand much about falling in love. I mean they all dress the same way." Wesley shakes salt onto his hand, sticks his tongue to it. "Don't you date nobody?" He looks at the salt shaker in his hand. We could use one of these back in the room, he thinks.

"Naw. That's the reason I'm in BOTA. I got charged with rape, convicted of assault."

"I didn't know that."

"You do now."

Mary brings the hot dogs, starts to walk away.

Ben says, "You think you could put a little more chili on there?"

"Mine too," says Wesley.

She picks up the plates.

Wesley waits a few seconds. "Rape?"

"That's what the charge was. That's what *she* said. And she had a lawyer and everything. But what happened was she called me up to come over to her house and then she started insulting the hell out me. Yackie, yackie, yackie, yackie." Ben stares at Wesley. "It was a nodnamned fight is what it was—we made love while we was fighting is what happened. And it ain't the first time we'd done it— that way. We'd just kind of knock over things and lose our heads and stuff. Lamps, tables. A lot of kicking each other in the ass, stuff like that. Nothing bad, you know. Just having a little fun. That's all it ever was, just having a little fun."

Wesley is visualizing the fight. "How did you . . . so I mean what happened after that?"

The waitress brings the hot dogs, heavy with chili.

Ben waits for her to leave, then says. "I got convicted of assault because she was kind of beat up. After I left, that same day, she hit herself in the head with a frying pan. I know that's what she did. She had to. One of them cast irons. That's all she had. That's all she had in her kitchen. She'd cook everything in it at the same time. Some stuff would be too done, other stuff not done enough. Man, I hated eating over there. But, hell, I couldn't take her out, you know, with the situation and all—her being married. I didn't have no money anyway." Ben takes a big bite of hot dog—talks with his mouth stuffed. "She called the nodnamn police. Can you believe that shit? It was the same chick I saved from the man with the gun, when I got shot." He swallows. "She called the police—on me—and they came to my apartment and got my ass, man, nass, and she'd done pressed charges. The only reason the assault conviction held up was because she'd beat herself up a little. Damn frying pan." He takes another bite of hot dog. "I told them I never touched her stupid head. The whole problem, see, was she just went kind of crazy, or something. She had these mental problems. Bad."

"So you don't date or nothing?"

"Naw. I don't date exactly, naw."

Wesley looks at the salt shaker in his hand. "Don't we need a salt shaker?"

"Maybe I should have wrote her a song, huh?"

"Yeah, maybe you should have," says Wesley.

"I don't know, man. Let me have that salt when you're through."

"I think maybe I'll write another Phoebe song."

I went down to the river, yesterday afternoon.
I went down to the river, yesterday afternoon.
And when I got down to the river . . . I went fishing.
And I sang this song:
I got the sour sweetheart blues. I'm gonna jump in
     the river and drown.
I got the sour sweetheart blues. I'm gonna jump in
     the river and drown.

134

I think my woman loves me, then she shoots me
  down.
I took her to the circus,
I took her to the fair,
I took her down to the river for some loving—
She wanted to go back to the fair.
I got the sour sweetheart blues, muddy water in my
  cup.
I wish my sweetheart ... I wish she'd sweeten up.

10

"AND COLONEL TRENT, IF YOU WILL, YOU CAN sit right here," says Ned Sears to Phoebe's father. He looks like Alexander Haig, thinks Ned. "Wesley, you and Phoebe sit right down there. Or, Phoebe, maybe you want to sit by your daddy, too."

"This is okay, right here."

"No, he hasn't seen you in some time. Here . . . I'm sure you all have plenty to talk about."

Ted Sears comes into the dining room from the restroom, where he's given himself a thrice-over in the full-length mirror he recently had maintenance install in there.

A camera flashes—Greg Stephenson, in charge of Ballard's PVA (Photo, Video, Audio) University History Program, is covering the new academic dean's first school function: the Project Promise banquet.

Stan Laurence, the new assistant treasurer, and his wife, Darleen, are standing back.

"Stan, you and Darleen come sit over here," says Ned. "There you go. Darleen, that's a beautiful dress. You certainly don't look like you've been taking care of four children all day."

"Thank you."

When they are seated, Darleen whispers to Stan, "Isn't that the boy from the halfway house—the one who was in the newspaper?"

"Where?"

"Beside that big redheaded girl."

"Oh, yeah. Without a tie. Benfield. Wesley Benfield."

"He doesn't look like he'd get along too well with the girl's father."

"No shit. You can say that again."

Wesley looks around at the heavy, leather-covered chairs back against the wall in this room, which he figures must be right under the cafeteria. It's a room he didn't even know about before tonight. To his right is Vernon, then Holister. To his left is Phoebe, then Phoebe's father. This is a big deal. Phoebe finally phoned him and said yes to his invitation. Even said she would drive. His song worked, and the note. She loved it. She called him up and told him so, and he was so happy he hopped all the way down the stairs from the hall phone beside his room, through the TV room in front of Linda and Carla, out the front door and around the yard. And to top off all this good luck, somebody has said the band is going on a little tour.

Darleen asks Stan, "What's this room for anyway?"

"It's where they bring the trustees and other people they want to get money from. They call it the University President's Eastern LinkComm Dining Room or something like that. Eastern LinkComm furnished it."

"Looks like they'd take donors to a shabby room, so they'd see the school needs money."

"Apparently it doesn't work that way." Stan decides not to go into the kind of thinking he's hearing in this administration: people give money where money is, withhold money from where it's not. Which seems to explain all sorts of things—like the president's salary versus faculty salaries.

Vernon punches Wesley on his shoulder. "Will we be doing this every week?"

"I don't think so. This is the kick-off dinner. The only one. How come? Don't you like it?"

"I don't know why we're doing it."

"For the Project Promise thing. The start-up."

"But I mean, ain't nobody going to learn nothing here."

"Well, that's right. That's sure right. You're just supposed to eat."

This is an unusual gathering for Ballard University. And Ned and Ted are not entirely at ease. Here are people of all stripes eating at the same table. Usually at dinners in the President's Dining Room, the people attending are in most ways alike. Men.

But tonight there are women here, and three mentally retarded youths—two girls and a boy—along with their three tutors from the halfway house, faculty members from the School of Social

138

Work, several graduate students from over there too, and a client from the Nutrition House—all these mixed in with administrators and a few trustees. Ted and Ned can't know with confidence that harmony and smiles will prevail.

Wesley watches the older black cafeteria workers and several white student helpers bring in salads—lettuce and tomato—and iced tea. Iced water was set out earlier and the ice has melted. The glasses sweat. "I was laying in bed this morning," says Wesley to Phoebe, "and my toe was itching and every time I scratched it with my other foot, my ear popped, kind of deep inside. When I scratched it with my hand nothing happened. It's connected to that acupuncture stuff. That stuff is true. If I could have found out about that when I was little I might have solved all those pisser problems." I shouldn't have said that, Wesley thinks.

"What was that?" says Colonel Trent, leaning forward from the other side of Phoebe.

"Nothing." He ain't going to like me, thinks Wesley.

Father is not going to like Wesley, thinks Phoebe. The camera flashes.

I don't think I'm going to like that boy, thinks Colonel Trent. He probably doesn't even *own* a tie.

Ned Sears clinks his glass with his fork as he stands. "May we bow our heads and return thanks," he says. He smiles, looks around at everyone, head held high, nose in the air, glowing. He closes his eyes tightly.

Vernon bows his head and prays aloud, rocking. "God is good, God is great"—Holister grabs Vernon's knee, Vernon keeps praying—"let us thank

139

Him for our"—Holister squeezes—"*food amen* what are you squeezing my leg for?"

Holister glares, hisses. "You're not supposed to—"

"That's what he *said*."

"Thank you," says Ned. Who in the world is that? he thinks, consulting the laminated seating chart beside his plate. "Thank you very much, Jules Jackson. It's good for all of us to pray, isn't it?"

"It's Vernon Jackson. It's good for me. I don't know about you. Is it good for you?"

"Oh yes, Vernon. Indeed it is."

"Shut up," Holister hisses to Vernon.

"Well, thank you for that, Vernon, very much," says Ned. "Now let us all bow in prayer to our Savior. Dear Lord, we praise Thee and offer thanks for Thy bountiful gifts. We praise Thee for blessing us in our endeavors to bring quality Christian education to the citizens of North Carolina, and we ask for Thy continued guidance as we initiate a new community program, Project Promise . . ."

"Wouldn't God already know what it's named?" Vernon whispers to Wesley.

"I think so."

". . . and make us ever aware of the Holy Spirit dwelling even within the least of us. Be with us as we welcome, tonight," continues Ned Sears, "a new member to the Ballard family, Colonel Hampton Trent. And now bless this food to the nourishment of our bodies, in the precious and glorious name of Jesus Christ, Amen."

Ned prides himself on his ability to say short but meaningful blessings. "And I'm sure it's no surprise to any of us here," he continues, still standing, "that we now, officially, have a new member of the Ballard family, a new dean, Colonel Hampton Trent." Ned claps his hands enthusiastically. Others clap.

Colonel Trent smiles, nods his head, rises to a stooped position, nods again, sits.

I was hoping he'd be wearing his uniform, thinks Ted.

"And now let's enjoy the fine food," says Ned, his chin held high, a smile on his face. He sits down and is suddenly stuck with cold panic. *I forgot to find out whether Trent is divorced.* How could I have *forgotten?* Surely Mrs. Trent is dead. How in the world could I forget to find out whether Trent is divorced or not? Please God, let his wife be dead. We *can't* have someone this high in this administration *divorced.*

Ned leans over toward Big Don, who is directly across the table. "What's the story on his marriage?"

Big Don turns up his hearing aid. It squeals. Everyone looks. He turns it down. "What?"

"Never mind."

"What?"

Ned shakes his head back and forth and frowns.

Ted is considering the way he must be seen and thought of by the older black women and men serving dinner, what they must think about him. I do eat with the help, he thinks. The first Monday, every month. And everybody knows it. I eat with them and they eat with me. We eat together. Break bread together. The faculty knows it. They know I get down amongst the workers. It's what Jesus would have done.

The camera flashes.

Ned tries again. He gets a business card from his billfold, writes "Is Trent divorced?" on the back and hands it across to Big Don.

Big Don reads the note to himself, whispering— "Is Trent . . . what's this, *choired*?" He looks at Ned and says loudly, "Is he what? 'Choired'? I can't read this, Ned."

"Nothing." Ned blushes. "Never mind."

Big Don turns up his hearing aid again. It squeals. "What? Does this say 'choired'?"

People are beginning to stare.

Ned holds up both hands, palms out. With slow, exaggerated lip movement, he whispers, "Never mind."

The greatest leaders mix with the help, thinks Ted. But why are these blacks so silent when I'm eating dessert with them? Why do they sit there through a whole dessert and not say a thing? Surely they're not like that all the time. Maybe I should tell them I grew up saying "nigger" with people who said "nigger" but I stopped. Maybe they're quiet around me because they're aware they don't speak the King's English very well. They've probably heard some of my speeches, which I imagine are bound to intimidate them. And why none of them will take our night courses in grammar, diet, and personal hygiene is beyond me too. "Yes, thank you, Carlyle, and some of those rolls when you get a chance." When I was growing up the black folk would take reading courses, talk to you, for heaven's sake. They don't seem interested in much of anything these days. But at least ours don't complain. At least I'm doing my part to give them work, and hospitalization. And this Benfield fellow. The only man, well, male, here without a tie. Even the retarded boy is wearing a tie. It doesn't go with anything, but he's wearing one.

We're doing a lot for that Benfield—a part-time job here on campus, and Project Promise. A whole new start in life. A second chance. And the newspaper article on him. It does look like he could wear a tie.

Wesley notices Vernon eating his string beans with his spoon. "Hey. Why are you eating those string beans with your spoon?"

Vernon looks at Wesley, at his plate, at the spoon, at Wesley. "I been eating my ham with my fork and knife. I been eating my rice with my fork. I been eating them there little things with my fork. I'll be eating that cake with my fork. That's everything but the string beans. Now, I figure they give me the spoon for something. So, I'm eating the string beans with my spoon. What do you expect? You expect me to use my fork on everything, and just leave the spoon sitting there? Why do you think they put the spoon there beside my plate if I ain't supposed to use it? They don't just put it there to put it there."

Wesley opens his mouth, but nothing comes.

"Greg," Ted calls to the photographer.

Greg rushes over and bends over the president's shoulder.

"Greg, do get a picture of Mr. Holister, down there at the end, with his son—the one beside him sort of swaying. Mr. Holister owns a small business just off campus." Let's see, thinks Ted, "Project Promise clients eat in the President's Room." Something like that. No, "dine" in the President's Room.

143

Maybe the *Baptist Review* would do something with a picture of a retarded boy in the President's Dining Room. Ballard wasn't in the last issue at all. Maybe if . . .

"Sir," says Greg, "maybe after the meal we can get one of you and the boy, or all four of the retarded people and you. You know."

"Four?"

"Well, let's see, that boy rocking back and forth, the girl with Down's syndrome, and the girl beside her, and then the boy without a tie beside the red-headed woman."

"The one without a tie isn't retarded. He just needs a haircut."

"Oh. Yes sir. Sorry. But, you know, perhaps we could get a shot of you and some of the retarded folks."

"Yes. Good idea." Greg is worth every cent we pay him. "And see if you can get some of these shots off to the *Baptist Review*. And maybe Royal will take a couple at the *Star*," says Ted.

"Yessir. I was planning to do that."

The camera flashes, then flashes again.

"Who does he work for?" Darleen asks Stan. "The photographer."

"PVA. Photo. Video. Audio. At Ballard. He's the head man over there. Mainly, he's the president's photographer." And with an eight-hundred-thousand-dollar budget, thinks Stan, a building with state-of-the-art dark rooms and developing equipment, video machines, closed-circuit TV for dog operations at the vet school, and who knows what else, and on call twenty-four hours a day to photograph everything that moves within forty feet of the president. "Have you ever picked up any newsletter or pamphlet around here and gone over two pages without seeing the president's picture?"

"I've never thought about it. You think about that kind of stuff too much, Stan. It's going to wear you out." Darleen lifts a tiny thread from Stan's knee.

"You can't help but think about it. I'm still thinking about being hungry too."

"It wasn't very filling, was it?"

After dinner, the guests are filing out the door and down the side steps. Ned grabs Big Don by the arm and pulls him away from the others to a spot under a tree. They are lighted by the street light. "*Divorced*," says Ned. "*Divorced*. Is Trent *divorced?*"

Big Don tucks his chin, pulls his head back. "No. His wife died several years ago."

"Thank God."

"What?" Big Don turns up his hearing aid.

"Thank God that ... we've gotten him and his daughter together down here."

Nearby, Wesley stands by the passenger door to Phoebe's car and watches Phoebe and her father talking, several cars away.

"When is he going to be able to drive?" asks Colonel Trent, almost whispering.

"I'm not sure."

"At some point we need to sit down and talk about this."

"Okay, but he's really very nice, Father. You just need to get to know him. The BOTA House is almost like summer camp. It's not really a, you know. They've got women there and—"

"Those two women they introduced tonight, right?"

"Yes."

"They looked like coal miners or wrestlers or something."

"Father. . . ."

"Never mind. Did you know President Sears was a Marine?"

"Yes. He talks about being one when he comes to the Nutrition House. He was a fighter pilot in the war—one of the wars."

"Really? I don't know how I missed that. He didn't mention combat to me." Trent looks at his watch—a diver's watch, good to two hundred feet down. "Do you have a curfew?"

"No, but they do at BOTA House. Nine o'clock on week nights—if they don't have demerits."

"It ought to be earlier, seems to me."

"What do you think about driving on out to the lake?" says Wesley, as Phoebe turns the car into the Nutrition House parking lot. "I got time. And, I mean, I've thought through everything and I just got carried away in the wrong way, and I'm really sorry."

"No. I don't think so. It's getting close to your curfew, and I told you last time, Wesley, I need to, you know, be careful about everything. I just can't rush into things."

"I know. I'm the same way. I just got a little carried away. I was actually kind of worried you might not ever speak to me again."

"I just have to be careful, Wesley. I need to do what's right, and safe." I don't want to lose you, thinks Phoebe. Nobody loves a large woman. No man. Unless he knew her when she was skinny first. I've found a kind of treasure in Wesley. A kind of diamond in the rough. A little boy trying to grow up. A little boy with a man's body who might be a kind of mysterious genius. He certainly knows how to be funny, and nice, at the same time.

Phoebe parks the car farther away from the Nutrition House back-porch light than she usually does.

Damn, thinks Wesley, we're down here in a dark corner. "Listen, I'm real glad you decided to come with me tonight. I mean, it was nice and all, your daddy being there and everything." Shut up about her daddy, he thinks. "How'd you like Vernon?"

"He's a very interesting person."

"He sure is. He can get on your nerves, though. Listen, if it's all right with you, I'm going to get out and walk around to that side."

"Wesley, we—"

"I just don't feel right over here. Look, I ain't going to do anything. I promise. Not one thing. I'll just sing you a song or something." You parked the car down here in this dark corner, thinks Wesley.

"Well . . ."

Wesley gets out. He's walking too fast around the car. He tries to slow down and not show his excitement. He opens the driver's door as casually as he can and waits for Phoebe to move over. Then he gets in and sits with both hands on the steering wheel. "This is better. I didn't feel right over there."

Phoebe's thigh rests against Wesley's thigh.

147

Wesley puts his arm up on the seat behind her. It's a long way around her.

Phoebe wants Wesley to kiss her, but she doesn't know how to arrange for it without seeming too forward. "Oh, boy," she says. "I'm tired." She lets her head fall onto Wesley's shoulder.

Yow, thinks Wesley. Yow. Yow. Yow. She's hungry for love. She's got to be hungry for love to do that. This is almost a complete turnaround.

"I usually get pretty tense around Father. He's a little bit worried," says Phoebe.

"About what?"

"Oh, about us."

Us? Us! What a good word, what a perfect word, coming from her lips, thinks Wesley. Us. The word fills the car, overflows through the crack in the window on the passenger side, over the front seat and down into the back floorboard, around the back seat, down through the seat cracks, and into the trunk. The word fills his chest, his ears. "Oh, well. He don't have nothing to worry about."

"That's what I told him."

"Maybe a *little* to worry about."

Phoebe turns her face toward Wesley and Wesley sees chastisement in her eyes. But it's light chastisement. His face falls slowly forward like wet clay falling. Their lips touch, hard. But. Something in his mouth—the partial plate. It'll slip back in place, Wesley thinks. It always does. But ... the angle of the touch, the force of the touch—Wesley feels a definite dislodgement. Oh, no, Jesus, please. He starts to draw back. I can't draw back now, he thinks. Phoebe's lips are opening. Oh Glory. Wait. The damn thing is, is turning inside his mouth—or something. The wire part is about to . . . he's got to move his head back, away. But Phoebe is already breathing hard. Maybe he can turn his head so that he can get the thing back in his mouth at a safe angle until the first break in this, this kiss. If she sees two teeth stuck on a wire, she'll . . . hold still, Phoebe. Jesus, please help this partial plate to—

Phoebe jumps back like she's been shot. "What was that?!"

Wesley turns away, drops his head, brings his hand to his mouth. "I lar ee in ahy outh."

"Wesley, what are you doing? Are you sick?"

Wesley has both hands in his mouth. He gets the partial plate back in place and coughs a couple of times with his fist to his mouth before he sits up straight and looks at Phoebe, who has backed herself against the passenger door.

"It was just, ah, a toothpick," he says.

"A toothpick?"

"Yeah, I forgot about it."

"How could you—"

"I carry them around in my mouth sometimes. You know, a little short one. I just completely forgot about it."

"Wesley. That was strange. It scared me to death—to be stuck like that while . . ."

"I'm sorry. I'm really sorry. It's gone now. See." Wesley smiles, opens his mouth wide. "It's okay," he says. "Everything's okay."

"I hope so." Phoebe reaches into her bag, pulls out a Kleenex. "A toothpick. Gross. I just . . . where is it?"

"In the floorboard."

"I don't want a toothpick down there. It's nasty."

149

"I'll get it." Wesley reaches down to the floor-board, pretends to pick up a toothpick. He rolls down the window and pretends to drop it outside. He rolls the window back up and looks at Phoebe. "Now. Where were we at?"

11

AT BAND PRACTICE ON SATURDAY AFTERNOON, WES-
ley leads Phoebe in by the hand. She's wearing a
black sweatsuit.

"This is Phoebe, y'all, " Wesley says. "She just
wants to sit in."

White tub of lard, thinks Shanita. When she sit
around the house, she sit around the house.

Phoebe smiles, looks around, finds a seat in the
corner.

She just flat-out do not care about her figure,
thinks Shanita.

Sherri Gold is late. When she arrives, Wesley introduces Phoebe and Sherri. Then he says to the
band, "I want to ask you-all about getting a bass
player. I know one. I want to start playing some

bottleneck while he plays bass so Ben won't have to be switching off. This guy plays keyboards too."

Is he black or white? thinks Shanita.

"Ben heard him play on tape, and he heard him play the piano downstairs. I just had to show him stuff one time and he got it. He's some kind of genius about music. He don't have to hear something but once and he's got it."

"White boy?" asks Larry.

"Yeah, but, I mean, he's good. I taught him some stuff, and his daddy said he'd buy him a bass."

Shanita turns sideways in her chair.

"That'd be five of us," says Larry. "Less money each."

"We ain't making no money anyway," says Sherri. "We might as well sound a little better with a fuller sound."

"What do you think, Ben?" says Larry.

"Well, Wesley's sounding good on bottleneck, this guy can play bass, and lots of places we play there'll be a piano we can mike. You can get some good sounds with a piano. This guy's pretty good. I think it's okay to maybe try him out for a few weeks. Don't promise him nothing."

Larry looks at Shanita. She turns away more. "I think we're okay like we are," he says.

"Look, this tour is going to give us some exposure and we need to have a big sound," says Sherri. "Seems like to me the bigger the better. I mean, not over seven or eight. There's just some stuff we do we don't get a full, big sound on. Y'all know that."

"How's the big sound going on that record deal?" Shanita asks Sherri.

"The record deal? Oh, well, Jake is waiting to hear from this guy at BirdSwim. They been talking on the phone and all. It's going to happen. I don't have any doubts about that."

"I want to make some money," says Larry. "I mean, I ain't doing this just to pass the time. What's that provost got on the tour so far, anyway?" he asks Wesley.

"The fair, two or three churches, high school, Christmas luncheon at Eastern LinkComm. We could at least try the guy out. I swear he'll learn every song we know in no time. And it'll fill us out. Now, he is retarded. I'll have to say that. But it don't normally show—specially if we comb his hair."

"Let's vote," says Sherri.

"How about we just vote on trying him out?" says Larry.

"Okay," says Wesley. "On trying him out. All in favor. . . . Okay, opposed? Three to one. I'll let him know."

"I be up smoking a cigarette," Shanita, standing, says to Larry.

Phoebe decides she'd like to step outside, too. It's warm in the basement. And she feels she should get to know Shanita. They're each dating a band member, and they'll be seeing a good bit of each other. She tells Wesley she'll be back in a minute, follows Shanita out the door and up the steps.

Standing outside on the ground at the top of the basement stairs, Shanita lights up, shakes out the match and tosses it away, looks off toward some bare tree tops standing against the late afternoon sky.

"Do you come to these practices often?" Phoebe asks. She leans back against the side of the house, her arms crossed. She's wearing her extra-large green down jacket.

"Most of the time."

"They sound real good. I got the tape they made."

"Yeah." Shanita draws on the cigarette, blows smoke.

"Do you ever play music with them or sing or anything?" asks Phoebe.

"Naw." What is this? thinks Shanita. The Spanish Inquisition. She does have a pretty face, if she'd lose two or three hundred pounds. "Nobody asks me."

"Do you sing?"

"Oh yeah, I can sing."

"I can too. I've been in several choirs. Maybe we can ask them if we can sing back-up on a couple of songs."

"I don't know about that." Shanita takes a drag, blows smoke, drops her cigarette, steps on it. "Well, I'm going on back down."

Inside, the band starts playing—"Jesus Dropped the Charges."

When the song is over, Ben says to Larry, "Larry, you dragging on that bridge."

"I ain't dragging."

"You are, too. Right where it goes into the bridge and after that. You dragging."

"Naw, I ain't. What's wrong with you? Shanita, you think I'm dragging?"

"Yeah, you was dragging."

"Why don't you ask me if you were dragging?" says Sherri.

Larry is still looking at Shanita. "What do you mean?" Larry frowns, looks at Sherri. " 'Why I don't ast you?' "

"I'm in the band. That's what I mean. Why didn't you ask me?"

"Listen, bitch. You was dragging yourself. That's why I didn't ast you."

"Don't you call me a bitch, goddammit, you son of a bitch." Sherri steps toward Larry, hits against a cymbal.

Larry stands up.

"Red alert, red alert, red alert."

Just a closer walk with Thee. Just a closer walk with Thee.

Sherri starts swaying back and forth with the music. Larry slowly sits behind his drums, singing, frowning, as if concentrating on his harmony part.

Ned Sears comes through the basement door, stands listening. The song is finished. "That's very good. But I didn't hear someone say the g. d. word, did I?"

"It was 'got down,' " says Sherri. " 'Got down' like you *slowed* down. I was saying Larry got down."

Larry's chin tucks in, his head pops back, his eyes open wide.

"Well, you-all should know," says Ned, "that we've had a few complaints about use of the g. d. word at BOTA House, and the last thing we want is a tarnished image for Ballard University. There are certain expectations of everyone in the Ballard family, expectations that are part and parcel of all the privileges. If this tour comes off, and I have every reason to believe it will, then you-all must be particularly careful about your language."

Talk to me, blabby-mouth, thinks Shanita.

"I just didn't know what to think of you, you know," Phoebe says to Wesley. She is driving him from band practice to visit Mattie Rigsbee so that she can finally meet her. "You were in BOTA House, of all places, and we all knew it was a half-way house. We used to sit on the porch at the Nutrition House and make jokes."

"You ought not to been doing that."

"I guess not. But I'll bet you-all did the same thing about us."

"Never. All I knew at Copy-Op that day was that you were pretty. Mighty pretty." Wesley slips toward Phoebe, puts his hand on her leg, looks straight ahead, waiting for her response, prepared for anything. She doesn't seem to mind. This kind of thing is okay for a Christian to do.

Mrs. Rigsbee's house is just ahead. "This is it. Right there. That porch is where I tried to get in and steal some pound cake one time. I mean, you know, I was planning to leave some money, so it wouldn't really be stealing, but anyway ... this is it."

Mrs. Rigsbee sits in her spot on the living room couch. Wesley and Phoebe sit in chairs. Wesley always chooses the chair he sat in that first night he was ever here. It's the green chair with the big fat arms.

Wesley tells about Vernon's screaming. "So a sliced tomato is what his daddy gives him every time. The second time it happened we were sitting in Dr. Fleming's office and in rolls this woman in a wheelchair. Her name was Tina Johnson Dillworth. Some woman was pushing her. See, what had happened was I moved this gold plaque that had her name on it beside this classroom. They got them things all over the place, I don't know, so I just got bored or something and unscrewed hers one day and screwed it in the wall right next to a broom closet. Well, somebody was rolling her on a little tour and she saw her plaque beside the broom closet and started having these hissy fits and got rolled right into Dr. Fleming's office and Vernon got to talking to her, and she asked him why he had to rock back and forth all the time. Well, everything got real quiet, but I seen his eyes getting big behind his glasses, so I said to Dr. Fleming, 'Do you know where I can get a tomato?', and she just looks at me funny. Then Vernon starts screaming. They had to roll the wheelchair lady outside, and I had to go all the way to the snack bar before I could find a tomato. They had to let out a couple of classes."

"It's just horrible the way some people get raised," says Mattie. "And spend all that time in front of a television set. My Lord. And buy all that junk they advertise on television. I declare, somebody ought to be put in jail. You take that Jimmy Jo Bathroom Cleaner. They go on and on about how it cleans this, that, and the other. Show it in the toilet bowl just a cleaning in one swish, and you go buy some for I don't know how much and it won't clean no better than dirty water. It's mostly lies. Just out and out lies. And people wonder why young people lie so much these days. Why, it's in

157

front of their faces, and everybody tolerates it like they think they ought to. Hitler and them used all kinds of propaganda in World War II. Lies. Well, this is the same thing. They all ought to be in jail, I tell you. Whoever it is that writes that stuff up. I use baking soda for all my cleaning. If people bought what they needed instead of what they wanted then some of those crooked concerns would go out of business.

"So. Anyway. And you been over in this boy's house? This retarded boy?"

"Yes ma'am. I cooked a meal."

"Well, good for you. What'd you cook?"

"Okra, cornbread, pork chops, potatoes."

"You didn't let the pork chips get dry, did you?"

"No ma'am. I put the water in and the lid on and all. They were tender."

"Good. Now, how about you, Phoebe?" says Mattie. "Are both your parents living?"

"No, my mother died four years ago, but my father has just moved down here from Michigan. He's the new dean at Ballard University, and is looking around for a house. I think he might want me to move in with him once he finds one."

"And you're at the Nutrition House?"

"Yes. They have a really good program. I've already lost a good bit, and I just started at the beginning of the semester."

"Well, idn't that wonderful? Appearance does count for a lot, don't it? That's one thing I tried to teach Wesley when he was staying here. And I did help him out with his teeth some."

"You did?"

"Phoebe teaches kindergarten at the church," says Wesley.

Mattie looks at Wesley. "I just wanted to tell her a little about your teeth," she says.

"Phoebe works at the church—Mt. Gilead."

"So, you work at the church?" Mattie says to Phoebe. She looks back at Wesley.

"Yes, I'm an aide in the kindergarten. I'm working on a degree in childhood education from Michigan State and so this has worked out real well."

"And your daddy's a dean?"

"That's right."

"What does a dean do?"

"Oh, he's an administrator. Administration things."

"I declare, it's all getting so complicated. It's getting so you don't know what to expect from college students. I guess they stopped teaching them anything about the Bible a long time ago."

"I had an Old Testament course last year," said Phoebe, "where we had to read the Old Testament. It was something."

"I been reading that stuff about David," says Wesley, "that I didn't know was in there. I asked you about that," he says to Mattie. "David had some little bastards, I think, and he slept with these women that won't his wives."

"Watch your language. God settled up with David."

"Where does it say that?"

"It's in there."

"Well, it don't bring it up in the place where it happened."

"Son, the Scriptures are there for inspiration. It's

all there. Don't you worry about that. You read Second Timothy. That will tell you. And the fact is—David got forgiven. That's what's important. Everybody knew David had done wrong. That's very clear. Maybe you ought to sit down and read the whole Bible. Not just jump around. You ought to sit down and start reading it straight through."

"Okay. Maybe I'll do that. But jumping around is what they do in Sunday school."

Phoebe is surprised that the conversation is heating up.

"I know," says Mattie, "but they got men working all that up so that it fits together. They got men preparing those Sunday school lessons. Do y'all teach Bible stories in kindergarten?" Mattie asks Phoebe.

"Oh, yes, that's about all we teach."

"You wouldn't talk to me about Song of Solomon, either," Wesley says to Mattie.

"I don't remember much about it."

"Just read it sometime. You do that—you read Song of Solomon for me, and I'll start at the beginning and read the whole Bible straight through for you." I don't want to get mad in front of Phoebe, Wesley thinks.

"Don't go too far before you read the New Testament," says Mattie. "That's what's important. Don't you-all want a little more tea?"

"This is just fine," says Phoebe.

"I'll take a little more," says Wesley. "I can get it."

"I'll get it. Give me your glass."

After Mattie leaves the room, Phoebe looks

around and says, "I can see how it would be nice living here."

"I gained some weight while I was here."

"What was that about your teeth?"

"Oh, nothing. A few fillings, stuff like that."

Mattie returns with fresh iced tea for Wesley. "Don't y'all want to stay for supper?"

"No ma'am," says Wesley. "We got to get on back."

"What about us stopping by the mall for a little bit?" says Wesley on their way out to the car.

That means the mall, then the lake, thinks Phoebe. "Okay, I guess so."

At the mall, Phoebe gets a bag of popcorn and they sit on their bench across from the pet shop.

"She's getting pretty old," says Phoebe.

"Pretty old, yeah."

"I wonder what's going to happen when she gets so she can't take care of herself."

"Oh, she can take care of herself. She'll be taking care of herself for a long time yet. She'll probably outlive me and you."

"She's what—eighty-six?"

"Yeah, but she's good for a long time yet." Wesley tries, but can't picture a really frail Mrs. Rigsbee.

"Does she have any children?"

"Two," says Wesley. "She kept wanting them to have grandchildren, but they wouldn't get married. So when they finally *got* married, they moved away. Idn't that funny? I figured ole Elaine—that's her daughter—would move away. She was weird. But I didn't think Robert would. But he married this

161

woman that was kind of like Mrs. Rigsbee, except she was meaner, and when she got ready to move, she moved and Robert went with her."

"It's a good thing she had you."

"Yeah, I guess it is. But that was all happening to her about the same time I was involved with the car business."

"You never told me about that. Why in the world would you steal a car?"

"I don't know. It was just something to do. What do you say, let's go to the lake."

Phoebe's nostrils are flaring. She's breathing hard. Wesley's hot fingers are under her blouse, moving back and forth. She opens her eyes. The moon shines on the water. She can't decide what to do with her hands. She's been moving them up and down slowly over the shirt on his back. But she doesn't want to seem too eager. She's got to maintain some control over all this. But her breathing. She can't control her breath. It's coming so strong she has to break the kiss, open her mouth for air to rush in and out. Oh God, it feels so, so good. His mouth finds hers again. He's doing things with his tongue, in her ear and on her neck. They had talked and then. . . . Now this. She opens her eyes, looks at the moon on the water, closes them.

A sticky sweat is working up on both of them. They work hard, they long for each other, long to be closer and closer and closer.

Wesley longs with a memory of what it was like with Patricia holding him within her while wild horses strained, stretched high into the air, suddenly left the ground twisting and turning, while they were shot through with pure hot molten gold, then dropped back, limp white fish—that memory of what it was like, the memory of what it was like before this, his new life with Jesus and real love; he longs for the hot gold here at the lake with Phoebe—somehow along with Jesus *and* real love.

And Phoebe wonders what finding Wesley within her could ever be like, what it could mean to her life. She wonders whether she, unmarried, should ever become totally intimate with him here at the lake no no of course not, whether she should maybe drink a lot of wine so she could be saved from deciding no of course not. Her daddy is still alive, the lights of right and wrong still shine into her life. She finds the window handle with her hand, turns it, feels cool air, saves herself again by fumbling upright in the seat. She straightens her clothes. "Wesley, we'd better get back."

"Phoebe, Phoebe, Phoebe . . . Phoebe, baby."

12

WESLEY, CARLA, AND LINDA HAVE BEEN RAKING AND bagging leaves—the last scheduled leaf-raking for the year at BOTA House. Now they are sitting on the front porch steps, taking a break.

Ned Sears parks on the side street and goes in the back door.

"Why does he always go in the back door?" asks Linda.

"Sneaking around," says Carla, taking off her work gloves. "Thinks he's going to catch something going on. He's a case, ain't he? Pure hell would be being married to somebody like that."

"Hell for me," says Linda, "would be being married to anybody."

"How you and Phoebe getting along?" Carla asks

Wesley. She leans back against the concrete step behind her.

"Good. Good."

"She's lost some weight, ain't she?"

"Oh yeah."

"She's got a real sweet personality," says Carla.

"Great skin," says Linda.

"Yeah, that's one thing I like about her."

"My skin is like the Sahara Desert," says Linda.

"You do have dry skin," says Carla, standing, slipping her gloves back on, picking up a rake. "If Phoebe's smart," she says to Wesley, "she'll write out a contract before y'all get married."

"We ain't planning to get married. Not right away, anyhow. Not until after I get out of here. And I ain't real sure about her old man and all. She might move in with him." Wesley locks his fingers behind his head, leans back on the steps. "When he buys a house it could get complicated. I don't think he likes me."

"Last time I saw my sister," says Carla, "she was about to get married and I told her, I said, 'You get you a contract before you marry him and you make it say something about where he's going to be spending his time, because if you ain't careful he'll be one hell of a lot more free after he's married than he was before.' You get a contract and a good lawyer to tell you what to put in it. I'll tell you one thing: love and marriage don't necessarily go together. What it is is love, marriage, and divorce, and I'll tell you one man never got over his divorce—my husband. He never got over it because I shot him before he had a chance to get over it. And that's why I find my young ass right here on this

165

porch. It was one big mess and I ain't no criminal either, which is why they got me here instead of behind bars, but this is what a life of hell can end up in."

"I didn't hear someone cursing, did I?" The screen door creaks. Ned Sears steps out onto the porch.

"I said 'hell' but I won't cursing, sir," says Carla.

"There's a thin line there," says Sears.

"I was talking about a life of hell."

"Well, the hell I know about is far worse than anything we can experience here on earth."

"Maybe so."

"Wesley," says Sears, "could I chat with you a moment inside."

Wesley looks at Sears over his shoulder. "Sure." It's going to be about the wall, Wesley thinks.

Inside, Sears speaks to Wesley from behind Mrs. White's desk. "Have a seat, Wesley. I just wanted to let you know that the Board of Trustees was happy about the plans for the band tour and about the fact that we'll soon be getting the Lord's music out into the community. This will be a unique outreach effort from the Ballard family. And all of us in the administration are happy with it, too. The president especially. We believe it may bring us new students, and new support of all kinds." Sears stands. "So I just wanted to express our happiness with all this. After all, if a person only hears what they're doing wrong, how are they ever going to know what to do right?"

"I don't know. I never thought about it." Wesley pulls at his ear, looks at his foot. So—it ain't the wall.

166

"I don't think they will." Sears moves around to the front of the desk, sits in a chair. "And there is one other item. We're going to need to move that wall one more time. But then that'll be it. Just one more time. My wife feels, and I agree, that we need to open up the space just a bit more there in the living room, and the perfect place for a reading area is at the top of the stairs in that little foyer. Mrs. White agrees. A brick wall will add a certain amount of privacy up there, I think. So we'll need to get right on that."

That afternoon, before supper, after tearing down half of the wall, Wesley balls up his pillow against the headboard on his bed, sits against it, and thinks about blues riffs on the National Steel. And he thinks about Mrs. Rigsbee, about Phoebe, about moving that damn wall again, Vernon, Project Promise.

If he can teach Vernon the band songs, then get him in the band, playing bass, then that will free Wesley up to play the National Steel all the time rather than just part of the time. People will be hearing him do the riffs, hearing him get down on some of the stuff he's been learning. He can work some of it into the gospel and then be ready for the blues.

Back at the orphanage, in his room in the afternoons, he used to listen to blues records—the ones given by the Civitans. The blue notes, the bass runs. The flatted thirds and fifths, sevenths. Bent notes. Rhythm-and-blues had it. Blues had it. Black gospel had it. It was like food. Blues music, good blues music, was like Mrs. Rigsbee's pound cake and apple pie, except he ate it with a different part of himself. He had to have it. He had to have the sweetness of it. Blues tasted sweet like her food and it was sad sometimes and there was something about it that sounded like a part of the feeling, the sweet ache in his body when the horses were twisting in the air, getting shot through with hot gold. And that's what he could have with Phoebe if he could figure it all out. He knows he's on the way—now he knows how to love a woman in her heart, whereas he hadn't known about that before. But somehow with Jesus it got more complicated. You give up all the other stuff until you're married. He thinks about the Bible, about reading it straight through. Figuring things out. He needs somebody to talk to about it once he does get started. Somebody to listen to him while he tries to figure it out. Somebody who don't know it all, who will help him figure it out.

Wesley opens the bedside drawer, gets out the Bible Mrs. Rigsbee gave him. Maybe he *should* read the whole thing like she said to. From start to finish. She'd been right about a lot of things. Find out for sure what all is in there. There's no telling. If there was that stuff about David and the concubines and all that, then there's no telling what else he might find. He thumbs through the first few pages, finds Genesis 1.

In the beginning God created the heaven and the earth. And the earth was without form, and void; and darkness was upon the face of the deep. And the spirit of God moved upon the face of the waters.

As he reads, Wesley suddenly sees himself—as if from below, from the front row of an audience— dressed in a white shirt, striped blue-and-white tie, and a navy blue suit, standing behind a lectern, preaching. He sees the sun shining through a window behind him, brightening the fuzz on his cheek.

At first it was all dark, he says aloud.

Ben's tape recorder is on a chair across the room. Wesley gets it, gets his bottleneck practice cassette tape from his bedside table, inserts it into the recorder, sits back down against the headboard, presses the record button, and . . . starts preaching:

At first it was all dark. God was in the dark. Then it was like God had a wand. Whammo here, whammo there. Stuff starts exploding all over the place. I mean it was all clommed together and he starts separating out stuff one from the other.

Wesley reads from the Bible. He looks up at the ceiling. Then he preaches some more, loudly.

Whammo. Light. Bright as day. Bright shining light.

Now the question is whether or not God could see in the dark. Well, He must not could have, because if He could there wouldn't have been no reason to make the light. If God could have seen in the dark it wouldn't have been called the dark. It would have been light, too.

Whammo: water. Whammo: land. Whammo: fruit trees and all kinds of green plants. He was on a roll.

Wesley reads, thinks.

Whammo: sun, moon, stars. But here is a problem it looks like. In the Bible, God made only one sun, one moon. When was all the other galaxies and suns and moons and all that done? I don't know. You don't know, dear friend. Do we need to know? No. It was probably all done at the same time. It's just that whoever wrote it down didn't know everything, it looks like. Else he'd been God.

Whammo: fish and animals.

Whammo: man and woman. And God said to the man and woman, You run the show, and increase, which means make love and have little children. And you eat the fruit and stuff that has seeds and you give the green leafy plants to the animals.

It took God six days to do all this and then he rested on the seventh day because he was pretty tired. And there was all these little animals and big animals running all over the place. And all these little fishes, and everything's fine.

Wesley reads, studies. He flips back to the beginning, reads, flips forward.

Now friends, that's the first version; and the second version is a little different. The second version comes in the Bible right after the first version and it says that God created man before the animals—instead of after. Did you know, friend, that there were two versions? I didn't. What these two versions agree on is that God done it all. What it disagrees on is in what order. This teaches us not to sweat the small stuff. This teaches us that if you believe every word in the Bible is absolutely true like some kind of steel trap, then you believe both of those versions are absolutely true, and if you believe that then you ain't using the brain God gave you and you should be making mud pies or something like that—keeping everything in neat little piles. Because on the earth God made, you can't have two different things happen at the same time with the same people. That's a truth in the universe.

The message of God Almighty is I AM, I put it all together, I put it out there.

Then God made a woman out of the man's rib. In other words, God made man along with the animals, then he made woman. God man woman from bone after he practiced on man and animals. He made man from dirt. What does that say? Well, I don't know.

Wesley hears the door unlatch as the knob turns. Ben comes in, walks to his bed, slips off his shoes. Wesley is reading quietly. Ben, his back to Wesley, starts to say something. "Did you—"

Now friend, we got the fall of man.

Ben looks over his shoulder. Wesley is pointing at him.

"What the—? You talking to me?"

And it ain't here just for a story. It's the core of all our problems, and what it amounts to is us doing something we ain't supposed to do. It happens all the time: You get the deep voice from somewhere saying you ain't supposed to do something, then you get this little shallow voice telling you it's okay. You forget the deep voice, then you put in your two cents worth, which is, you go with the shallow voice, figuring out how it's right, not paying any attention to the deep voice which you heard a long time ago, which is the voice of God. What you do is think about all the good little deeds you did last week and that means you don't have to do what the deep voice is saying. Oh yes, brother!

"What are you . . . ?" Ben sits on his bed, pushes back until he's against the wall, facing Wesley.

The shallow voice is a snake, but you listen any-

way. And you got trouble, brother. The problem with all this about the serpent is we think it's something that happened only one time with Adam and Eve but the fact is it happens every day, and we're stuck with it because Adam and Eve started it all.

Wesley looks straight at Ben.

They had been walking around naked and they didn't even know what naked meant, and they could do anything they wanted to do except eat the fruit off that tree of knowledge. This gets complicated, friend. In fact, it gets so complicated I can't figure it out. Do we need to figure it out? No, we don't.

"What the hell you talking about?" asks Ben.

"I'm preaching."

"I know that. I ask what you talking about?"

"I'm talking about the voice of God. It just got jolted into me."

"Yeah, it sound like you got jolted," says Ben, getting off the bed. "I'm going to fix a samitch."

"I'll be on in a minute. I got to finish this."

"You crazy, man."

The voice of God is loud and clear all the time. Today. This Adam and Eve stuff is going on with you today, maybe this very minute. And friends, the voice of the serpent is talking to the PREACHER. It's telling him to put all the stuff off on the ones he thinks is the mean people in the world. Friends, sometimes the PREACHER is mean. YOU are mean. I am mean. The voice of the serpent is in all our ears, but it's also in our blood. The voice of the serpent is true. All the voices in the Bible are true.

Wesley stands.

Oh sinner, sinner, sinner, you preacher sinner, you place yourself above mean people, the robber, the whore, the kind lady whore with a cat she feeds every day on the way out the door to work. And she gives him fresh water. The serpent speaks from the tree of knowledge, and you think you've got the tree of knowledge in your head. That is why you preach and rant and rave. You put people down. You say don't do this, don't do that, don't do the other. And, oh friend, out there in radio land, know that the voices from the Bible are the voices in your head. You're okay. You live now, then, and forever. Learn the difference between the deep voice and the shallow voice. And if you're comfortable in life, if you have food and warm clothes and a nice mama and daddy and you hear a voice that says, What's still wrong in the world?, that's the shallow voice ... no, no, I got it wrong—it's the deep voice. It gets complicated. The deep voice is the voice of God. Oh voice of God, speak to me, speak to us here together now so we can figure out one from the other. Oh voice of God, speak that I your humble servant may hear.

13

LARRY IS SETTING UP HIS DRUMS, MOVING A CYMBAL away from his seat, touching it with a drumstick, moving it back where it was.

Shanita looks at Vernon Jackson and then at his father, Holister. Two more pasty-faces, she thinks. My God. She leans toward Larry and whispers, "This thing getting to be like the city council."

Larry moves another cymbal away from him a few inches. He slides his chair forward one-half inch.

"Y'all, this is the bass player I was telling you about, Vernon, and this is his daddy, Mr. Jackson. And this is the band—Larry, Ben, and Sherri. And this is Shanita."

Holister says, "Howdy" to Shanita. She says, "Fine," looks at a far wall, scratches her calf.

Holister is thinking, In music, race don't matter.

Sherri Gold is late. When she comes in Wesley hands her a sheet of paper with tentative dates and times for the tour.

"Sears wants to talk to us about the tour," says Wesley, "but he couldn't come by tonight. On this first gig we can't have any instruments because we'll be on this hay wagon—at the Hansen County fair. About seven songs is all we need. Larry, you can bring a snare and use your brushes like you did on the front porch the other day. Ben, you could bring the acoustic guitar from the TV room. It'll have to mostly be good singing songs, acapulco stuff."

"Do you all know 'I Need Your Loving Every Day'?" asks Holister. He's sitting near the door with his elbows on his knees and his chin in the palms of his dirty hands.

"Gospel tune?" asks Ben.

"No, it's a love song. But it's a lot like a gospel tune. It's got good back-up singing."

"Bring a tape of it and we can learn it. One won't make a difference," says Ben.

"You going to be coming to every practice?" Larry asks Holister.

"Oh, no."

"Gets crowded down here."

Crowded ain't the word for it, thinks Shanita. Turded-up is the word for it.

Hanging from the side of a long wagon pulled by a large green tractor is a banner: Ballard University Musical Hayride. It's a bright fall day, seventy-one

175

degrees, warm for November, puffy white clouds. The wagon holds the band and about fifteen passengers, and there are at least twenty waiting to ride. The word has spread. Good music. The wagon takes on a load, and the tractor starts out bumping along the side of a small field at the edge of the county fairgrounds.

Larry starts a vamp with brushes on the snare drum he holds between his legs. Ben strums a chord and starts singing "Jesus Dropped the Charges." On the chorus he has six back-up singers—the original band, and Vernon, Shanita, and Phoebe. They are all seated on two small benches, facing the listeners, who are sitting on the hay. On the first chorus a woman starts clapping her hands.

The tractor cuts across the corner of the field. The band does "I Am a Pilgrim" and "This World Is Not My Home," both spiritual style. The tractor rumbles down a trail which leads between the twelve county fair Dempsey Dumpsters, six on each side. A suit of clothes hangs from a clothes hanger on the side of one. Flies and bees are all around. The air is suddenly thick with the smell of garbage, sour food. Several people in the wagon hold their noses.

On the long home stretch Ben stands and starts singing; "Whoa-whoa, whoa, whoa, whoa, whoa, I need your loving every day." Shanita, Phoebe, and the others sing back-up: "I need your loving every day."

Vernon, out of the blue, starting singing a bass *guitar* part—a bass line—"Boom-ba, boom-ba, boom-ba, boom-ba." So that behind Ben's voice is acoustic guitar, drum brushes, harmony back-up, and bass. It's full and clean, on pitch.

When the song is over, the audience applauds loudly. Larry reaches over, pats Vernon on the back, catches himself, looks at Shanita. The audience wants more. The tractor is back at the starting point and people are waiting.

"You think you could drive this thing somewhere else this time?" asks Ben. He's standing on the ground, looking up at the tractor driver. "That garbage stinks, man."

"I have to stay on the trail."

"Who says so?"

"Dr. Sears."

"You're driving."

"I don't make the rules. I'm just the driver."

"Can't you just turn around and come back this way before you get to the Dumpsters."

"No way. You tend to your part and I'll tend to mine."

"Don't your nose work, man?"

"Yeah, my nose works." Uppity nigger.

"This is the smelliest gig I ever played. And I played some stinking gigs."

"I drive the tractor where I'm told to. You sing like you been told to."

"Shit, man," says Ben. "Sh-nit."

Last night Vernon dreamed about building a wall. His tools were in the grass and Wesley would say, "Trowel." Vernon wouldn't be sure if he was pointing it out or if he was asking Vernon to pick it up or if he was asking Vernon to pick it up and do something with it. When he would bend over to

177

pick it up, Wesley would say, "Striker," but Vernon wouldn't be able to decide which was which. Then Wesley said, "Edger," then "Chisel." Vernon knew the chisel. He picked it up. He handed it to Wesley and Wesley stuck it in Vernon's ribs. Vernon had cried out, waking himself up.

This afternoon after the fair gig, Vernon is driving his Plymouth to BOTA House to help with the wall.

Wesley is in his room, alone. He places an earphone plug in his left ear. A cord runs to Ben's recorder, which holds the recording of his sermon. He pushes the play button, listens for a minute and then joins in, saying the words as he hears them—about a half-second delay, same tone, pitch, force. The regular volume knob is off so the only sound in the room is Wesley's voice, preaching, just as he preached the first time.

Later, Vernon holds a hawk with mortar. He is rocking back and forth. He scoops mortar with Wesley's trowel and plops it on a brick. His tongue is curled out over his upper lip. "I think I'm getting it. How does that look?"

"Looks pretty good, actually. Not bad at all."

"I dreamed about all them things last night. Chisel and edger and all that. You stuck me in the ribs with a chisel."

"I wouldn't do that, man."

"I know that. But that's what I dreamed."

"Listen. I've got this idea I want to try out when we finish working. All you've got to do is come up to my room for about ten minutes."

Upstairs, Wesley pulls the cane-bottomed chair from against the wall into the middle of his room.

He faces it toward the door. "Sit here," he says to Vernon.

"What for?"

"Just sit down. Here. I'll show you."

Vernon sits.

"Now, all I got to do is hook all this up."

Wesley pulls his bedside table to a spot in front of the door, places the tape recorder on it. He faces Vernon. A cord runs from his ear to the recorder. "Now. Everything is ready. All you have to do is pretend you're in church. I'm going to preach you a sermon and I want you to listen. Okay?"

"How long is it? The only ones I ever heard were too long."

"This is about ten minutes. Just a practice. Here goes."

Wesley pushes the playback button.

At first it was all dark. God was in the dark. Then it was like God had a wand. Whammo here, whammo there. Stuff starts exploding all over the place. I mean it was all clommed together and he starts separating out stuff one from the other.

Wesley looks into Vernon's eyes as he preaches, locks in, moves his arms, leans forward, back, then leans in and holds—as if leaning into the wind.

Wesley is hearing and saying the words, but at the same time he's thinking: he stopped rocking.

Whammo: water. Whammo: land. Whammo: fruit trees and all kinds of green plants.

And finally, *Oh voice of God, speak that I, your humble servant, may hear.*

Wesley turns off the recorder, pulls the earphone from his ear, moves the table back to where it was. Vernon starts rocking slowly again, quickly getting back up to speed. "That was good preaching," he says. "I didn't used to ever understand any I heard before."

"Did you understand this?"

"No. But it was short."

"Well, I just needed to do it for somebody. I'm kind of deciding on a long-term career after I do music for a while."

"You'd have to get some new clothes if you're going to be a preacher. And them two shoes don't look too good, either."

"Shoes wouldn't make no difference. You'd be standing behind a thing. I'd probably have to wear a suit." Wesley thinks about the sparkling coats he could wear as a professional musician, the white doctor's coat he would wear as a doctor, one of those dermatologists.

"How'd you learn how to preach?"

"It all started with this old lady that took me in."

"In what?"

"Inside. I was a orphan."

"You was from England?"

"No. No. I was a orphan. I didn't have a mama and daddy. I was raised up in an orphanage."

"I thought all orphans was from England," says Vernon, "and it happened to them in War War One and War War Two."

"War War One?"

"Yeah."

"You mean 'World War'?"

"I don't know. Ain't that where orphans come from?"

"No. That's crazy."

The rocking stops.

"Wait! Wait!" Wesley stands, holds out his hand, palm up. "You ain't crazy. You ain't crazy!"

"AARRAAAAAAAAAAAHHHHH."

Wesley is out the door, running for the kitchen.

"Did you know that Lot slept with his two daughters?" Wesley asks Mattie next day at Sunday dinner.

"Here, eat some more of these," says Mattie, passing Wesley a bowl of corn and butter beans. "I want them all gone. I've had them in the refrigerator I don't know how long."

"Did you know he did that? Slept with his two daughters?"

"We're going to talk about this again?"

"I mean 'slept' like he had sex with them."

"I think I might have heard something about that."

"It's in the Bible."

"Well, there's lots in there, son, that's more interesting than that."

"I think that was pretty interesting, myself."

"There are all kinds of things in the Bible."

"I know that. Now. But you didn't—"

"Here, eat the rest of these. There ain't enough to save."

"I was reading all that stuff and, I mean, man, it's something."

"Do you read any from the New Testament?"

"I did. I started reading the red print, then I read it all. Jesus comes out different when you read it straight through. He caused a lot of trouble. Did you know that?"

"That's one way to think about it. But it was a whole lot more than just causing trouble."

"It just seems like causing trouble is more like Jesus than staying out of trouble. And all I been hearing for the last six or eight years in church is stuff about staying out of trouble. I'm thinking about writing a song about Jesus."

"Oh? A hymn?"

"Not exactly. But something, something that shakes people up maybe. Actually, I've already got one started about what Jesus might dream. See, I have these drea—"

"You don't need to be shaking people up. Especially when you're in a halfway house."

"I'm just thinking about it."

"Did you say you're thinking about preaching?"

"It went through my mind. I even did a little sermon into a tape recorder."

"Well, I pray for you every day, son. That you get a good occupation. I pray for your health. I pray that you will serve God and be happy in your work, whatever it is, and that you will hear His call for whatever it is He wants you to do."

"Well, I've been thinking a little bit about maybe becoming a skin doctor. I was reading something about that. A dermatologist. But right now I'm happy doing music and masonry—and eating creamed potatoes. How do you get those little lumps in there?"

"You don't overcook the potatoes to start with, and then you don't mash them up all the way. But listen, you ought to consider moving up to something else. I think it would be wonderful if you did

182

become a preacher—if you were really called to do that."

"I don't know. I'd have to get ordained. I'm not sure I'd like the ordainers."

"I've always prayed that my children could maybe live out some of the dreams I couldn't live out because I didn't have time—bringing them up. Elaine did teach for a while but now she's in that other work, computers. Seems like computers ain't nothing but speed. They just do stuff faster. I'd be afraid if I worked on them things I'd die sooner."

"Die? You ain't ... what dreams did you have?"

"Oh, nothing. Eat that last piece of cornbread. I'll tell you some other time. It's time to clean up this mess."

"I don't think I could preach the stuff I been hearing. And the Sears twins are always bringing up America and stuff at the same time they bring up Jesus. It's like they think Jesus was an American or something. Which he won't."

"Son, listen, you can't judge your own life by what you don't like in somebody else's. Those twins have a big place to run. They have to be concerned with stuff you never have to think about. Now sometimes I think they're a little too big for their britches, but that's not one of the things I was put on earth to worry about. You've got to learn not to get quite so upset at other folks' ways."

"I think they're too big for their britches, too. The problem is, everybody's afraid to tell them. Next time that Ned tells me to build that wall again, I'm going to tell him to do it hisself."

"You had to build that thing again?"

"Oh yeah."

"Well, I don't blame you."

"It don't make no difference to him that somebody's got to do it. He just wants to see results. You know what they do when somebody dies? Like one of the professors or something?"

"What?"

"They send their family a rose for every year they've worked there, or something like that, but if it's more then twelve, they send them a dozen roses and a bucket of Kentucky Fried Chicken. Something like that."

"That Bojangles is good, too."

14

Wesley, Ben, and Vernon are eating french fries in the Columbia Grill.

"We could use that bass singing, like a bass guitar, I mean, on all the stuff we do straight—without instruments," says Ben to Vernon. "That sounded pretty good, man. What made you think of that?"

"I just pretended I was a bass guitar and made sounds I'd be making with my fingers."

Mary, the waitress, asks, "Y'all want some more fries?"

Ben and Wesley are sitting across from Vernon. "You got any money?" Ben asks Vernon.

"My daddy don't let me carry money."

"I got some," says Wesley. "Yeah, we'll take another order." Wesley pulls out his billfold. "I think

185

I got some more." He looks. "Yeah, I got two dollars."

"We need to work up some more songs, too," says Ben. "That thing at the Activity Club is supposed to last a hour—just gospel stuff. I'm getting tired of that crap. That's two gigs we've played without any instruments, too."

"Four months and we can be doing all blues," says Wesley. "We might even have that album behind us."

Vernon is trying to read the small print on his can of Coke.

"I believe that when I see it," says Ben.

"Anyway, I been writing this song about Jesus in a kind of blues style," says Wesley. "I just read all this stuff about Jesus straight through, the red ink and all that, and it's something, and I figured I would write a new Jesus song, figured I could put in some stuff about Jesus being in the world today because it's like whatever he'd be would be kind of weird."

"Sing it," says Vernon.

"Well, I just started working on it. But, see, I figured I could turn everything around in the song and have Jesus be what he wouldn't be. Something like—get kind of a blues vamp going—dada, dada, dada, dada, *Jesus was a banker with a white Continental, joined a country club in 1962. He had a house*—let's see—*he had a mansion on the lake, played golf once a week, da da da, da da da*, something rhymes with 'two.' *Watched Monday Night Football*. Something like that. I don't know. I hadn't got it worked out. But you get the idea."

186

"What the hell's wrong with Monday Night Football?" asks Ben.

Vernon clunks his Coke can down on the table and sings, *Jesus was a ugly nigger woman.*

"What you *say*, man?" says Ben. "What the hell you *say*?" Ben glares at Vernon, snatches his Coke can, crunches it in his hand. Coke pours out on the table, flows toward Wesley. Wesley moves back, grabs napkins from the napkin holder and starts blotting it up.

"He said it's what he *ain't*," said Vernon. "He didn't say it's what he was. It's about what he ain't. Why you getting mad because I'm—"

" 'Cause you saying 'nigger.' That's what the problem is."

"I said what he ain't. If I was saying that's what he was, you ought to get mad, but that ain't what I was saying."

"Listen here—"

"Wesley said it would be about what he ain't and I just thought that up, so why are you getting mad at me about saying what he ain't?"

"Shut up, man. You don't go asking me questions."

"Well, I didn't mean nothing."

"I don't care what you mean. Besides that, Jesus was a honkey."

"Hey, watch it," says Wesley.

Mary sets the french fries on the table, looks hard at Ben, says, "You got to be kidding me," and leaves.

"But maybe," says Wesley, "see, maybe we could do that—maybe we could say all of that in the song."

"You crazy?" says Ben.

"Don't you see?" Wesley gets a french fry, the salt shaker, salts it.

"Salt them all, man," says Ben.

Wesley salts the fries.

Vernon gets one, dips it in the ketchup left on the already used french fry plate. "I like to dip mine," he says.

"That's too goddamned bad," says Ben. "You got a lot of nerve, you know that?"

"Wait a minute. Look, Ben, he's right," says Wesley. "It's like Jesus was at the bottom of the barrel. People were spitting on him and stuff, like if somebody was to call you a 'nigger.' "

"I don't want to hear it, man. From neither one of you. Especially in no god—nodnamned song."

"But see, the song could be about how people hated him at the end," says Wesley, chewing on a hot french fry, then holding his mouth open. "That's all. I mean it was a bad time. And that's what they would say. And see, we could say that too. That don't mean you believe in it."

"Forget it, man, it's a crazy idea. I ain't singing no song that says 'nigger' in it. You crazy. You better be glad Shanita ain't here."

"Well, we could write that in about 'honky' too. Then we could say he was a Jew somewhere in there. What do they call Jews, anyway?"

They are quiet for a minute.

"Jews, I guess," says Ben.

"Well, I'm going to write it anyway. Jesus driving to work in a car or something like that. Let's get out of here. I got to work on that song."

Wesley leaves a quarter tip.

* * *

Ben has a letter waiting on the table by the door when he and Wesley get back to BOTA House. He opens it and reads as they start up the wide stairs to their room.

"My damn sister, asking for money," he says.

"Where is she?"

"Memphis, out of work."

"Why don't she ask your mama and daddy?"

"Ha."

"What do they do?"

"My mama and daddy? They play cards and drink. When my daddy ain't propped up in a corner in the floor with vomit all over him, he'll have people over and they sit around a card table, playing cards and drinking Winn-Dixie wine, or liquor if they can get it."

Ben sits in his chair by the window, lights up. "They start playing cards about four o'clock in the afternoon and play until there's a fight or somebody falls down, passes out or something. When we was little there'd be so much noise we couldn't sleep. There was four of us, and we slept on couch cushions in two little closets. That's no shit—nit, man. We had coats for covers. And Sears asked me why I ran away from home and why I didn't stay home and help my mama and daddy get out of the conditions they was in. I can't remember exactly how he said it, but that's what he meant. Nod-*namn*."

Wesley thinks about the orphanage. He sees long, empty halls.

"I tell you," says Ben. "I'd like to kill that son of a bitch."

"Sears?"

"My old man. He used to—hell, Sears too. Anyway, my old man used to get drunk and piss in the closet on them couch cushions and we'd have to sleep on it. There's the wall, the dark wall with crayon marks and no light in there, and I'm sleepy, man, I mean sleepy, and there's that smell and I touch my hand down there and it's damp and so I turn it over,"

"Namn."

"Yeah, that's right. You just turn them over and hope it ain't seeped through. Some hot day in July or something my mama would soak them in water and let them stay in the sun one at a time for a few days till they dried out. At that orphanage at least you didn't have to sleep on piss, did you?"

"Not 'less it was your own. We had a lot of little boys peeing in the bed. They'd have to hold their noses in it for two minutes. Two minutes is a long time."

"He'd get drunk and he didn't know the closet from the bathroom. He actually pissed on us, man. More than once. I'd hear it splattering on somebody. Or feel it on myself. Then he'd get to crying and stuff.

"That pamphlet thing Sears put in our box on Father's Day. 'Honor thy father and mother' and all that. Ain't that a gas? See, that's the way he think. That's the kind of head he got. Sears, I'm talking about. That's what in his head, and don't make no difference what goes on out there in the world, you know, what's really going on, that's just the way he think, the way he made up his mind to think no matter what's going on. Yeah, I could kill his ass too. You sleep on piss for fourteen years, see you don't want to kill somebody that didn't."

"I didn't sleep on piss for fourteen years. That won't get you nowhere—you kill me."

"Naw, I mean, you know, somebody that comes along and tells you how to think about your own stuff, talk, how to talk nice. That's what I mean. You at least got your rule—some kind of compromise. You ain't, you know, weird about it. This dude talks to me like I'm some little baby. You know what I mean?"

"Yeah. I know what you mean. What are you smoking anyway?"

"I got some good stuff. Whew."

Wesley pulls off his socks, throws them onto his bed.

"Yeah, man," says Ben. "They'd play cards. And if they didn't have enough people my mama would play. And there'd be cockroaches and stuff. And they'd just sit there having a good old time. I mean, they'd be laughing and . . . having a good old time."

"What about fourteen years—did you leave when you were fourteen?"

"Yeah. Two nights after my little sister did."

"Who put the plaque on the broom closet door is all I want to know." Ted is presiding over the Monday executive committee breakfast meeting.

"I put it in the right place to start with," says Coach Guthrie. "I don't know what happened after that. I know I wouldn't put it up beside no broom closet." He looks around at the others.

"Well, we got her calmed down, thank goodness," says Ted. "Hampton," he says to the new
191

dean, "you did a good piece of work on that. A-plus."

"Thank you, sir. I've had some experience with hysterical women in my time."

"I'm glad you called over there and got all the details. I couldn't imagine who'd been doing all that screaming."

"I heard it was one of them retarded people in the Project Promise?" says Big Don. "Is that right?"

"Yes, the one that prayed out loud at the banquet, which worries me a bit because it illustrates how risky this kind of thing can be. Mrs. Clark's trust fund holds over two million dollars, as you-all know. But, she seems to understand finally, thanks in large part to you, Hampton.

"Now," Ted continues, "the band thing—this little tour—is going to work for us, I think. I been getting some very positive phone calls about their performance at the fair. People are excited. We need to get as much publicity out of it as possible— recruiting, et cetera. Look toward something bigger."

"We've already got a problem on it," says Ned. "I talked to Herb Bolling this morning. He was driving the tractor at the fair, and he said the band was doing some kind of long song about 'making love' or something. I don't know what it was. Anyway, one of the band members cursed him. It was something about the route they were taking around the fair grounds. The boy actually cursed Herb. One of the blacks."

Ted frowns, wipes his fingers across his mouth. "I want to know who that was. We can't have that,

not with Ballard's name on it. Get right on that."
He's looking at Ned.

"I certainly will." Maybe this is something we can assign to Colonel Trent, thinks Ned.

"I told the *Pilot* to cover the Christmas luncheon," says Coach. "They called and said they were working on another article on that Benfield boy, about his 'transformation' or something, living with that old Rigsbee lady, attending church, getting that retarded boy playing in the band."

"He's in the band too?" asks Big Don.

"Oh, yes, and we do need to get Benfield in a grammar course," says Ted. "Can we do that now?" he asks Ned.

"Not before spring semester."

"Well, as soon as possible in any case. That'll make our ties to him more definite. In fact, maybe he can give a little testimony at the LinkComm Christmas luncheon—the nursing home thing." Ted turns his Parker fountain pen—tip to tip— between his fingers. "Maybe we could write something out for him. I think both we and LinkComm could get some good exposure on this, this time around. Snaps agrees. And of course those people at the rest home need all the support we can give them."

Ned is realizing that the band-impropriety matter is exactly the place to test the new dean's loyalty. "Hampton, would you talk to the gospel band about these improprieties?"

"Sure. I don't mind handling it." Well, I'll be damned, Trent thinks. I didn't know this was the kind of thing I'd be asked to do. Talk to a gospel band about cursing. This is some kind of test or else Ned is afraid of it.

"How much weight has your daughter lost, Hampton?" asks Coach. "She's sure gone down some."

Trent draws up a little. "I don't know exactly, but she's happy with the program." He glances at Stan, the assistant treasurer, the very quiet one. Why isn't he talking?

"It is a good program," says Ted. "It is a good program." He checks his hair in the mirror. "Oh yes, Mysteria, do you have those PVA schedules for next week?"

"Yes sir."

"How about bringing them in."

Each member of the executive committee looks over the PVA schedule. Coach reads silently with his lips moving.

"Ned, we need to schedule Greg to videotape the LinkComm luncheon. Be sure he's not covering dog surgery that morning. What kind of coverage are we getting for the luncheon, anyway?"

"Good. Very good, so far. This band idea has actually already helped some. Good Morning Charlie is going to cover it. We got a tentative TV promise, and one from the *Star*, so it looks good. And I think it's a very good idea to have Benfield give a little testimony. Something about Ballard's influence on his life, how he became a Christian. Something short. Why don't you bring that up to him when you talk with the band, Hampton? I'm sure he'll agree to do it. He's quite outgoing. 'Course you'd know about that—him dating your daughter and all."

"Yes. He's outgoing." Hampton's eyebrows come up, the corners of his mouth go down.

Stan is wondering if the president is going to mention the memo sent from the faculty senate to the president. Someone mailed Stan a blind copy. There are several requests on it. One is for clarification on whether or not an airport expansion is in the works.

"What about the senate concerns regarding the airport?" Stan asks Ted.

Ted is viewing his reflection in the polished surface of his desktop. If he tilts his head just right, he can see if his rooster tail is holding down. How does Stan know about that memo? he thinks. "What about it?"

"The senate was wondering about it, I think. Wondering if there was—"

"Yes. That's also something we need to discuss this morning. As all of you know, nothing has been decided on any airport. There haven't even been any official discussions of it. Of course, when it is decided, if it is, it could be one of the best boosts for businesses in Summerlin imaginable—and in Bethel and Listre, too. And students could get out and in of here lots easier. Speakers too. We could get that American Eagle commuter service in here. I've already checked on that. And with growth of this area, we of course get growth of Ballard University.

"Now, since you asked, Stan, we at this table, and some of the folks at Eastern LinkComm, and another company or two are the only people who knew—I thought—about any possible expansion of the airport. And be advised if that decision ever is made, it will be a wise move. So, that's that on that. Don't leak it. Don't even leak that there was a leak. In fact, there is nothing to leak. There are no plans in existence to expand the airport. If anybody asks, that's what you can say and it's the truth. There are no plans. Now, I got a memo from the faculty senate—which you apparently also received, Stan. Who from?"

"I don't know."

"You don't know?"

"Yes sir?"

"You *do* know?"

"No sir."

"You said, 'yes sir.' "

"I meant yes sir, I don't know."

"Oh. Well, anyway I got a memo from over there, the senate, asking among other things that Ned and Hampton no longer be voting members of that group. Weren't you-all there at the last meeting?"

"Ned was, weren't you, Ned?" asks Hampton.

"No, I thought you were."

"Neither one of you was?" asks Ted. "Listen. Try not to let that happen again. If one of you had been there, I don't think this memo would have been considered. I want you and Hampton to get on top of who's stirring up trouble over there. So. That's that. Any other questions, Stan?" This is your last year here, son, Ted thinks. We made a mistake. Your loyalty quotient is lower than dirt.

This is my last year, thinks Stan. I'd rather work at a grocery store.

Big Don is looking out the window at his white Cadillac. "Is anybody else getting his car door chipped in that parking lot?" He turns his hearing aid up.

Nobody says anything.

"Well, I am, and there ain't nothing to do but get rid of that handicapped place and widen those four places across the side there. Put the handicapped space somewhere else. Mysteria, are you on?"

"Yes sir."

"Would you get maintenance on the phone, and get that done?"

"Yes sir. Right away."

Jesus, where do you park, when you drive your car to town?
Jesus, where do you park, when you drive your car to town?
Do you park by the bank, or down where people are down?
Do you drive a Cadillac?
Do you drive a Pontiac?
Do you park at the mall?
Do you drive a car at all?
Jesus, da-da da da, da-da da da, da-da da.

15

WESLEY SPOONS BLACK-EYED PEAS FROM A BOWL, AT Mattie's.

"You were a little hungry, won't you?" asks Mattie.

"I guess I was. Could you pass that cornbread?"

"That was certainly a nice article about you in the newspaper. I want to hear your band sometime."

"You can come to that luncheon they wrote about. Miss Pearl will be there."

"Yeah, she cut out three copies of the article. They put one on the bulletin board. They get free newspapers a day late." Mattie squeezes lemon in her iced tea. "What was that about a song you're writing about Jesus? Is that what you were telling me about the other day?"

"Yes ma'am. It's a song about what Jesus would be like if he was alive today."

"He is alive."

"Well, you know. I mean if he was in the world and all."

"He would be Jesus. Put your napkin in your lap."

"I know that. But see, I told you I started reading all the red print in the Bible, you know, Jesus talking, and that got me reading the rest of it—around the red print—and it's amazing stuff. He'd get mad at these people following him around. He'd just get real tired and have to drop somewhere. And he hung around with these women some, too. Talked to this prostitute and stuff. No joke. It's right there in black and white. And red and white. Anyway, they were a kind a gang or a posse or something, you know, these thirteen guys sort of hanging around without jobs. So I figured he'd have a hard time of it today. We got to talking about it in the band and so I'm writing a song about it. About whether or not he'd drive a car."

Mattie frowns, leans her head back, looks at Wesley for a few seconds. "Well, you need to be careful about that songwriting. You did that Texas song with that ugly word in it."

"That was before I stopped cussing. Oh, one other thing I found out: you know what Jacob did? He slept with all these different maids of his wife and had all these children, and he slept with his wife's sister—and God was involved in that. I know where it is." Wesley stands, walks over to the chest of drawers in the dining room and gets Mattie's Bible. "Here it is ... somewhere. Here it is. 'And God harkened unto Leah, and she conceived.' And

199

all the time God knew that Leah was Jacob's *wife's sister.* Did you know about all that?"

"Some of it, yes."

"And somewhere in there Jacob told God, 'If you expect me to do such and such, then you ought to do such and such.' It was like he was talking back to God, kind of standing up to him, somehow. . . . What's the matter? It's in there."

Mattie is staring at Wesley—hard. "You be careful how you talk about God."

"It ain't *me,* it's the *Bible.* One of them things they never preach about. Here, I'll show you. It's right here somewhere. I tell you, it's like there are two Bibles—the one in church and the one between the covers. The one between the covers is better, but some of it don't go together. Like those two different creations and all."

"Well, you be careful. There's one important word you better remember, if you want to stay out of trouble."

"What?"

"Respect."

Wesley is looking in Genesis. "It's in here somewhere. Oh, well. I can't find it. But just about everything else is in here, too. Everything you ever thought about."

"You just remember what I said." Mattie stands, walks over to the stove. "About respect. And read some Psalms, for heaven's sake. You sound agitated." She moves a pot off a hot eye. "I forgot to turn this off. Your teeth doing okay?"

"Fine."

"Don't you want some more of these black-eyed peas?"

"I'm about stuffed, but I'll eat a few more."

"When we was living on Prichard Street in Raleigh back when I was about fourteen, me and Pearl ate black-eyed peas in the middle of the night one time. Do you want some more tea?"

"Sure. I can get it."

"No. Keep your seat."

Mattie pours Wesley more tea. "You need some more ice," she says. She opens the freezer door and gets out three cubes of ice, drops them in his tea. "What was I talking about?"

"Eating black-eyed peas in the middle of the night."

"Oh yes. Well, Pearl had got up and packed her bags to run away. Merle what's-his-name was going to pick her up. Merle and Pearl. I didn't know anything about it. She was sleeping in the same room with me and when she got up, she woke me up, but she didn't know it. So I stayed real still and watched her pack in the dark and leave the room. Well, it scared me to death. I didn't know what in the world was wrong. I got up when she was out of the room, and what she did was go sit out on the edge of the front porch beside her bag, waiting for somebody. I could tell she was waiting for somebody. There weren't any street lights back then and I could see her through the window from the light of the moon. I didn't know what to do. She was going somewhere and hadn't even said goodbye. For all I knew I'd never see her again as long as I lived. I didn't want to be without Pearl, you know."

Mattie reaches for and stabs two cucumber slices with her fork. "I went back to my room, got dressed very quietly, got the cardboard box I kept under the bed, cleaned it out, and put some of my own clothes in it, went back to the living room to wait for whoever it was coming after her. I figured what I'd do is go with her, but I wouldn't show myself until whoever it was come. I didn't know it was supposed to be Merle Bogart. Bogart, that was his name. It never crossed my mind that whoever it was would mind me coming along.

"Pearl had this pocket watch that Merle had give her. She had it in her dress pocket, and she kept taking it out and looking at it in the light of the moon. I can see her now, holding it up to the light of the moon, reading the face of that pocket watch.

"She came back in when it just started getting light. When she saw me, she put her face in her hands and started crying, just sobbing like nobody's business. Then she looked up and said, 'What are you doing up?' and I said, 'I was going with you,' and she said, 'I ain't going nowhere. He didn't come,' and she started sobbing again. I said the only thing I could think of—'Don't you want something to eat?' And she said yes, and so we went in the kitchen and the first thing I grabbed in the ice box was a bowl of black-eyed peas and we spooned us out some on two little flat plates, staying as quiet as we could so as not to wake anybody up. Pearl kept looking at me, crying, saying, 'He didn't come. He didn't come,' while we ate our little piles of black-eyed peas, ice cold."

"Didn't anybody wake up?"

"No. We got back in the bedroom and lay there awake for a little while before anybody got up. Then Mama wanted to know who'd been eating. I don't remember what we said."

"We used to get up in the middle of the night at the orphanage and do things," says Wesley. "But we didn't ever eat any black-eyed peas. They locked up the food." Wesley takes a drink of iced tea. "What happened to the Merle guy?"

"You know, I don't know. He was never mentioned again, and I never saw him again. Wouldn't it be interesting to come across him somewhere and ask him what happened."

"I guess he chickened out."

"I guess he did. You about ready for dessert?"

Phoebe and her father are eating supper at Brad's restaurant in downtown Summerlin.

"But, Daddy, I don't think you know how serious he is about things. He's not a bit like Pete or Randy. He's really very nice. He's had a lot of hard knocks in his background, and I wish you could meet this elderly lady he used to stay with. She's something."

Phoebe watches the butter—left out long enough to be soft—spreading over her father's bread, thick and even. She's down twenty-five. About seventy-five to go.

"That's all fine and good, but the problem I'm confronting is a problem of assimilation. You've got a group of people who aren't used to certain institutional norms, and they've got to conform or the institution suffers, the purpose suffers. The purpose of Ballard University is—in a nutshell—Christian Higher Education. It's a higher goal, a higher cause. And can you imagine a more noble cause, or purpose, in today's world?"

"No, I don't guess so."

"You don't guess so?"

"I was just trying to talk about Wesley. And I heard some of that conversation between Ben and the tractor driver. The tractor driver wouldn't listen to anybody. He kept driving between those smelly Dempsey Dumpsters when he didn't have to."

"I know, I know. But you're missing the point. I'm not talking about the past. I'm talking about the future. This band thing can either be very good or very bad, and it's up to the administration to see that it supports the college's purpose. I am now a part of this administration. They pay me, Phoebe." Trent lines up the salt and pepper shakers, side by side. "I'll talk to the band. If they're smart, they'll heed what I say."

"What do *you* think about Wesley?"

"What do *I* think about him?"

"Yes."

"Well, he's got a way to go."

"Before?"

"He's just got a way to go, don't you think?"

"I don't know, exactly."

"Honey, I can't tell you what to do. Who to date. But there is a fine student body on campus— eligible young men. And a fine ROTC."

The band members sit around in the basement. Vernon rocks. Shanita picks a spot on the wall to stare at. Larry turns his drumstick in his hand, scrapes its tip with his fingernail.

"We've gotten all kinds of good reports," Colonel Trent, standing, tells the band. "But we've had a couple of problems, and that's why the president has asked me to share a few ideas with you." He sits. "First, which one of you is Ben Ashley?"

Ben raises a finger.

"One more instance of your cursing or demonstrating other negative behavior while representing Ballard University and you will no longer be on any tour we sponsor. Is that clear?"

"What you talking about?"

"The hayride at the fair. The tractor. The driver was Herb Bolling from the religion department. You cursed him."

"You know what he did to me?"

"No. And I'm not interested. No more cursing. Is that clear?"

"Yeah. That's pretty clear."

"We've got to be clear. We've got to understand each other."

"Why are *you* the boss of BOTA House?" asks Vernon.

"It's not a matter of being boss, son. It's a matter of a relationship involving a lab setting within Ballard University's School of Social Work that we—"

"You're talking like a boss."

"You're the young man in Project Promise, is that correct?"

"Yep. Are you my boss, too?"

"I'm not anybody's boss—here. But I do need to make a couple of points that I do have the authority to make. If you don't mind. Now, secondly, in any organization—"

"I don't mind, if you ain't my boss. My daddy's the only boss I got."

Trent, sitting very still, looks at Vernon for a few seconds. This young man is retarded, he thinks. Patience is due. "You see, hierarchy is necessary in any organization. In fact, it's the cornerstone of

205

American democracy and the rise of so-called equality has been at the expense of excellence in our society—a point missed by not a few intellectuals, and others. There's no need for me to get into all that, I suppose, but the way that pertains to this band is this: On this tour—and as long as you're affiliated with Ballard University—it is necessary that (a) you do only gospel songs and (b) there be no use of profanity on tour. I can't control your thoughts or your language off tour, but on this tour there will be no profanity. In fact, all the rules of BOTA House, those posted on the bulletin board, apply at all times on the tour. This way we all win. We're in this together."

Vernon squints through his glasses at Trent. "That other song is the one my daddy likes. It's about 'everybody needs somebody to love,' and God is love, so it seems like to me that it's a song about God. If God is love. Because it's about God and the Bible says God is love."

"Well, I don't know about your theology there, but first, God is about more than love, and second, as I mentioned in (a) above, this group is to do *no* songs that aren't strictly gospel songs. It's very simple. What you do on your own time is of course up to you, but on this tour and subsequent tours, if we continue to recruit this way, the music is to be strictly gospel music. We just can't afford any negative feedback. That's the bottom line. And, by the way, we're finalizing plans for a Christmas dinner over at Eastern LinkComm—something that's been a tradition, I understand—for the folks at Shady Grove Nursing Home. It's going to be on radio, and maybe TV. The president will be there and he's suggested that—and this is my last point—Wesley, he's suggested that you might like to give a brief testimony about your Christian faith, and perhaps a short tribute to Ballard University."

"Sure," says Wesley. I'll do anything you ask me to do, he thinks. Me and you get on bad terms and my love life might be in trouble.

When I sleep in class I drool all down my desk.
When I sleep in class I drool all down my desk.
I like to sleep in Math, but I like to sleep in English
  best.

I don't bother nobody, and nobody bothers me.
I don't bother nobody, and nobody bothers me.
I been a graduating senior since 1983.

16

"ALL RIGHT," SAYS WESLEY. "I'LL LET YOU DO the whole thing from start to finish. First you got to open these cans."

On the counter beside the sink at Vernon's house are a can of soup, cans of tomatoes, of corn, of butter beans, four small red potatoes, two onions, one wrapped beef bullion cube, a large cooking pot, and a half-head of cabbage.

"I can open cans." Vernon gets a bottle opener from the drawer and starts putting triangular holes around the top of a can of vegetable soup—Campbell's.

"No, no, no. Here, give me that. Here." Wesley looks in the drawer, finds a can opener. "You've got to use one of these kind. Ain't you ever opened a can?"

"Hundreds."

"I mean the right way."

"I got everything out of every one I ever opened. Why ain't that right?"

"I mean—look—here's all you do."

"My way's just as easy."

"No, it's not."

"I'll race you."

"No, no, no. If you do it that way you get them little pieces of metal in there. This is what this is, a can opener. What you got is a bottle opener."

"Looks like if you open a can with it, it's a can opener, too. Something that opens a can is a can opener, it looks like to me. All you have to do is—"

"Listen. You could run over it with a car and open it. That don't make a car a damn can opener."

Vernon pauses, looks at Wesley. "It would for just a second."

"Vernon. Open the cans any way you want to. I don't care."

"You don't have to get so upset."

"I ain't upset. Okay? Now pour in the tomatoes first because you've got to cut them up some. I'll help you open the rest of these cans."

"I can do it."

Vernon slowly opens the other cans with the can opener while Wesley stands back and waits. Then Vernon pours the tomatoes into a cooking pot. "Do you leave all the juice in there?" he asks.

"Yeah. That's what this is, man. Soup. Now just cut them up some."

209

Vernon cuts up the tomatoes, holding the knife by the blade and getting his fingers in the juice. "Looks like you wouldn't mix all them juices together."

"Why not?"

"I don't know. It just don't seem right."

"Now, you got to ... I'll peel the potato while you cut up that cabbage. Can you cut up cabbage?"

"I don't know."

"Here. I'll just do one slice. This cabbage is the secret of the whole thing." Wesley cuts off a slice of cabbage, sections it, chops it.

"Who taught you all this?"

"That Mrs. Rigsbee I used to live with."

"You going to live with her when you get out of that house?"

"Oh ... I don't know. I don't know. I probably will until I get my job figured out. My career. You know. Then I'll probably live in Myrtle Beach for a while. She ... ah, she taught me about shaking people's hands, too—looking somebody in the eye and shaking their hand." Wesley lays down the knife, wipes his hand on his pants. "Like this. You walk into a room, see, and you see somebody standing over there that you want to meet. You walk up like this, look them straight in the eye, stick out your hand and get a firm grip like this, see, and say, 'How do you do? I'm Vernon Jackson.' Pump it a couple of times, turn loose, and that way you get along better in the world. Now, why don't you go in there, walk back in here and do the same thing. Practice."

Vernon looks over at the door. He doesn't move. He stands, rocking slowly. "I don't want to meet

210

anybody. I already know everybody I want to know."

"Well, I mean . . ." Wesley rolls his eyes to the ceiling. "Like, you might need another music teacher or something when I'm gone."

"I don't want you to go."

"I got to go sometime."

Vernon stops rocking.

Wesley feels funny. Why did *he* say that? He's got a whole daddy, who lives with him in a house with four walls.

"You going to peel them potatoes?" says Wesley. "No, I'll peel them. You know, you never know when it might be a good idea to meet somebody. Like what if we were having a gig and you had to meet somebody."

"I'd just have to play the music right. I wouldn't have to shake their hand no certain way."

"You're hardheaded, man." Wesley is peeling a potato. He looks to see if Vernon is clouding up, if his eyes are getting bigger. They're not. "But you're all right."

"I'm a killer diller," says Vernon.

"Just pour that in there. . . . All of it, get it all. Now do the onions the same way. This will be good stuff. You won't believe how good it is. There ain't nothing better on a cold day. See, what gives it a little bite and makes it so good is the cabbage and the tomato, and then the onion makes it sweet and, man, it's good stuff. It'll be about ready when your daddy gets in. . . . Yeah, just go ahead and dump that in there. Right. Now, put it on the stove. I'll turn on the stove. You just turn it to medium-high and when it starts boiling you turn it almost off so it just simmers for a long time. It'll be ready when he gets in and then every day it'll get better until you finish it, and by that time you'll be tired of it, unless it goes real fast."

"You're a killer diller," says Vernon. "You ain't dull in your head."

That night, just before lights out, Wesley and Ben are in their beds talking. It's raining hard and lightning flashes.

"Vernon's old man has got over thirty tapes of blues he's recorded off old albums and stuff. That's how Vernon learned to play piano. Maybe I can get you over there sometime. There were some good ones we listened to tonight. One was that 'If It Looks Like Jelly, Shakes Like Jelly.' Our version is a little bit too fast. And Vernon, you know, will say that. He'll be standing around in the shop and his daddy will ask him to get something and he'll be fumbling around in this tool chest over there on a table going, 'If it looks like jelly, shakes like jelly . . .' "

"That's what I think about Sears and them."

"What's that?"

"If it looks like a asshole, smells like a asshole, then you got to believe it's a asshole. Nasshole. Nasty nasshole."

"Did you know that Ted, the president, was a fighter pilot? Flew jets."

"So what?"

"I don't know. He just flew jets. I'll bet that was fun."

"There's somebody in the hall," says Ben.

The wood in the hall floor creaks, then creaks again. "Wesley," calls a voice. It's Carla.

"Just a minute." Wesley gets out of bed, slips on his jeans, opens the door. "What is it?"

"You got a call at the front desk."

There is a black phone on the table by the front door. It sits on the phone book beside a big desk calendar where the duty schedules are written. The receiver is lying on the calendar.

"Hello. . . . Yeah. . . . When? . . . Where is she now? . . . No, I, I got curfew, but I can come in the morning. First thing."

Back in his room, Wesley asks Ben, "You think you could drive me somewhere in the van?"

"What you mean?"

"My grandma's sick. She had a heart attack. She's in the hospital."

"It's after curfew, man. We locked in here."

"Yeah, but I . . . I need to get on over there to see how she is. She probably needs to talk to me."

"You have to wait till tomorrow, unless you want to jump off the roof or something. Why don't you just wait till tomorrow? It's raining. Hard."

"Oh, I don't know. She could die. She's pretty old—I told you." Wesley needs to do something for Mrs. Rigsbee—get on over there and see her no matter what, even if he has to dress up like a doctor and sneak in the hospital.

"I ain't going to give you no ride, man. The van keys is locked up and I ain't leaving this place during no curfew. Not to take you to no hospital. But you do what you got to do. I got to go to the bathroom." Ben throws back his cover and gets out of bed.

213

Wesley looks up at the water stains on the ceiling and thinks. She might need him more right now than she ever has in her life. He could go down and talk to Mrs. White, see if she'd say okay, or he could just leave through a window or something, borrow Vernon's daddy's truck. He'd say okay.

Ben comes back in.

"I could go out through the window there—then jump or climb down," says Wesley.

"You're crazy, man."

"I'm going. That rain is easing up. Can I borrow your raincoat?"

"Well, I guess. Don't leave it somewhere. I ain't got but one."

"I'll go down that downspout on the side."

Wesley puts on his denim jacket, and then Ben's raincoat—a very old navy blue London Fog. He pulls up the window, unlatches and opens the screen. The rain suddenly starts coming down hard again. Lightning flashes.

"Why don't you go to bed, then get up in the morning and go like you supposed to?" says Ben. "She ain't gon' die."

On hands and knees Wesley crawls out onto the porch roof, stands, and looks back in at Ben. His hair is already slicked down wet.

Ben latches the screen, lowers the window not quite all the way and sits down in his chair. The rain spatters in through the open window. He reaches to close the window and as he lowers it he hears a low, metal-moaning sound, then sharp raspy scraping sounds. He pushes the window back up. Something bad is happening. He opens the screen,

214

climbs out and stands on the porch roof, looking for Wesley. The rain is cold through his shirt.

Wesley is not in sight—gutter nails are popping out of the gutter one after another on toward the front of the house and on toward the back of the house as the entire gutter system begins to move, as a piece, out and away from the house. Then it stops. Lightning flashes and lights up Wesley, out about six feet from the house, on top of the long metal downspout. He is looking down. Gutter nails are holding somewhere toward the front and back of the house.

Ben steps over to the edge of the roof, near Wesley. "Hey."

Wesley looks. Lightning flashes. Ben and Wesley's eyes lock. In Wesley's eyes is a great hunger to be over there where Ben is.

"Don't move," says Ben.

"I ain't."

"I told you not to do it."

"I know you did. That ain't important now."

"There ain't but a few nails at each end holding this whole thing onto the house. You better not move."

"I ain't. Don't worry. Can't you get something to pull me in?"

"Well, yeah. But I don't think I'm going to have time. Like I say, you hanging by about two or three nails. Maybe if you get a good tail wind you'll blow back in."

The rain suddenly slows almost to a stop.

"Well listen." Wesley is breathing hard. He allows himself to look down again. Far below, almost three stories down, the quiet light from the front porch reflects from puddles in the grass. "Maybe the ground is soft."

"You gon' be going pretty fast when you hit. You might just drive on down to the dry part."

"Stop talking. Do something."

The rain picks back up.

"Maybe you could kind of pump yourself on back toward the house."

"I ain't moving, man. Go get something to pull me in. Now."

"Pull you in? Like what?"

"I don't know. Oh, God, help me get back over to that house."

"I can get them extension cords and lasso you."

"Okay. Anything. Just do something. *Now.*"

"Or I could kind of pull these gutters back in and hope you'd come with it."

"Don't touch those gutters. Get the extension cords."

"Okay." Ben starts back in through the window and says to himself, "Now we gon' hang his ass."

Ben crawls under the bed and unplugs one of the three or four extension cords that are around somewhere in the room. There's another one in the end of this one, or is that the lamp cord? No, that's an extension cord. *That's* the lamp cord. Okay, two. Now. As he slides back out from under his bed, a blast of thunder tumbles and rumbles away, far away, and dies to the sound of the rain picking up again. Under Wesley's bed, Ben unplugs another extension cord from the wall and then from a lamp cord. He slides back out from under the bed, stands, then moves the dresser out from the wall and gets

216

the last one. He plugs them all together and heads back out into the rain. Wesley hasn't moved.

"You want me to make a lasso?" says Ben.

"Yes."

"Why don't I just throw it to you."

"I can't catch it, Ben. My God, I can't move or this whole thing will fall. Can't you see that?"

"How do you make a lasso?"

"Ain't you ever seen one on TV?"

"Well, yeah, I *seen* one, but I ain't ever seen how to *make* one."

"You got to make a loop. And then put a loop through that. Make a little loop, tie it, and then run a loop through that. Oh God, please save me."

"Okay, let's see." Ben starts working with the cords. "Wait a minute," he says. The rain has slowed to a soft drizzle—in the dark. "This ain't going to work."

"Why not?"

"When I get you lassoed, and start to pull you in, they'll just unplug."

"Tie the goddamned extension cords together, Ben."

"Hey, watch it."

"Just *tie them together*."

"Give me a minute."

"I don't know whether I *got* a minute or not."

"You'll be all right. I told you not to do it. Okay. Here we go. Okay, all set. Can you kind of stick your neck out a little bit, so I'll sort of have a knob to aim at?"

"Ben, lasso me. NOW."

Ben steps to the edge of the roof. Lightning flashes, but it seems to be far away. The rain has stopped. Drops of water fall from the big, old oak tree in the yard out behind Wesley and down onto its hard, gnarled roots.

Ben tosses the lasso. It misses. He pulls it in, tosses, misses. He slides his toe out over the edge of the roof, and on the third try the lasso lands around Wesley's neck.

"Now, pull me in, but do it slow, Ben."

Ben pulls. There is a metal-groaning sound toward the front of the house, and instead of moving toward Ben, Wesley is slowly moving away. A nail pops from a gutter somewhere.

Now there is no slack in the cord.

"Turn loose," says Wesley. Ben does, as Wesley's weight starts him picking up speed on the inevitable quarter circle arc toward earth. Sections of gutter break loose and fall along beside him.

Halfway down, Wesley turns to face the ground. Now he is going as fast as gravity will allow and his movements to somehow change his fall into a jump have no effect on anything. Lightning flashes, and Ben sees, trailing in the wind, the tails of his raincoat, wet blond hair, and an extension cord—all streaming out behind this white boy as he heads on down toward the ground below—toward those hard roots, as a matter of fact. The gutters, and Wesley, face down, with his legs still tight around the downspout, crash. Then all is still in the wet night. The drizzle falls. Thunder rumbles far, far away. The porch light shines out across the quiet mess. Ben watches from above. There is no movement at all. Then just as Ben turns to head downstairs there is movement. He sees Wesley's right arm rise slowly into the air. The fingers snap once, then again, then again. The arm drops back.

Downstairs, Ben is pounding on Mrs. White's door. The message for the week is BLOOM WHERE YOU'RE PLANTED.

17

*I*T'S THE NEXT MORNING AND MATTIE RIGSBEE IS
propped up in her bed in Intensive Care. A person
walks unsteadily into the room. The head, completely wrapped in white bandages, is wearing mir-
rored sunglasses.

Lord have mercy, thinks Mattie. It's something
come to get me for good.

The head speaks. "It's me. Wesley."

"Wesley? Lord have mercy. What in the world
happened to you?"

"I fell off BOTA House and broke my face and
some ribs." Wesley can see that Mrs. Rigsbee looks
pale and drawn.

"How?"

"I was trying to come see you—coming down a downspout after curfew."

"You know better than that, son."

"Well, no, I don't. It's all right. Ben told them I was after a cat. How are you doing?"

"Oh, I don't know. Somebody said a heart attack, but I don't know if that's right or not. Did you break anything?"

"My nose and my cheek in three places and two ribs and I got maybe a concussion and some cuts and they can't hold the bandages in place unless they wrap my head. The ribs hurt worse. I have to breathe deep so I don't get pneumonia. And man, that hurts. I'm on some medicine I'm not supposed to walk around with but I wanted to get down here to see you. They don't guard you very much up there. I wanted to get a wheelchair but I couldn't find one. I always wanted to ride in one of those things."

"How about your teeth?"

"They're fine. They're all there. My partial is okay. That thing could of got drove up in my brain. Here's something I brought you." Wesley hands Mattie an oatmeal cookie.

"Oh, good. It don't seem like they believe in food around here. Hide it in that drawer. Thank you. Well, Lord have mercy. Don't you hurt anywhere?"

"Not much, now. My ribs, like I said. I did hurt. I snapped my fingers until my hand gave out. But they gave me something for pain. I got a room upstairs. I'm supposed to be in bed. They're going to give me some tests or something."

"Why don't you sit down over there."

Wesley sits in a chair against the wall. "Are you hurting in your chest or anything?" he asks.

"Not really. Did Elaine tell you about it? Is she out there—and Robert?"

"They're out there. She said congestive heart something. They said I could come in for a couple of minutes. They said they don't get but five minutes every hour. I probably better get on out."

"Wait. Let me tell you what happened. Alora was over at the house and I just started coughing. And couldn't stop. I've never had anything like it. It was like nothing you ever seen in your life. It took all my breath and I couldn't stop and what it was was congestion of the heart—fluid, like you hear 'congestive heart failure,' you know. I think that's what they finally figured out. I guess they know."

"Does it hurt?"

"No, not now, not bad. There's some soreness from the coughing, and I do feel pretty wiped out. Did Elaine tell you what I did last night after they got me up here?"

"No ma'am."

"Well, they give me something to take, I don't know what it was or why for, but it sent me out of my mind, got me thinking I was home, and down the hall out there was the kitchen and you and Elaine and Robert were down there trying to cook some fish. And y'all didn't know how, so I had to get up to show you because y'all were fussing about it, so I did, and the nurse came in, put me back in bed, and put up these sides to the bed here—all four of them—and I tried to explain to her but she wouldn't listen. So I ended up crawling over the railings, and they all come in here and got mad at

222

me. I pulled all these tubes and things loose. It's just wiped me out bad. Whatever it was they gave me did all that to me—sent me out of my head."

"You look kind of wiped out."

"Well. The doctor said he wanted me to get a long rest after I get out of here—some place I could rest." Mattie closes her eyes, doesn't open them right away.

"You okay?"

"Oh yes." She opens her eyes. "I always wanted to play the violin. For a long time I wanted to, then I stopped wanting to." She closes her eyes again. "Oh, me, me, me."

Wesley looks at her—her face is pale, and her hair is all spread out on the pillow behind her head, not combed. And he's beginning to feel a little bit nauseated. But all of a sudden he feels he needs to ask Mrs. Rigsbee a lot of questions. He's never really known a lot about what she thinks about besides Jesus and food. What she used to think about.

Mattie opens her eyes, looks at Wesley. "I always wanted to play violin. And go to Carnegie Hall. That's what I dreamed until I was too old—one of the things. There was a house, a big white house down the street when I was little, and a woman, a beautiful woman used to practice in a back room. We'd sneak down there, and—"

The nurse comes in. "I think I'll have to—" She sees Wesley's head, takes a step back. "Oh, my goodness. I'll have to ask you to leave now."

"Oh, okay." Wesley stands, staggers, steps over to Mattie's side. "When you think you'll be getting out?"

"The sooner the better. Unless they're planning to send me to the nursing home."

"I'll be up here a few more days myself. I'll come back, unless you're out jogging, then you can come by my room."

"Oh, yes. Okay." She laughs.

As Wesley starts out, he hears Mrs. Rigsbee say to the nurse, "He ain't really mine, but I've thought about him that way for the last eight or ten years."

The next afternoon, Ben peeks into room 4217 and sees someone with a wrapped head sitting up in bed, wearing sunglasses. "Hey man. Is that you?" Ben is carrying Wesley's National Steel in the yellow bag and also his own cassette recorder with a practice tape inside.

The head turns. "Oh yeah, it's me. I was asleep. Come on in."

"You look like a mummy."

"I feel like one, too. They're going to wire me up this afternoon so they can see what my brain waves are like while I'm asleep."

"I tell you one thing, it sounded like, I don't know, it sounded like, loud, when you hit the ground."

"It felt loud. Sit down."

"When I saw that hand come up and them fingers start snapping, I said, 'Thank God, the boy is alive.'" Ben sits in a chair against the wall. "I was surprised you woke up as soon as you did. The stranded cat was Carla's idea. What all did they find out was broke?"

"Nose, cheeks, ribs. I'm sore all over. I tell you,

man, these ribs. I thought about your ankle. You know, when you had the cast on?"

"Oh, yeah, I know."

There's a knock on the door. "Wesley?" Phoebe sticks her head in.

"Phoebe?"

"Wesley! Good gracious. Hi, Ben."

"Hey."

"Come on in," says Wesley. "I messed up my face, but the doctor says I'll be even more handsome than before. If that's possible."

"I don't know if you can stand to be any more handsome than you were. I'll just sit on the side of the bed here." The poor, poor darling, she thinks. After a cat. That sounds just like something he'd do. Phoebe sits near the foot of the bed, and puts her hand lightly on Wesley's knee, under the edge of the sheet.

Keep your hand on there forever, thinks Wesley. Oh, Phoebe, you're here on my bed with your hand on my knee under the sheet. Don't ever take it off. I'll stay real still, just leave it there with that little bit of pressure.

"You look terrible," says Phoebe. "What I mean is you look like you'd look terrible."

Wesley removes his sunglasses. The wrapping is split so that both eyes are visible. One is purple but open, the other purple and swollen shut. "That's what my eyes look like, and other than that there are some cuts. They gave me some shots in the face. They didn't want to put me to sleep because they said I had a concussion, whatever that is. I heard of them all my life but I don't know what it is." The glasses go back on.

"I think it means it's just a very hard blow to your head, one that shakes up your brain."

"It must of been bouncing all over the place in there," says Ben. "It's so little. I *told* you not to go down that downspout."

"You lie."

There is another knock on the door. Holister and Vernon come in. Holister is holding a ball cap in his hand.

"You *did* have a little accident," says Holister.

"It's crowded in here," says Vernon, walking over to stand by the window. "Why you wearing sunglasses?"

"It's kind of cool. I like the way they go with these bandages." Wesley's blond hair sticks straight up out of the top of the bandages.

"And people don't have to see those poor eyes," says Phoebe.

"I got to get on back," says Ben, standing. "I'm supposed to pick up some vacuum cleaner bags. Carla did the vacuuming las' week and she always throw away the bag whether it's full or empty. See you later. Don't be going out the window."

"I won't." Wesley looks at Phoebe and smiles, then realizes that nobody can see him smile. She can't tell he's looking at her either. There she is, sitting there on his own bed. With him in the bed. She hasn't moved her hand. If we were in here alone, maybe.... Now if Vernon and Mr. Jackson would just leave we could be in here alone.

A nurse comes in. "Looks like you've got some

226

visitors. Let me just check those bandages and get your blood pressure and temperature."

Vernon edges over toward Wesley, gets himself where he can see the nurse checking the bandages on Wesley's face.

"Is there anything we can do for you, get for you?" asks Holister.

"Oh, no. I just got to take a nap in a minute. This medicine makes me sleepy and I didn't get any sleep last night." Take a hint. Take a hint. Take a hint.

The nurse sticks a thermometer into Wesley's mouth.

"I'll be going on then," says Phoebe. "I need to set up a science center this afternoon."

Wesley grabs for her hand under the sheet, finds it, and holds on. He's looking through his sunglasses. None of them can see his eyes. Nobody saw him grab Phoebe's hand. She is looking down, and OH HAPPY DAY squeezing back, sort of blushing. The world is good.

Vernon is bending over the nurse's back staring at Wesley's bandages, and Holister is shifting his hat from one hand to the other.

"We better get on back, boy," Holister says. "I got a bunch of cars waiting."

"I want to see if he's got a temperature," says Vernon.

"Let's go. Now."

"See y'all later," says Wesley, with the thermometer in his mouth. "Thanks for coming by. I'll be all right."

Wesley holds Phoebe's hand tightly under the sheet. It's as if, behind the sunglasses, he can

227

squeeze as long and as tight as he wants to, he can almost do anything, and everything. He's hidden away.

Wesley's first visitor next morning is Ted Sears.

"Wesley?"

"Yessir."

Sears approaches the bed, reaches out his hand to Wesley. "Wesley, how are you?" He looks at the Bible in Wesley's lap—the Gideon Bible that was in the drawer in his nightstand. "I'm glad to see your priorities are intact." He looks around for a mirror.

"I just thought I'd read a little bit."

"Looks like they've got you wired up there."

"Oh, yeah. They did that last night before I went to sleep. They're checking my brain waves. Actually, I feel pretty good. I'm just sore all over, mainly my ribs. It's hard to sit up by myself."

"How long before you'll be up and about?"

"Just a day or two, they said."

"That must have been quite a fall. I was shocked to hear about it. I think the fact you were trying to save a poor cat makes the event all the more meaningful. You might find Palmer Royal at the *Star* giving you a little call about it. And I must add, Wesley, that I can't tell you how much your Christianity means to all of us at Ballard. It's far more than a publicity thing, but on the other hand, these newspaper articles and this tour have given us a little boost, and the Christmas dinner at LinkComm will afford us an opportunity to recognize your contributions and make some announcements about the future. I think you'll approve."

"That's good."

Ted checks his watch, reaches for his billfold in his back pocket. "Unfortunately, I don't have a lot of time, Wesley." He is opening his billfold. He takes out a five-dollar bill and lays it on Wesley's nightstand. "I'm going to leave this with you in hopes you might find a use for it, and then I'm on my way. We've got a faculty member out here I need to see, and I also thought I might drop in on Mrs. Rigsbee. She's such a charming little lady." Sears puts his billfold back in his pocket. "Does she have any heirs, by the way?"

"Airs?"

"Children."

"She's got two."

"Oh. Well."

"Why?"

"Just wondering. Son, listen. Don't ever abandon that book," he says, nodding toward the Bible. "It's true cover to cover. Cover to cover or nothing, I say. And it's being attacked from all quarters. We've even got *Baptists* now denying its literal truth. So, son, you're important to us. You're helping the Ballard family fight the secularization of Christian higher education—through your example. And, by the way, I hope someone has mentioned that we'd like for you to give a little testimony at the LinkComm Christmas luncheon—about what Jesus means to you, what Ballard, the Ballard family means to you. Something short and simple—no need to worry about it. We can even jot down a few notes for you. We understand the radio and TV station might cover it. And now before I go." Sears kneels. "Dear God, bless this Thy faithful servant.

Heal his incisions, his broken bones, ease his pain. Guide and direct his thoughts and deeds. Bless all the sick and afflicted here in this facility, and help this young man to find Truth through your Word. In our Savior's precious name, Amen."

Sears stands. His knees pop. He pats Wesley on the shoulder. "Fight the good fight."

"Okay. I will." Airs? He's after her money.

Wesley picks up his Bible, turns to Leviticus, and starts reading in the Old Testament where he left off last time. Not very interesting. He decides to go back and pick up where he finished his sermon. In pain, he slowly props an extra pillow behind his back, inserts his tape, and listens to the sermon. Not bad. Not bad at all. Maybe he can do another one, and then keep doing them all the way through the Bible until he's read the whole thing, and then stick that ear thing in his ear and go around and preach on anything anybody wants to hear about. Sort of a weekend job.

He reads again about Adam and Eve's sons: Cain and Abel.

God asks Cain, who has just murdered Abel, "Where is your brother Abel?"

Now here is God, thinks Wesley, who on the one hand has just knocked out a whole universe in six days, but on the other hand doesn't know where Abel is. He ought to know *that* much. This doesn't exactly make sense, he thinks. How can I preach about something that doesn't fit together? Or maybe God is just asking Cain so he can put Cain on the spot, see if he'd tell the truth. That's probably what it is.

For sure God knew where Abel was.

Someone brings Wesley's breakfast, then a nurse comes in and takes his blood pressure. He stays with the story, reading while he eats.

Here's a bunch of killing and revenge going on and this great-grandson is killing people for hitting him, and then all of a sudden Adam lays with Eve again, and they have another boy while they already had these great-grandchildren.

And here it says Adam was nine hundred and thirty years old when he died. He must have been right dried up, thinks Wesley, out there in the desert and all.

Then we have a whole bunch of people having babies and them growing up to have all these babies who live to be hundreds of years old and finally we got Methuselah, who lived nine hundred and sixty-nine years, and was for sure ready to die. They had to be counting different back then. How old would Mrs. Rigsbee be compared to Methuselah?

Methuselah's grandson was Noah. Well, that's news.

But they don't name many women through here. Times are different or something. Maybe the custom or something didn't allow them to talk about women, because they all wore veils. I wonder if they had dreams like Mrs. Rigsbee's. There were those women who hung around Jesus. Maybe it was men doing all the talking, and they naturally talked about theirselves. Here's all this eye-for-an-eye stuff. Jesus came along and changed the whole eye-for-an-eye part of the way they used to live. I know that.

Then Wesley reads about Noah.

He sees himself in a huge auditorium, before a large audience, behind a microphone. He is wearing his navy blue dress suit, white shirt, and tie. People are looking up at him with a kind of yearning in their eyes.

He presses the record button on the recorder.

And the whole bunch of people on Earth were rotten, except for Noah. God was so mad, he was going to get rid of the birds and bees and beasts. I don't know what they had done, but anyway God was fixing to flood everything and everybody. But, listen. Noah's wife and sons and all them got to go along with Noah on this ark. And—and they were bad *people, because the Bible says Noah was the only good man on Earth. So you see, friends, it pays to have connections. I've had connections in my time, but I've not had connections too, and I'll tell you what: if I was the next door neighbor of one of Noah's sons and I hadn't done no more wrong than that son had, I'd be a little upset to see him floating away in a dry boat while my lungs were filling up with muddy water just because God was mad. I'd say to myself, Now, why does my neighbor get off scot-free and I have to drown?*

"Mr. Benfield, I need to take your temperature," says a nurse.

"Okay." Wesley clicks off the recorder, takes the thermometer in his mouth.

"Are you in the ministry?"

Wesley nods his head yes.

She removes the thermometer when the box beeps. "Normal. Is everything feeling okay?"

"Yep. Except for my body."

"Well, you give us a buzz if you need anything." She leaves.

Wesley presses the record button on the tape recorder.

Wouldn't it have been nice to be Noah's son back in them days? God says, "You go along on the ark too, son. You're one of old Noah's boys." It would have been good to be a daughter-in-law. "You come right along, honey." Noah was good and if you was in his family, you had the right connections, and friend, you could have been robbing and beating up little people all your life, but you'd still float away safe and free.

Family connections have always been important, Wesley thinks.

So, here's old Noah floating around up on top of that water, in his boat—homebuilt—and can you imagine the folks on logs and in trees and on roof tops screaming and that water getting higher and higher?

Can you imagine being left off the boat and seeing your very own grandma in the top branch of a tree, and water up around her shoulders, and you can't even see the tree no more, except that one branch above her which she grabs and gets herself up a little higher, and you're across a field in a taller tree? Or maybe it's your own buddy, or your own little boy, or little girl—your own little girl, and you raised her up and fed her and rocked her to sleep, and even though you're mean, you can't help but love her.

"Mr. Benfield?"

"Yes."

"Hi. I'm from sleep analysis. Is this a convenient time for me to remove your wires and ask you a few questions?"

"No."

"Oh. It's not. Well, I guess I can come back later."

"Okay. See you."

And she's holding on, with the water moving up her shoulders, around her neck, chin, and mouth, one inch every five or six seconds, and now she's breathing through her nose because the water is over her mouth, and she's starting to suck a little of that red, muddy, smelly water in through her nose, knowing full well that when she turns loose of the limb it's all she wrote. She can't swim. She knows it. She'll be dead and gone to hell. And I wonder if, on account of her mean parents, she ever had a chance to know what God wanted, if her mean parents ever had a chance because of their mean parents, all the way back down the line to the first mean parents that started it all. They had to be real mean.

You swim over from your tree and she grabs on to your neck and you're kicking your legs under water and the water keeps rising higher up over that tree branch and you finally hold her up over your head with one hand the best you can and she's screaming because of what she's just seen in your eyes when you looked up at her.

So anyway, after everything settled down and all these dead corpses were floating all around, you can tell God was pretty rattled himself because he said, "Never again will I do this." He had some regrets, and I do too when I look back on it. I agree with God about those regrets.

Wesley stops for a breather and reads for a while longer.

Then God made a deal with man. He would never again flood the earth, and the rainbow was a sign of the covenant and it would remind God of the deal he'd just made, which goes to show you that God could whammo, whammo, create the earth and moon

*and stars and it shows you He could learn something:
to be a little more patient with man. Not to get mad
so quick. It's like when you learn not to kick your
dog. Give him a little more time. The rainbow was a
reminder, and God fixed it so it occurs all over the
place because I see one on the white enamel in the
bathtub sometimes.*

"Are you through with your breakfast, Mr. Benfield?" says a young woman.

"Yeah. Take it on out. Thanks."

*Then Noah went out and got drunk and naked.
Now ain't that something?*

"Excuse me?"

"Nothing. I'm preaching a sermon."

"Oh."

*—and Noah, instead of feeling bad about it, got
mad at his son, Ham, for seeing him. For seeing him
drunk and naked. Noah was the one that got drunk.
Ham was the one that saw him. Something Ham
didn't have no control over. God said, "That son's
descendants are going to be slaves." All Noah's sons
had children but only Ham's were the slaves. This is
one I ain't figured out because all of this was because
Ham saw his old man, Noah, drunk, and got his
brothers to go in the tent and cover him up. Noah is
the one ought to have been in trouble, it seems to
me, for laying around drunk with all his clothes off.*

"Excuse me. Do you mind if I listen to a little of
this?"

"I don't care."

"I'll just sit here."

*But it didn't work that way. Noah didn't get in any
trouble for laying around drunk, so one of the problems to figure out is why getting drunk is such a big*

deal today. Well, it can probably be figured out. It's all in here somewhere. Then the story settles in on the names of countries as the same as the names of kids, and Ham's kids, the Canaanites, spread around and included places like Sodom and Gomorrah, which I have heard about.

Wesley turns off the recorder. The young woman sitting across from him is distracting him somehow. She's sitting at perfect attention, not moving, but she's too something—paying too much attention— and he needs to preach this out alone. "That's all," he says to her.

"What denomination are you?"

"Baptist. I guess."

"I am too, but that sounded different from what I usually hear. It was sure interesting." She leaves, carrying Wesley's breakfast tray.

Wesley wonders whether or not he should keep preaching what's on his mind. Here was Noah— after the rainbow—laying around drunk and naked. Seems like the whole problem was due to *Noah*, not *Ham*, for heaven's sake. What's going on here? It's got to have something to do with how whoever was writing this down was seeing things, thinks Wesley. For sure me and him have the same God.

He goes back to Genesis 6:4, reads again. Angels making love with giant women. For sure they won't married when they did that. How'd they get by with all that?

His phone rings. It's Mrs. Rigsbee. "I got a room—7221. Can you come up?" she asks.

"Yeah. They said I could get up and go to the bathroom. Maybe I can find a wheelchair."

"I got a little something for you."

"I'll be right up. I been preaching."

"Preaching? Who to?"

"Myself."

"Oh, well. Come on up for a little visit."

Wesley rolls into Mattie's room in a wheelchair.

"You can't walk?" she asks him.

"Oh, yeah. I can walk. I'm just doing this for something different. It was sitting in the hall." Wesley speaks like an old woman: "Did I tell you? I used to have everything I wanted."

"Lord have mercy. That's not funny. I wonder how she's doing. But listen. Guess what I got for you."

"Pound cake?"

"How'd you guess?"

"Where is it?"

"Over there in that bag. Don't eat it all at once. There's enough there for two times. They don't have you on no diet or anything, do they?"

"Oh no. I think I'll eat a little bit right now."

"Well, get something to put it on—a paper towel from over there. Does it hurt to stand up?"

"Yes, it does." Wesley stands up from his wheelchair, gets a paper towel from over the sink, comes back, sits down in the wheelchair, breaks off a piece of cake and starts eating it. The cake is wider than the mouth passage. Crumbs are falling.

"Good health is just about everything, ain't it?" says Mattie.

"You can damn sure say that again. How'd you get this cake up here?"

"Elaine brought it."

"*She* cooked this?"

"Oh, no. I had it at home. What were you preaching about down there?"

"Noah."

"And the flood?"

"Yes ma'am. And getting drunk. And did you know about these angels making love with giant women?"

"Lord no. What in the world are you talking about? You find some of the oddest things."

"They ain't written up like they were odd. They're written up like they were normal. This is good cake."

"I thought it was pretty good myself."

Wesley finishes the cake, balls up the paper towel and tosses it into the trash can. "Did Dr. Sears come by to see you?" he asks.

"Oh, yes, he did. He asked me to join the Ballard family."

"Did he say what it would cost you?"

"Why no. He didn't mention that."

"Mrs. White, at BOTA House, joined. When she kicks the bucket Ballard gets her car and whatever else. They'll do all the maintenance on her car if she leaves it to the school. They cut the grass at her sister's house and keep it up till she dies and then that's theirs."

"They couldn't have my house but it wouldn't be such a bad idea, leaving a little something to the college."

"What about Elaine and Robert?"

"Oh, they'll be fine. I said a little something. If everybody left a little something to the Christian colleges, then maybe there wouldn't be so much lying on television. And maybe I could get my TV fixed without taking out a loan. I'll swanee. Will they keep your TV fixed if you will that to them?"

"I don't know. Probably."

"The way people overcharge and lie and misrepresent is a crime and if Christian education can't do something about it, I don't know what can."

18

A UNIFORMED GUARD, IN A LITTLE HUT, LEANS through a window and asks for a pass. A long wooden arm with black stripes blocks the road in front of the BOTA House van. Ben is driving. Wesley hands Ben a pass he received in the mail from Ms. Clark, the woman they're supposed to meet here at Eastern LinkComm. Ben hands the pass to the guard.

The guard takes the pass, leans back into his booth, slides his window into place and makes a call on his phone.

"What's he doing?" says Ben. "What do they make in this place, anyway—atom bombs?"

"Telephones, I think." The skin beneath Wesley's eyes is light yellow, and the cuts have almost healed.

The guard opens the window. "You both with the band?"

"That's right."

He hands the pass back. "First door up there. Under that green panel."

They park the van and go in.

Pale pink tiles reflect bright lights. A uniformed woman wearing a badge stands behind a dark pink chest-high counter to their right. "Pass?" she says, glancing up, then looking back down to a list of numbers which she's checking against another list.

Wesley hands her the pass.

"Pass?" she asks Ben, glancing up. She goes back to the lists.

"He just gave it to you."

She looks up. "Where is *your* pass?" she asks Ben.

"That's mine too."

"Both of you have to have a pass. Two people—two passes. You can't get in without a pass."

"We both just got in the gate," says Ben.

"That's the gate. You might get in the gate, but you don't get in the building without a pass. I'm the building guard."

"What the hell are y'all guarding?" asks Ben.

The woman looks at him. "Information."

"You think I'm going to steal information?"

"You might. Listen. I don't make the rules. I just work here."

The woman pulls out a different list of numbers and checks it against the number on the pass. "Sign in. Right over there. What's the name of the person this pass was sent to?"

"Me—Wesley Benfield."

"No, you don't sign in," she says to Wesley, "just him. Once we get him assigned a pass he'll need to sign in again since he didn't have a pass to start with. *Your* pass signs *you* in. Do you know who sent this pass?"

"Miss Clark. In public something."

"Public Relations?"

"That's right."

"I don't have this pass number on my master sheet."

A man comes in from the outside and hands the guard a large white envelope. "Personnel," he says.

The guard makes a call on the phone. "Package, gate two . . . Darnell." She presses and releases the receiver button, presses two numbers, looks at Wesley's pass as she waits for an answer. She hangs up. "I'm going to have to call back. Y'all can wait in there." She nods to a small waiting room across the hall.

Three people have come in and are waiting their turns.

Ben sits in a chair in the waiting room. Wesley sits at the end of a couch. He looks at his watch. "We're already ten minutes late."

"I got to take a leak," says Ben. He gets up, goes out to the desk, comes back.

"You don't mean you got to have a pass to go to the bathroom?" says Wesley.

"You got it. I'll tell you one thing. If we have this much trouble getting back out of here, we're gon' dry up and die."

They wait five minutes.

The guard comes to the door. "Did you say Miss

Clark? We got two Miss Clarks. We got Miss Deborah Clark and Miss Georgia Clark."

"I don't know. It was in Public Relations or whatever that was you said. We play in a band. We're supposed to be meeting about setting up a gig for week after next."

The guard turns back to her little room. There are now six people waiting for her.

Wesley looks at his watch. "This is crazy."

Ben picks up the receiver to the phone on the table beside his chair, pushes the zero. "Yes, this is Security. I need Public Relations. We got a little problem down here. . . . Thanks." Ben hands the phone to Wesley.

In three minutes Georgia Clark stands in the doorway. "Well, hello," she says. "You had a problem getting in?"

"Yeah, we did," says Ben.

As they walk to the elevator, Ben says, "You think you could show me where the bathroom is?"

Ms. Clark's office is one of twenty-eight honeycomb cubicles set off by lightweight, head-high dividers. Ben and Wesley listen as she describes plans for the Christmas luncheon that LinkComm and Ballard are giving for the clients at Shady Grove Nursing Home.

"My grandma's out there now," says Wesley. "She had something like a heart attack, and they got her resting."

"Wonderful. She'll get to see you perform then. How nice. When we have an opportunity to do something for the community, we do something for the community. Mr. Snaps, the president, is really behind it. And the president at Ballard is also very interested this year—Dr. Sears. The media will be here and all. Let's go over to the dining room and I'll show you the setup."

As they leave her office, Ms. Clark says to Wesley, "You know, I always wanted to be in a band."

Ben rolls his eyes.

On the way home, Ben and Wesley stop at McDonald's for supper. They each get a Big Mac, large fries, and a large Coke. "Let's go outside and eat," says Wesley. "It's got to be seventy degrees— and it's near about Christmas." He carries a salt shaker out with him.

They sit outside at a small table. Several children are playing on the kiddie playground.

Ben watches the children playing. A little boy picks up a piece of bark beneath a swing and throws it at another little boy. "You marry Phoebe," he says to Wesley, "you'll have a little redhead."

"Yeah, probably. My problem with Phoebe is her old man don't like me."

"What's he got to do with it?"

"He's her old man."

"She don't have to do what he say."

Wesley chews, watches the children. "I want you to go out to that nursing home with me sometime."

"Why?"

"I figure maybe we could figure out a way to get Mrs. Rigsbee out of there. Spring her. I bet she would do it."

"Ain't she sick?"

"Naw. She can take care of herself. She ain't that bad off. She don't want to be out there. Like we don't want to be in the BOTA House."

"I been thinking about that." Ben sips Coke through his straw.

"What?"

"Running."

"You ain't got that much longer, man."

"I got three months. And that's a long-ass time you be wanting to go somewhere."

"Where do you want to go?"

"Anywhere."

"What about the band?"

"I don't know. We could all meet somewhere after you get out."

One of the children—a little boy—starts crying, sits down on the bark shavings. A man comes out of the door and goes to him, picks him up and talks to him quietly. Wesley wonders how Holister treated Vernon when he was a baby. He thinks about Phoebe and her daddy, what it would be like to have a colonel as a daddy.

"Ever since the fair they been after my ass," says Ben, "and Mrs. White been writing all them drug things on the blackboard, and she's been in the room twice when I come in, snooping. I think she's after my ass."

"You got paramania. That's all. But, maybe they are after you. You better quit smoking in there."

"You wouldn't run?" asks Ben.

"Not me. No way. I'm running out of second chances."

The Monday morning breakfast meeting has just broken up and Stan, still known as the new assistant treasurer, is seated at Mysteria's desk talking on the phone to his wife, Darleen, about how to handle the afternoon trip to the pediatrician. Their youngest has an ear infection. He has just seen Ted and Ned go back into the president's meeting room. Everyone else is gone. Mysteria is away from her desk. Stan notices Ned closing the meeting room door.

"I'll come on at three-thirty," says Stan to Darleen. "If there's any problem with me getting away I'll call you. I'll ask Big Don at lunch—when he's happiest. Call me if it gets unbearable. Bye."

Stan hangs up, looks at the buttons on the phone. He presses *intercom*, picks up the phone quietly. He can hear every word:

"But if it *is* marijuana and we don't do anything—"

"It looks like it. Don't you think?"

"I'm sure it is. It wouldn't be in the plastic bag if it was something else."

"It was in a pair of balled-up socks. She said there was only one pair of balled-up socks and that's how she knew to check. The rest were just loose."

"The bags?"

"Socks."

"Oh. And we can trust her. Right?"

"No question."

"We can't do anything now—with the luncheon tomorrow."

"No, we can't."

"We got big coverage on it. Snaps is going to be there for the announcement and all. This would throw a wrench in everything."

"We could always discover this stuff next week, or maybe even a bit later, depending. Wait, I just had an idea. There may be a way to maximize on this thing. Every part of it. In fact, this could be a blessing in disguise. Listen." A chair scrapes. It sounds like they're moving to another part of the room. The voices are lowered. Stan strains to hear. "Cla cou dar drug bust and whefen ter ha bun Benfield comes out of it clean ah ah junt de bour the Ashley boy and besides that we oper in aye morn of Benfield's faith and our influence. Listen iglit ar lee up seqen to the barm then close that place down and if Snaps to leggit of the option—"

Mysteria opens the office door and backs in with a tray of clean coffee cups. Stan presses the intercom button off. "Okay," he says into the receiver. "I'll be there about three-thirty. Goodbye." He hangs up. "Hi, Mrs. Montgomery. Just borrowing your phone to call Darleen."

"Oh, that's fine."

"One of our kids has an ear infection."

"It's that time of year, I guess."

"Sure is. Here, I'll let you have your desk back."

At the snack shop, Stan orders coffee. He sits at a table, opens his yellow legal pad to a clean page, pulls his Bic ballpoint from his shirt pocket and starts writing:

Dear Wesley Benfield,
    You don't know me, but I enjoyed your music on the radio a while back and I think I know something you need to know.

He puts his hand to his head, flips to a new page.

Dear Wesley Benfield,

I've been working at Ballard for some time now, as an administrator. But my time as an administrator here is over. I am familiar with your music and I've just come across some information I think you might need to know about.

"It sounds like to me you're headed for trouble," says Mattie Rigsbee to Wesley. She is dressed and sitting up in a chair in her room at Shady Grove Nursing Home. "Just because he's your friend and got in trouble ain't no reason for you to go messing up again. What you need to be thinking about is finishing your time over there and getting a job and settling down. Around here, somewhere. You've got a good job skill and you're starting to get some roots around here. I don't know what you'd get into without any roots."

"I got roots."

Wesley tries to believe that Mrs. Rigsbee looks better than she did in the hospital.

"You go running off and you won't. You need to settle down, have a kitchen and a wife and children. You can't have roots where you can't cook. That's one reason why this place is so horrible. I can't live nowhere I can't cook. And they won't let me go home. It's the saddest place I've ever been in my life and nobody won't listen to you. They cut you off in the middle of what you're saying or else they walk out on you. It's just . . . I don't know. But, son, you listen here. You put this running-off business right out of your mind. It's dangerous and plum foolish, you go running off for no good reason.

You're twenty-four years old, son. Your life ain't even started yet. They're liable to lock you up sure enough."

"Can *you* escape?"

"Escape? Me?"

"Yeah, escape. From here. You can figure out ways to get out of places like this. I've gotten out of places a whole lot harder to get out of than here. You could probably just put on a overcoat and hat or something and walk out."

"Well, I don't know. I don't think it would be so easy."

"Do you want to escape?"

"I hadn't thought about it, really. But, you know, maybe I do. I think maybe I do. I hadn't thought about it before." Mattie looks at Wesley and smiles. "I think maybe I do."

"Well, let's figure us out something. Do you want to go to Myrtle Beach?"

"No, I just want to go home where I can be by myself and cook."

"Wesley," says Phoebe, "it'll be the biggest mistake of your life." They're sitting on their bench at the mall. "I almost wish you hadn't told me. You're leaving *me*, too. And Mrs. Rigsbee, just when she needs you the most."

"Phoebe, I don't think you understand."

"I think I do understand."

"No, you don't. They're playing around with us. See? They're playing around with Ben. It ain't fair. I can't just sit there and watch him get carted off after we finish that gig."

"Wesley, you're . . ."

"He's a good man. We're making a plan. Myrtle Beach. And listen. I want to ask you . . . to go, too. Did you know my mama and daddy were *married* in South Carolina?"

"Wesley. Wesley, my father . . . Don't you see? Don't you see that you're . . . Wesley. I can't just make a decision about that right here in the mall, now."

19

into the jar. The fingers snap once, then again, then
again. His eyes reach back

WESLEY STANDS WITH VERNON JUST OUTSIDE THE
door to the garage and scuffs at the oil-packed dirt
with the toe of his shoe. Holister is inside the garage, preparing some spray paint.

Vernon stands, rocking. He is frowning at Wesley
through the thick lens of his glasses. "I wish I didn't
have to go to school. I never been on TV. Why
couldn't they have this thing at night? Looks like
they could have it at night."

"It won't be but three songs before lunch and
then three afterwards. But I don't know exactly how
it's going to go." On the ground is a canvas bag
holding Wesley's trowel, hawk, chisels, and other
masonry equipment. "I figured you might like to
borrow this stuff. Just don't say anything about any

251

of this to anybody. The mortar tub is in the shed behind BOTA House. Tell Mrs. White I said you could have it."

"I don't want, I don't, I don't want you to leave. It's the first band I ever been in." Vernon looks down at the ground. His rocking slows. He looks in the garage at his father, who has a mask over his face, spray-painting with green paint over the last orange on the hood of their old GMC bus.

"You got a whole . . . a whole garage, here," says Wesley. "And your daddy, and a house and everything."

"Yeah, but . . . what about the band? They're supposed to vote me in."

"I don't know. Maybe *you* can start a band or something." Wesley sticks out his hand. "Besides if I do go anywhere, I'll be back. You remember how to shake hands, don't you? You take it easy."

Sherri carries a cymbal and a snare drum. She hips open the swinging door into the upstairs dining room at Eastern LinkComm. "Where you want us to set up?" she asks Santa Claus, who is lifting small wrapped presents from a cardboard box and arranging them on a table.

"Ask her," he says, nodding toward Ms. Clark.

"Hi." Sherri shifts a cymbal to under her left arm, extends her hand to Ms. Clark. "I'm Sherri Gold, with the band. Where do you want us to set up?"

"That corner there in the back. We don't want the music to be overwhelming, you know."

Ned Sears is standing by the window, looking out. "They're here!"

"Who?" asks Ms. Clark.

"The folks from the nursing home. And there's no press here. Have you seen any press?"

"No, but there's a camera in my office," says Ms. Clark.

"We don't even have chairs in here yet," says Ned. "Where's the maintenance man?"

"Yes."

"I said, where is he?"

"Gosh, I don't know. He was supposed to have all the chairs in here by ten A.M."

"Get your camera," Ned says. "Then we'll worry about the chairs. I will be darned." Ned's hand is on top of his head. "I wanted some shots of them getting off the elevator."

Downstairs, Wesley walks outside. There are four blue vans parked in a line. He sees Mrs. Rigsbee getting out of the second one. She's wearing her old brown sweater, and she's sure moving slower than usual. The drivers are standing in a group nearby, smoking and talking. Attendants are helping the old people. Wesley walks over to Mattie. "Hey," he says to her. "You got here okay." He lowers his voice. "Come on up with the rest. I'll tell you what to do."

When the elevator doors open upstairs near the dining room, Wesley rolls out Miss Emma. Ned Sears is down on one knee, holding Georgia Clark's Pentax ME Super to his face. Behind Wesley, residents from Shady Grove begin to unload slowly. The automatic elevator doors keep hitting old people, who then stagger in little short steps, are clutched at by other old people, who then get hit themselves by the doors, closing again. There are many little grunting noises. The camera flashes. It flashes again. Ned advances the film, stands, reaches down his hand to Miss Emma—in her wheelchair. Miss Emma picks up several M&M's from her lap, and places them in Ned's hand. Ned withdraws his hand, gives a half-bow, pockets the M&M's.

"I used to have everything I wanted," says Miss Emma.

Santa Claus takes a present from the stack on the table and hands it to Miss Emma.

"I used to have everything I wanted," she says to Santa Claus. "Do you know who you are?"

"Excuse me?" Santa turns up his hearing aid.

"I said, Do you know who you are?"

"Well . . . yes, yes I do. I'm Santa Claus."

"That's right!"

The elevator opens again. Ned twirls, drops to his knee and flashes light into a full elevator. J. D. Smith, a twenty-two-year veteran of Shady Grove, standing in back, wearing soiled khaki shirt and pants and an old, wide red tie with palm trees, yells "Japs!," faces into the back corner and covers his head.

Wesley rolls Miss Emma into the dining room. Two men in overalls are placing folding chairs around long tables.

The maintenance supervisor is standing in a doorway and holding two fold-up chairs. "I didn't know," he says to Ned. "I thought it was going to be in the dining room downstairs. They've changed their minds three times on this already."

"These chairs were supposed to be in place at ten A.M., sir," says Ned. "It's now eleven-thirty A.M. I am making notes of this for Mr. Snaps. I think he'll be interested in the foul-up."

The maintenance supervisor tucks his chin, stares at Ned.

Ned starts toward the band, stops, looks around, puts his hand to the top of his head, then continues on over to the band. "Who told you-all to set up here?"

"Ms. Clark."

"Is it too much to ask you to move to the other corner?"

"It's right much," says Larry. "But it ain't too much. I don't think it's too much. Does anybody else think it's too much?"

Santa is shaking hands with J. D. Smith. J. D., backed into a corner, draws up each time the camera flashes.

Ms. Clark is on the phone. "If they have any kind of press credentials let them in. . . . Credentials. . . . *Credentials*. Something that shows they work for the press, for a newspaper. . . . Well, read it to me. . . . Yes, that's the radio. That's *Good Morning Charlie*, for heaven's sake. Let him in. . . . Yes, I did send them a pass. . . . *Let them in*, goddammit."

Good Morning Charlie and Jake Davis arrive and begin setting up to record the luncheon speakers and the pre- and after-lunch music for playback on "Weekly Happenings in Christian Higher Education."

A reporter and photographer arrive from the *Star*.

The Channel 9 television crew arrives with their equipment. They set up and test their lights. The room turns blue-white. Some of the old people turn to look. Their faces have turned bright gray and yellow.

Now the pre-lunch music, performed by the Noble Defenders of the Word—"Swing Low, Sweet Chariot," "The Time Is Near," and "Do, Lord"—is over. Ms. Clark has made several remarks, Ned Sears has said the blessing, and everyone is eating.

The band has their own small table. "It's going to be at least a week before Shanita and me can get there," Larry says to Wesley. "We can't leave before I get my paycheck."

"Look," says Ben to Wesley, "if you just talk a little bit it ain't going to give us time to load all the equipment. We need to be loaded and cranked and ready to go when you come out."

"Don't worry. It's going to be more than what they wrote up for me to say. Y'all will have plenty time to load up."

"What did Phoebe say?"

"She said that if she's not on the front porch waiting, she can't go."

Over at the next table, J. D. Smith, recovered from the camera flashes, is wrapping brownies in napkins, and putting them down inside his shirt and into his shirt and pants pockets.

Wesley stands, tries to move slowly, take his time. He puts his hands in his pocket, fingers his bottleneck. He starts around a long table, speaking to Miss Emma as he passes her. Then he bends over and whispers to Mrs. Rigsbee. He goes on out and waits for her. Together they go into a little alcove.

Mattie sits down heavily in a chair. "You sure this is going to work?" she asks Wesley.

"Yes. All you have to do right now is just go downstairs. Then when you get home, go in and lock the door, and don't let anybody in. You got a key?"

"Oh yes."

"Then get straight in bed. You're looking kinda washed out."

"But listen, son. You need to serve out your time and then settle down. They've been pretty patient with you. Do you understand? What are y'all going to do, anyway?"

"I don't know for sure. But I'll be seeing you before too long. Now, just go down those stairs and wait in the lobby part—where the guard is—and leave everything else to me."

Mattie gets up, straightens her skirt, holds on to her pocketbook, and starts off, a little wobbly, for the stairs. She stops, turns. "You be good."

"I will."

"I've done all I can with you."

"Yes ma'am. I know. You sure have. Bye."

"Bye."

Wesley reaches into his pocket for the note he's written in wobbly handwriting. It's not there! The other back pocket. His front pocket. He pats both front pockets, both back pockets, looks around. His shirt pocket. Ah. There. He goes into the dining room, hands the folded note to Ms. Clark, and speaks to her before heading towards the band table. Ms. Clark walks across the room and hands the note to Santa Claus and whispers in his ear. Santa turns up his hearing aid and listens again, then reads the note.

My name is Mattie Rigsbee and I am here today visiting my sister Pearl Turnage who is in Shady Grove rest home. My visit is over and I need to go home. I am interested in talking

257

about leaving my will to Ballard University. I am downstairs in the lobby wearing a dark brown sweater and am wondering if you could give me a ride home instead of a taxi. I know that you are the treasurer at Ballard from your pictures in the paper about all your fund raising activities.

Thank You,
Mrs. Mattie Rigsbee

Ms. Clark has approached the microphone up front and is introducing Ted Sears to the guests. A very old, short, happy woman, returning from the bathroom and looking for her seat, stands back to let Sears by.

Santa Claus slips over to Ned Sears and whispers in his ear. Ned gets his car keys from his pocket and hands them to him.

"So it's my pleasure," says Ms. Clark, "to introduce one of Hansen County's most important leaders—"

Why can't they ever say "North Carolina's," thinks Ted.

"—for a brief statement, followed by several songs from the band and then Mr. Wesley Benfield will give a short testimony."

He shouldn't be part of my introduction, thinks Ted.

At the lectern, Ted pulls a folded piece of paper from his gray pin-striped suit coat pocket, and ad-libs as he unfolds it. "I can't tell you how happy I am to be here today. It's always a pleasure for me to visit those folks in our community who are making this world a better place. Eastern LinkComm's record in bringing jobs to our community is an enviable and proud record. Their outreach to our community is symbolized by this fine lunch for those among us who have, in many cases, fought the good fight, run the good race, climbed the highest hill."

In her mind Miss Emma is out on the freeway in her wheelchair, running the good race, climbing the highest hill, then—down the far paved incline—she hears her bright spoked wheels whine and whisper in high, soft tones. She feels the constant light breath of the whirling wheels against her thin, ghost-white thighs.

Ted is reading from his prepared statement.

"How the Ballard family meets the world's present critical challenges will not only determine how we propel ourselves into the twenty-first century, but also the role the Ballard family will play as Christian witnesses to the citizens of this state, indeed, to the world.

"How exciting it is to be near the heart of an industrial geoplex giant, Eastern LinkComm, headquarters for some of the world's most influential and far-reaching decisions in this Age of Information. But especially, from our point of view, how exciting to be able to impact on this and other Hansen County businesses—large and small—in a positive way beyond what we are now doing.

"Consider how much more we can do with the addition of modern air facilities in our community. The possibilities far exceed the risk of liabilities and we . . ."

* * *

On route 24 near the college—one mile from Eastern LinkComm—Santa is driving Mattie Rigsbee home in Ned Sears's white Continental. "And we'll be mighty happy to make you a honorary member of the Ballard family, Mrs. Rigsbee," says Santa. "We'll keep your grass cut whether it needs it or not. And—my, my, I wonder where *he's* going?"

"Who?"

"That boy in the glasses that we just passed—running down the road, the other way. He looks familiar."

"And so our trustees," continues Ted Sears, "have approved a five-year plan for an expansion of our airport here at Ballard, to be named—at the insistence of our trustees and against my wishes—the Theodore B. Sears Regional Airport. A modern airport. What a bold move for the Ballard family! We will merely extend and pave the Ballard airstrip now in place, adding, of course, the appropriate facilities as we go.

"In the immediate future, we will begin a telethon to help raise necessary funds from our friends and family. In these times of secular expansion, there is no greater need than that of the positive influence of Christ on the lines of transportation in and out of our beautiful, spiritually and economically rich Hansen County. We will all benefit. We will all grow together as we witness by our example. And as we grow and sow, so shall we reap.

"Thank you and may God bless you all."

Scattered applause. Six or seven nursing home clients are asleep. Camera flash. Flash again.

Ms. Clark introduces the band.

The band stands. Ben looks around at everybody, counts it out, "One, two, three," and Wesley sings, *Do you drive a Cadillac? Do you drive a Pontiac? Do you park at the mall? Do you drive a car at all? Jesus, where do you park when you drive your car to town?*

After a few lines, Ted looks over at Ned. Ted has an odd smile on his face—his lips are upturned at the corners, but there is an element of fear in his eyes.

At the end of the song there is enthusiastic applause from the audience. The happy lady who was looking for her seat earlier stands and approaches the band. She walks up to Wesley and asks him if she is allowed to dance. Wesley says yes. She dances through "Jesus Dropped the Charges." Then while the band sings "I Need Your Loving Every Day," eight or ten Shady Grove residents are up and dancing.

The odd smile that is still now on Ted's face is on Ned's face also. He's wondering if this is a case of blatant rebellion from a musical group that has been clearly told what is appropriate and what isn't.

When the song is over, Ms. Clark calls Ted Sears up to the lectern to introduce Wesley. Sears is thinking about those songs. What in the world kind of music was that, anyway? he thinks. We'll have to huddle about that. He fingers the knot in his tie—yep, up over the button—tugs at his coat in back, straightening it. He looks at Wesley. And why in the world would anyone be without a tie to give a testimony?

Sears approaches the lectern.

The other band members quietly unplug the sound system, wind up cords, put away their instruments and begin carrying equipment out through the back doors and down the stairs.

Ned is thinking, That music! For heaven's sake. We can't have that stuff played on the air. I thought Colonel Trent took care of this secular business. I'll have to call him in for a little talk. This was his area. And I'll have to corner these media people before they get out of here—ask them to edit out those songs. For crying out loud. I should have known better than to turn this band loose. They're going to cause more harm than good.

Ted is introducing Wesley, reading from a note card. "And I would just like to say that this young man has, through his faith in Jesus Christ, risen above difficult times, and we have come to know that Wesley Benfield is a shining example of what Christ can mean to one who has been in trouble. Wesley will be on the rolls of the Ballard family this spring. He will be a student at Ballard University. A fine student. A bright student. A Christian student. And we are proud. I present Wesley Benfield—to give a short testimony about what the Ballard family has meant to him. Wesley?"

Scattered applause. Wesley touches his collar. The cord is in place. Linda's Walkman is in his pants pocket and the cord runs under his shirt to his ear where the earphone is hidden by his hair.

The TV camera, silently running, is on Wesley. It is hot in the room. Wesley tells himself to take his time—to wait just a minute before starting. Downstairs, the van will be warming up. He puts his hand in his pocket, presses the start button, stares blankly for a second, and then speaks:

At first it was all dark. God was in the dark. Then it was like God had a wand. Whammo here, whammo there. Stuff starts exploding all over the place. I mean it was all clommed together and he starts separating out stuff one from the other. Whammo. Light. Bright as day. Bright shining light. . . .

The guard at the gate, sitting in his little hut, reading *Soldier of Fortune,* does not hear the soft padding of tennis shoes as Vernon skirts under the lowered wooden arm.

Vernon heads for the first door he sees—one under a green panel.

In the pink-tiled foyer, the guard says, "Pass?" to the funny-looking boy, who stands before her, out of breath, rocking back and forth.

Out back, Wesley jumps into the waiting, packed van and the band is off.

Vernon, back outside, dismissed from Eastern LinkComm, watches the BOTA House van heading for the gate. It's the *band.* He starts running after it, but it's going too fast for him. They're gone. Without him. He is suddenly stopped short by the sight of Santa Claus—right there in front of him almost—getting out of a big white car. Santa closes the door and heads inside. Santa Claus. The van is way out there past the gate and turning onto the main highway. Vernon looks inside the big white car. The interior is tan leather. He looks at the ignition switch. The keys are in it. Santa Claus' car. Santa Claus won't mind.

The van, followed by a white Continental, pulls into the parking lot at the Sunrise Auto Repair Shop and parks. In twenty minutes a school bus, painted a fresh dark green, emerges from the garage. Holister steps out of the garage and watches as the bus turns onto the dirt road. The rear wheel almost slips into the ditch, causing it to sway. A drum cymbal is visible through the emergency door window in the rear, and on the side of the bus in bright white letters is written: THE WANDER-ING STARS.

The band is on the road.

"Good Evening. Welcome to Eyewitness News. Sparks flew this afternoon at Eastern LinkComm after an impromptu sermon preached by halfway house resident, Wesley Benfield. More, after this word from Caldwell Chevrolet."

After the commercial, Kim Creston, local news anchor, continues:

"In ceremonies at Eastern LinkComm today following a luncheon for selected members of the Shady Grove Nursing Home, Wesley Benfield preached a sermon on the creation story in Genesis."

Viewers see a silent close-up of Mr. Wesley Benfield on camera, preaching, suddenly thrusting his arm wildly over his head. A voice-over by Miss Creston breaks the brief silence. "In his sermon, Mr. Benfield pointed out that there is not just one, but *two* creation stories in Genesis." The camera zooms to Wesley's face. The sound is now his voice. *If you believe every word in the Bible is absolutely true like some kind of steel trap then you believe both of those versions are absolutely true and if you believe that then you ain't using the brain God gave you.*

20

THE WANDERING STARS ROLL SOUTH ALONG I-95. Wesley is dozing, dreaming, waking, dreaming. He dreams that the bus pulls into a little church along some long straight stretch of single-lane road. Behind the church is a woods of pine trees that stand apart from each other. Pine straw is thick on the ground. It's night and there are lights on inside the church. People are singing.

They all get out of the van and go in. They're standing at the rear of the sanctuary. The ceiling, painted white, is only about seven feet high. Pews, under bare, bright white light bulbs, hold two hundred black people. A man in a maroon robe, standing down front, motions for them to come on down and sing a song. They all walk down, turn and face the audience. Ben pushes Wesley out front to sing.

Wesley starts singing quietly, moving slowly to the side of the church. "*Is there a place for me in heaven—is that my seat?*" he sings. He points to an empty seat on a pew.

The band charges in, singing backup, no instruments. "*Is there a place, is there a place for me-ee-ee? Is there a place, is there a place in hea-a-ven?*"

Wesley starts down a side aisle. "*Is that my place?*" he sings, as he points to an empty seat near the aisle. He moves in front of a couple of people— toward the seat—starts to sit as he sings, but just as he's about to touch the pew, he quickly stands back straight. "*Oh no, oh no, oh no-o-o. That's. That's. That's somebody's else's place, somebody's else's place, somebody else's place.*"

Backup: "*Is there a place for me-ee-ee?*"

He dreams on—now of a sunset cruise. He's lying on the bow of a sailboat. It's going up and down, up and down through clear light green water. Phoebe lies beside him, resting against him. He looks back to land, a thin line of dark green trees. He points and Phoebe looks.

Then after a while, when they can't see any land at all, they look at the red sky holding the red-orange sun just over the horizon. There is a warm breeze and the boat, a large white sailboat, moves on the gentle breeze, up and down slowly, up and down. The sun is almost ready to set; there's only a little space between the sun and the water. The boat slows, and slows, and stops facing into the light wind. The sail flaps gently like Mrs. Rigsbee shaking out a tablecloth, as the sun touches the water and begins to melt, spreading on the surface of the water like an egg on a frying pan, then slipping, slipping down, down, down, nobody saying a word, and finally a tiny orange spot and blip, out of sight smoothly, moving right on to where it's going. Not a sound. Nobody says a word.

Wesley moves along the aisle, points to empty seats, singing the question, on around to the back of the auditorium. Down the center aisle. He almost sits again.

The backup sings, "Is there a place, is there a place for me-ee-ee?" The band members down front are swinging loosely back and forth together, snapping their fingers. "Is there a place, is there a place in hea-a-ven?"

Seven or eight people near the back suddenly rise to their feet, clapping their hands. Then four others stand up down front. Others join them. Now everybody is standing, swinging, clapping.

Wesley dreams on. *He stands in Mattie Rigsbee's yard. He sees her coming out onto the screened porch, opening the screen door, shaking out her dust mop, closing the door, going back in. He walks up the steps, looks around, grabs the door handle and pulls. It is hooked. He rattles the door, looks for the hook: there. It is a simple hook, without one of those gadgets. Easy. He pulls a book of matches from his pocket, opens the cover, inserts it down low in the crack of the door, and starts sliding it upward. It is about one inch below the hook. He hears footsteps inside. The house door opens. Wesley instinctively knocks.*

Mattie squints. "How do you do?" she says. She walks across the porch. "Why, you're the young man from the prison: Wesley. I been thinking about you!"

The whole place is beginning to move. Wesley is halfway down the middle aisle, pointing, singing the question, moving down a row, starting to sit down, sitting down, then jumping up, singing: *"Oh no, oh no, oh no, that's somebody else's place, I said, somebody else's place, oh yes, now, somebody else's place."*

"Is there a place, is there a place for me-ee-ee? Is there a place, is there a place in hea-a-ven?"

"Look up," says Phoebe.

Wesley leans back on the bow of the boat, looks straight up into the sky, and right up there, right up there past all of the air in the world and out there in empty, cold space—as if lying on the air, not too far away—is a bright, thin new moon. And right next to the moon is Venus, bright.

"It's Venus being shot from Diana's bow," says Phoebe.

"Who is that?"

"Oh, Wesley."

The sky in the west over the water has turned to a deep, darkening orange. The boat sits, facing into a gentle wind. The other people on the boat are very quiet.

"I been thinking 'bout you too," says Wesley to Mrs. Rigsbee. He looks down the road toward Patricia's car. The sun reflects off the front windshield. The matchbook he is holding does not move. It is stuck in the crack of the door. He turns it loose. "What you doing?" he says to Mattie Rigsbee.

"Oh, just cooking a bite to eat. Here, let me unhook this. Here, let me unhook this. Here, let me unhook this."

The hook seems to be stuck. Wesley pulls on the

door handle. Mattie works at the hook. "Here, let me unhook this. The hook is stuck."

Wesley needs to get in there on the porch with Mrs. Rigsbee, this woman who might be his grandmother, whose blood might be in his veins. So he punches a fist-sized hole in the screen, grabs the hook. It is stuck.

"Its seems to be stuck," says Mattie. "Don't tear the screen, son."

Wesley starts tearing away the screen. He's got a fairly large hole in it now. About the size of a basketball. He will climb in through the screen.

But his feet will not pull up from the steps. He's stuck to the steps. He reaches down and pulls on his feet. They are stuck.

The low western sky is turning a deep brown. Stars are coming out all over everywhere. Wesley is lying on his back on the bow of the boat. They are headed back in to shore. Up and down. Up and down. Water hisses as it's cut by the boat's prow.

The whole place is standing, clapping, smiling, laughing, crying, hands over heads, people in the aisle, watching him, watching him sing his song.

Wesley points to a seat, puts his hand behind his head. The back-up singing stops just as it's supposed to. The clapping spatters and stops. Wesley holds his pointing finger in place. "I believe, I believe, I believe I found it. I believe I have found my place. I believe I have found my place in heaven. Oh, yes, let's sing the song. I believe, I believe I have found my place. I believe, I believe I have found my place." He sits in his seat, raises his hands over his head, as everybody stands and claps and sings the song with the band.

The sky above is dark. The low western sky holds

a line of deep purple. Wesley lies on his back and looks straight up. The moon is so bright it almost hurts his eyes. Phoebe is moving her hands up and down Wesley's legs. Up, down, up, down, then slowly up. He puts his arms around her and pulls her to him. She holds herself tight against him. He presses back.

Mattie Rigsbee is walking away, toward the kitchen. She's wearing her brown sweater hiked up in the back. Wesley is trying to get his feet out of his shoes. His shoes have toes, toenails. His shoes are his feet. They are made of brown leather, with long pointed toenails. They begin to change to flesh—flesh with bright blue blood vessels.

Mattie stops, turns, looks at Wesley. "I think I'm going to put together a little bite to eat."

The bus slows for a turn-off, jostles Wesley. He awakes, looks around, reaches for some popcorn in the bag in Phoebe's lap.

"I want some," says Vernon, reaching his hand over Wesley's shoulder.

THE END

While the World Sleeps, CLYDE EDGERTON Creates More Great Novels . . .